A FIRM PLACE TO STAND

LORI ALTEBAUMER

Scripture quotations taken from New International Version® and New King James Version®.

Scripture is taken from the Holy Bible, New International Version®. NIV®. Copyright © 1973, 1978, 1984 by International Bible Society. Used by permission of Zondervan. All rights reserved.

Scripture taken from New King James Version®. Copyright © 1982 by Thomas Nelson. Used by permission. All rights reserved.

Print ISBN: 978-154399-108-6
eBook ISBN: 978-1-54399-109-3

TO JOE

Thanks for believing I could and enduring the process. Your prayers and your patience did not go unnoticed.

I waited patiently for the Lord;
He turned to me and heard my cry.
He lifted me out of the slimy pit, out of the mud and mire;
He set my feet on a rock
And gave me a firm place to stand.
Psalm 40:1-2 (NIV)

CHAPTER ONE

Journalists traveled light—especially the unemployed ones running from a tsunami of poor choices. Of course, she wasn't exactly running since she had nowhere else to go.

And now no way to get there.

She watched the flames perform interpretive dance over her 1967 Ford Falcon against the backdrop of the night sky. The interpretation wasn't encouraging.

Her eyes darted to the silhouette of her material possessions now piled in the dark just beyond the edge of the road.

Two medium sized cardboard boxes labeled Fresh Peanuts, an overstuffed Army Surplus duffel bag, and a backpack. She looked like a Hurricane refugee—which wasn't far from how she felt. *But when you're the hurricane, it's hard to escape the destruction.*

Somewhat telling that at age twenty-six everything Maribel owned had fit into the back of a car.

Pressing a hand against her stomach, she exhaled, but couldn't rid herself of the uneasy premonition things might go from bad to worse at any moment. She stared over her shoulder into the dark. Even if something—or someone—were there, she'd never see them. The itchy feeling she was never alone crept up her spine.

She staunched the flow of rising unease. A job at a simple country camp should give her the chance to get her head emptied of the shadows haunting her.

No one knew she was here.

Shaking the feeling off, she looked at the car and flinched.

For a reason she refused to acknowledge, she'd never bothered to paint the car, leaving it exactly as it had been given to her. Unfortunately, the coat of faded gray primer gave off a deathly sick glow in the flames licking against its exterior. She glanced at the scorched "Life Is Good" t-shirt in her hand—a birthday present from her aunt. She'd used it to swat at the engine inferno before the lack of success and singeing arm hairs made her give up and shift her efforts to rescuing her possessions that weren't yet smoking.

Annoyed the shirt wasn't more useful for fire suppression or proclaiming the truth, she tossed it into the overgrown grass lining the side of the sticky-hot asphalt. One less thing to unpack from her duffel bag when she got to the Pool of Siloam Camp. Not that she planned to unpack. She'd labeled this job temporary.

Her Falcon sat there, calmly letting the fire devour its little body without a fight. But who was she to pass judgment?

Pulling her cell phone from her back pocket, she checked again to confirm it hadn't miraculously acquired a signal since the last time she checked. The battery level blinked a fading five percent. Not encouraging.

The dread of night and a deserted road through the thick cedar backwoods of central Texas was the exact point on the map a woman didn't want to be stranded. Alone. With no cell service.

Nothing new in the life of Maribel Montgomery.

A firm believer *Thou Shall Not Litter* should have been the Eleventh Commandment, she blew out a frustrated breath and retrieved the shirt.

Nothing but stars and a thin sliver of moon pierced the dark above. By her estimations, she was at least seven miles from the camp outside Turnaround, Texas. Doable on foot, unless she factored in the black of an almost moonless night, snakes, wild hogs, coyotes, and other predatory animals, not the least of which might be of the human species. And did she mention snakes?

The correct protocol for abandoning a flaming vehicle had never been considered. Uncertain, she watched as the last of her net worth nosedived toward negative oblivion.

The car meant more to her than an entry on her list of assets. The Falcon knew her comings and goings and didn't judge. It just waited in the parking lot for her to return—good days and bad days. Always there, always the same. Always keeping her secrets. Friends like that were hard to come by.

She didn't want to be here to watch it become another of her victims—or explode. She took a step back.

Running her fingers through her wind-whipped hair, compliments of driving with the windows down, she lifted the tangled mane from her skin. The warm night air brushed against her neck, turning the damp skin into gooseflesh.

Maybe she did need to find a farmhouse with a phone. She couldn't spend the night out here alone—especially if she wasn't alone.

She picked up her backpack and spun to meet the glow of headlights punching through the night a quarter mile up the road. Relief lasted no longer than the moment of surprise. If there had been anywhere to go, she would have stepped aside from the beam that grabbed for her. At five feet, three inches, Maribel's best defense wasn't intimidation, but showing fear wasn't going to be her ally either. She tucked a sweat dampened curl behind her ear, then crossed her arms, trying to recall why she hadn't bought a gun for protection when she first felt watched.

Oh yeah, fear she'd accidentally shoot someone who didn't need shooting—such as herself.

That she spent too much time scanning police reports for news stories and evenings alone binge-watching true crime shows until the wee hours of morning didn't help. It was the heroism and self-sacrifice, not the wickedness, that inspired her. But it proved to be an unhealthy habit currently feeding her sense of helplessness and paranoia.

The truck picked up speed, hurrying toward her flaming vehicle. Braking hard against asphalt still hot enough to cook Spam, it slid to a stop several yards away. The smell of rubber tires added another layer of acrid stench to the smoky air.

The headlights blurred Maribel's vision, but not enough to hide the bulk of a man who got out. He reached behind the seat of the extended cab truck and pulled out something she couldn't see.

He would help her, right? Nothing to fear.

She drew her shoulders back, inching her spine up to its height of maximum menace.

Striding toward the flames, the man popped the pin on a fire extinguisher and sprayed the engine. He gave Maribel a quick glance but kept his attention on the area under the hood, then searched the grass for stray embers. Satisfied the fire was out, he shifted his full regard to her.

"You okay?" His sandpaper voice rasped across the night between them.

She swatted at a blood-sucking mosquito and nodded, unwilling to extend the scepter of friendship simply because he carried a fire extinguisher in his truck.

The world was a wicked place. However . . .

"I'm good. Thanks."

His untucked faded denim work shirt stretched tight over the expansion of a waist that wasn't as young as it used to be. Gray hair, silvery in the light, stuck out from beneath his straw cowboy hat. Mid to upper sixties she'd guess, although his deeply lined and tanned face made it hard to tell. Long hours of hard work in the bipolar Texas weather had that effect. But his right hip concerned her most, where the sharp angled bulge beneath his denim shirt divulged the holstered gun strapped to his side.

"You all alone?" His voice scratched the night again.

Maribel ran a dry tongue over drier lips and nodded.

CHAPTER TWO

He stared at her for a moment, a hint of skepticism skimming the air between them. He set the fire extinguisher a safe distance away and returned to pull a flashlight from the cab of his truck. Maribel's first job as a reporter required her to cover the police beat, and she recognized the tactical flashlight often used by those in law enforcement.

She carried the same one herself. If she had money to spend on batteries, it wouldn't be lying uselessly beneath her back seat.

Her hand shot up to block the light he shone in her direction, but he was quick to move it, changing to the wider setting, instead of the blinding beam used to disorient the disorderly.

He ran it over the Falcon before settling it on her pile of belongings several yards away. "Yours?"

She nodded again.

"Not too much traffic on these back roads this time of night except for those up to no good. Lucky I was out."

That remains to be determined. Although no longer having her car charbroiling was a definite plus.

"Also lucky we've had a wet summer or else you might have started a grass fire." He stooped to double check the ground beneath the vehicle for evidence of stray embers. "Of course, these older model cars don't burn as fast as the newer ones. Don't have as much electrical wiring and such, so guess we're lucky there too."

A lump the size of a lumberjack's fist wedged in her throat at the thought she could have been responsible for a fire. Careless mistakes brought her here. She'd vowed to never make another.

"What brings you out this way tonight?" The headlights backlit his body, hiding his face in the shadows. She didn't need to see his face to feel the scrutiny.

She hesitated to give away too much information but understood her circumstances didn't allow for much negotiation. "The Pool of Siloam Camp. I have a job there."

His shoulders lifted, as if an insect had crawled under his shirt and bitten. He might have rocked back as if surprised, but it was hard to say. Everything held a sinister edge standing on a deserted country road in the middle of the night with a complete stranger—a stranger wearing a gun.

"Sheriff Rock Griger." He moved the light to his left hand and offered her his right. When she refrained—self-defense training 101—he dropped it back to his side, apparently unbothered by her lack of trust.

A name helped, but she'd need more before she felt safe. She stated her name and glanced at his unmarked truck. She must have conveyed her skepticism because he added, "Off duty."

He pulled a badge from his shirt pocket, holding it in the light for her to see. Nice try, but she was aware of how easy those were to come by these days.

"Found out you don't have any cell phone service here, I reckon." He stared at her disabled transportation, leaned over and spat, then nodded his head again, as if answering his own question. "I better give you a ride. Wouldn't be right to leave you out here alone."

She hesitated. It wouldn't have been her first choice if the other options weren't just as unsavory. She tried to cipher the statistics in her head, estimating the probability Big Bob the Backroad Butcher with his fake police badge and fire extinguisher would happen by in her moment of need, but math wasn't her thing. Chills rippled over her skin and took her breath away. *Too far, Maribel. Get control of the imagination.*

"Sure." The word erupted on a wave of false bravado. "But what about my car?"

"Nothing you can do about it now." He loaded her few belongings into the bed of his truck next to a muddy shovel and a random assortment of crushed aluminum cans.

She faked a smile as she opened the passenger side door. A day's worth of exhaustion topped off by a car fire—her car fire—must have been messing with the accuracy of her intuition. She didn't picture her demise would be this interesting, though. She believed it a much stronger possibility her end would come from slipping and hitting her head while cleaning the toilet.

The sheriff reached across the seat from the driver's side to clear out the pork rinds packages, beef jerky wrappers, and half-empty roll of antacids currently riding shotgun.

"I usually travel alone." His tone said he preferred to keep it that way.

No wedding ring on his finger, but law enforcement often didn't wear one.

Although the windows were down, a sickening aroma filled the cab and Maribel froze halfway in.

He observed her frowning face and followed her gaze to his muddy boots. "Got off in a little stagnant mud and water while I was fishing. Not a very pleasant smell, huh?"

Settling into the seat, she hugged the door, squeezing as much space as she could between the local sheriff and herself. A sheriff who spent his off-duty time fishing in the dark—without a pole or tackle box. She took a quick glance at the backseat. No fishing gear there either. The inside of her mouth suddenly felt as moist as the worn leather gloves lying on the dashboard.

An older model scanner lay on the seat between them, silent. "Gonna work for Peg Moreland, huh? You and Peg known each other long?"

"Not exactly. We've never met in person, that is." She ran her hands up and down the tops of her jeans, her thoughts bouncing between an inventory of the truck's contents and her odds of getting away if necessary.

Slim to none.

"You got your license handy? Just a quick check. Routine, you understand."

He flipped on the interior lights while she dug through her backpack. Something that might have been a smile flashed over his face. It didn't look natural, or reassuring.

He skimmed over her driver's license and returned it before extinguishing the lights again. Maribel fastened her seatbelt, noting the faint scent of perfume clinging to the shoulder strap. Apparently, he didn't always ride alone.

He headed toward the camp and the tense energy humming through her body eased.

"You have friends around here who can help you? With the car, I mean."

She faltered. She didn't, but he didn't need to know that.

"Is there a repair shop I can have it towed to?" She wouldn't think about repair bills right now. There was no way what needed to happen and what she could afford would be within waving distance of each other.

The scanner crackled, and a female voice joined the conversation. "Sheriff, just giving you a heads up. Conner called again to see if you'd found anything yet?"

Before he could answer she continued, "And before you say anything, I know you told me to keep him out of your hair, but he's very ... persistent."

Sheriff Griger rolled his eyes. "By persistent, I believe she means sweet talking and easy on the eyes." He paused, giving Maribel a mysterious glance before picking up the handheld and pressing the talk button. "You tell him I certainly did find something and to keep his schedule open for tomorrow. But tell him, too, if he calls me about this again, I'm going to take a very personal interest in every minute of his every day—and the fact that he has a taillight out on that Chevy truck he drives."

"Yes, sir." The woman signed off amid a fit of coughs.

"Wish she'd cut back on the cigarettes. You smoke?" He dropped the radio back onto the console.

"No." At least that was one vice she had no trouble resisting.

"You quick to fall for sweet-talking men? If so, you might want to be careful around here. Last thing I need is another lovesick female falling over that boy."

A question she didn't want to answer. She didn't plan to be a lovesick female ever again. She was more like a *sick of love* female. Her success rate for avoiding sweet-talking men was not as impressive as her success with other vices such as tobacco products. "So, about my car, is there a repair shop around?"

"Depends on how particular you are about the definition of a repair shop, but I think I can get it arranged for you."

Maribel tried to relax. Seven miles in the dark with a suspicious stranger could equal the agony of a journey across the state of Texas—the Texarkana to El Paso part.

The trees grew thicker along this section of road, stretching their limbs across the pavement until they locked arms above her. The tunnel of death. Darker and even more eerie. A metaphorical portal for the way her life was turning out. It would only take a small light to be a beacon.

Rounding a corner, they dipped down into the open. The narrow country road crossed a low water bridge. The opposite bank belonged to the Moreland Ranch, home of the Pool of Siloam Camp and, for now, her home. Temporary home, she reminded herself. A starting over spot. But at this moment the glow from the lights of the property were a relief to see.

A breath she didn't know she'd held escaped her lungs, releasing the pressure squeezing her chest. She found the beacon she needed, at least for the moment.

She recited the directions Mack had given her, and the sheriff rolled to a stop in front of the cabin fitting the description. Even in the dark, it would have been hard to mistake the blue tarp stretched across the roof.

A little too eager, she hopped out of the truck. Perhaps she should have at least waited until it came to a complete stop. Without asking, he helped her carry the small pile of possessions into the cabin.

"Looks like the storms did a little damage out here." Sheriff Griger deposited the last box on the cabin floor. "Been an awful stormy year."

If you only knew.

He stood in the doorway and faced her, his hand resting on the doorknob. "What is it you're going to be doing here?"

"Social media and marketing for the camp." That's what Mack told her to say, although they'd assured her there was more to the job.

"Social media. Don't have much use for it. I prefer the face-to-face method myself." He removed his hat and scratched the top of his head before setting it back on his head. "Kinda late at night to be showing up. They expecting you?"

"They are." Not until tomorrow, but her previous landlord hadn't seen the point in putting off the inevitable eviction.

"You never answered earlier, you know anybody around here?" To his credit he kept his tone neutral, but still it made her wary. Her reporter experience said the sheriff was digging. A reasonable thing for a sheriff to do, if only she didn't have so much to keep buried.

"Not really. Mack Stapleton contacted me about the job, but I've never met him." Mentioning the local pastor couldn't hurt.

He nodded without a word—a mannerism she was growing used to. "You show up late at night in a place where you don't know anyone? Darlin', that's either gutsy, desperate ... or something else I'll be sure to find out." He pulled the door part way, then paused, jiggling the knob, a peculiar expression on his face. "You might want to get this lock fixed."

She waited for the sound of his truck door slamming before examining the lock for herself. It spun unhindered. Broken. But most people in the country didn't lock their doors.

Besides, this was a girls' camp in the heart of nowhere.

A remote campground and no one even knew she was here.

Except for Sheriff Griger.

How dangerous could it be?

CHAPTER THREE

Maribel arose far earlier than she wanted after a long day of driving and a short night's sleep, but not because she was anxious to start her new job. The Pool of Siloam Camp wasn't a place she would have chosen to work under any other circumstances. But her life drifted further from normal each time the sun popped up to shine on a new day. It was time to stop rowing her boat in the wrong direction and start searching for an anchor.

Swinging her bare legs off the edge of the bed, she rested her feet on the cement floor. The contact was both jarring and refreshing as the chill soaked into her soles. It soothed her feet and grounded her soul. She flipped on the small light attached to the wall above the bed and inspected the living quarters not observed upon her arrival. She'd pitched her belongings on the floor, jammed a chair under the broken doorknob, and gone straight to bed, thankful someone had prepared her new home in advance. And thankful Sheriff Griger had arrived in time to put out the fire consuming her car. The arrival at her new job had not gone as planned, and her departure would now be a non-issue until she could get the car repaired.

She yawned and reached her arms toward the ceiling, hoping neither the kinks in her body nor the knots in her brain were permanent. Coffee would be great, if she could have afforded to buy any for the coffee maker packed somewhere in a box.

Caffeine would be nice, but her body told her a run would serve her better. And not only because she'd been taking comfort food to the extreme since Alexander's death. She needed the motion of running to unknot her thoughts from last night, last week, last—well ever.

Maribel took her time putting on her running shoes, arranging the laces until they were even, and the tension was right. Perfectionism was a hard master. The need for control, an even harder one.

She flicked at the edge of a sole coming loose and examined the bottom where the tread wore thin. She needed new shoes, but she needed food more. And now a car. New shoes would have to wait until she got her feet on solid ground.

Outside, she stretched tight muscles, her eyes adjusting to the dim light leaving everything around as odd shapes, dark and darker. The camp slumbered in the predawn calm, wrapped in a stillness so thick it had a tangible presence. The only things moving were moths bumping around in the artificial glow of the security lights standing like sentinels across the camp. For a moment, the world belonged to her.

And the moths.

The surroundings filtered through her senses. Inhaling, she drew in the earthy perfume of summer. Hope swept into her heart. She might find a sense of peace here she'd been missing.

Instead, the paranoia that was becoming a habit made her study the shadows.

Was this what a guilty conscience got her? A lifetime of looking over her shoulder?

Ignore the thoughts. Just run. She began a slow jog around the camp.

The coolest, calmest part of the day, the moment before the sun broke the horizon. The cusp of perfection, a day yet unmarred by problems—other than a self-inflicted lack of coffee and running shoes falling apart on her feet. Also self-inflicted.

By the time she returned, the sun would be up, baking everything with the unrelenting heat of Texas in July. The day would simmer, problems bubbling up in a slow boil. But until then, only the cadence of shoes striking pavement in the tempo she determined occupied her thoughts.

A catharsis—that's what it was. The steady, rhythmic pounding of her steps against the ground, muscles burning, lungs laboring, and mind demanding more until it thought about nothing but the movement, every nerve synapsing with determination. Will ... not ... quit.

And she would flow, like a stream of liquid silver. Running filled her with confidence and stripped the doubts away, making her believe nothing could stop her, and she might keep flowing forever.

Running was escape.

She increased her pace as her muscles warmed, then headed to the drive leading to the river as the pale light of dawn chased away the night.

The grass along the sides of the road was mown short, leaving it barely taller than the asphalt it bordered.

The morning chatter of scissor-tailed flycatchers clacked through the calm, the noisy birds unconcerned that, in the distance, the resonate tones of a whip-poorwill stole the spotlight.

A faint trace of moisture lingered in the warm air, stirring the pungent scent of horsemint and the sweet-smelling aroma of drying summer grasses.

This was a safe place. She could almost believe it.

Her stride found the place where she best heard the music, her steps settling into an unchanging meter. Without thinking, she began counting, letting the pointless sequence of numbers capture her focus, unwinding the thoughts in her head from the tight twist holding them.

Dark shapes morphed into recognizable things: immense oak trees, pecans, cedar elms, and cottonwoods. Briars tangled their feet while the broad leaves of wild grape vines draped their branches in graceful, leafy swags.

The driveway passed under the arch with the welcome sign and made a sharp left to parallel the river. A thick growth of vegetation covered the long slope to the river beyond, keeping the water hidden from view. The road ran straight for two hundred yards, then split, jaunting off to the low-water bridge to the right, or continuing around the hill to the home of her new employer, Peg Moreland.

The whippoorwill's call rose again from somewhere farther along the river. Enchanting and clear, its cry rose across the lowland, breaking through the stillness of the early morning. An alluring sound, yet lonely. A mating call in all its primal glory. Regrettably, she'd succumbed to those same alluring and lonely notes from her own species too many times.

She crossed the bridge, welcoming the uphill challenge on the opposite side. Ambitious since she hadn't run in weeks, but the searing burn in her muscles purged her thoughts.

The sky grew brighter, a swath of brilliant colors splashed above the horizon. A new day offering a new start. Pushing herself up the incline, she ran on, thankful for the level road when she reached the top. When her muscles felt soft and stretchy, she sprinted hard, trying to burn away the rest of the tense energy that never managed to leave her. She stopped, doubled over, hands on her knees for support. Her breath came in labored jerks, sweat dripping from her face onto the asphalt.

The runner's high. Maribel savored the fleeting feeling of strength and success she received when it kicked in. She'd hold on to the sensation for as long as she could.

Her breath returned to normal, her pulse slowing. She couldn't outrun the day. But at least now she might be ready for it.

She jogged back, stopping to enjoy the disappearing sunrise and its tranquility from the bridge.

Wildflowers dotted a field of native grasses bordering the river, flecks of color popping out, as if a painter flicked his brush across a green canvas. Mid-summer flowers in Texas had to be hardy and determined.

A short, metal guard rail lined the bridge, only a few feet above the river. She placed a foot on the rail and stretched, repeating the process with her other leg.

Unease prickled the back of her neck. Wary, she straightened, eyes scanning the distance while her mind berated her for the constant and unfounded paranoia.

A turtle stuck his head above the water. When she stood, he shot under and vanished, sending ripples over the river. Widening circles stretched toward the banks as she watched him swim away beneath the surface. One small movement troubled the water far from where the turtle had been.

The water looked cool, if not terribly clear, and inviting to her hot feet—feet already aching from lack of support in the worn-out shoes.

Leaving the road, she walked to the river's edge near a place shallow enough for wading.

A discarded Styrofoam cup bobbed by a stand of cattails. Nearby, a plastic shopping bag floated, caught on a log stretching out into the river like a mangled arm. Her belief in environmental stewardship was the final incentive to kick off her shoes and step into the water. Her feet sank into the loose gravel, the smooth pebbles and grit massaging her toes as she wiggled them. A pleasant coolness worked its way into her tired extremities, radiating up her legs.

Any tension leftover from the run drifted away in the dawdling current as she savored the peace that washed over her.

She eased over to retrieve the cup from among the cattails, then reached for the bag.

It floated further out where the water ran deeper, and she leaned against the log as she grasped at the plastic. Something soft and skittering tapped against her ankle. She smiled at the feel of what must be tiny minnows tickling her legs. The bag didn't move when she pulled. She tugged harder. The log shifted as the bag gave way.

The sudden release threw her off balance. She stumbled. Something smooth and thick slid against her leg. Snakes topped her list of phobias. Snakes she couldn't see were off the chart.

She screamed.

Not a snake, but a ghostly pale mass emerged from beside the log, rising toward her.

Swollen and grotesque, a woman stared up through dead eyes.

CHAPTER FOUR

Maribel flew backward as if hit by the concussive force of an explosion. A second scream stuck in her throat, choking her. She stumbled, falling in the shallow water, lurching away from the hideous thing bobbing towards her. Digging her heels in, she shoved hard against the water and shifting gravel. Splashing, she put distance between her and the bloated body.

She staggered on solid ground. The cup in one hand, plastic bag still clutched in the other, she flung both from her.

Her palms slammed against her forehead as she reeled from the river and the secret it no longer hid. *No, no, no, no!*

Frantic fingers raked through her hair, gathering it into her fists, eyes squeezed shut, trying to erase the specter tattooing itself to her eyes.

Shock dissipated with a steadying of her breath. She looked again, clinging to a thin hope it wasn't a human body she'd seen.

The corpse remained, a grisly princess resting on a bed of green satin. Leering at her and taunting her with memories and accusations of things it shouldn't know.

Not again.

A cold shiver ran over Maribel, knotting itself in her middle, squeezing the air from her chest. Wrong again.

This was not a safe place.

A sound from behind her broke loose the scream stuck in her throat. She jumped to find a man scowling at her from the top of the riverbank. She searched for an escape. Between the bridge and a thick snarl of briers, she had nowhere to go. Back in the river was not an option. Alive or not, someone else already had dibs on that.

"You're doing an awful lot of screaming for this early in the day." His words came breathless, his chest heaving. Sweat darkened his hair, dripping from spikey tendrils and shining on the skin of his bare torso. His drenched t-shirt hung limp in his hand, leaving him clothed in only athletic shorts and running shoes. A nylon holster, complete with a gun, was strapped around his waist. Was there a dress code in these parts she was unaware of?

Maribel didn't need to see in a mirror to know her eyes were wide. Every aspect of the scene rushed toward her. A thousand tiny monitors simultaneously playing details in her head. No time to sort them. No time to choose which needed her focus. Her mouth hung open, but there were no words.

"I didn't mean to scare you." The t-shirt clung to his wet skin as he worked to get it on while he moved toward her. His expression held a mixture of concern and suspicion—heavy on the suspicion. "Are you all right?"

He eased toward her as if trying to befriend a wild dog. His shirt hid the gun now, but the fact he let his hand hover near it made her wary as he closed the distance between them.

Her bare feet anchored themselves to the ground as he moved toward her, reaching. So much for flight or fight. Freezing was the only response she could muster. She swayed and he gripped her arms, bending so his eyes were level with hers, his gaze penetrating. Did he think he could see behind them to read her mind?

He leaned closer and sniffed.

Okay, not a mind reader. He thought she was intoxicated—a drunk or an addict wandering delusional on the riverbank.

She wilted, the surge of adrenaline roaring through her veins evaporating as quickly as it came. His grip tightened, fingers digging into the soft underside of her arms as he kept her from falling.

"I'm not gonna hurt you. Tell me what's going on. Are you hurt?" He lowered his voice, his speech calming. Maribel let the concern on his face eclipse all the other screens jumbled in her head. She focused on the features in front of her. Focused, and saw the worried lines above his brow, the bewildered parting of his lips, and the sincere and steadying warmth of his troubled gaze. And then it hit her in a crushing wave.

She swallowed, and her stomach fell apart. Everything in her dissolved into a gritty mass her body wanted to expel with force.

Clamping her hand against her mouth, she jerked free from his hold.

"I'm gonna throw up."

She twisted away, staggering a short distance before falling to her knees. Burn hit the back of her throat like a flush of lighter fluid an instant before the bitter acid of her empty stomach exited her body. She knelt there, panting and drooling, aware of the stranger's unwanted and far too scrutinizing attention.

Once she could breathe and swallow again, she wiped her mouth on her shirtsleeve and worked herself back to standing.

The last body she'd found had made her shake so uncontrollably no one had understood anything she said. She concentrated on breathing—in, out. She had to stay calm or the shaking would begin. And that would render her incomprehensible—and defenseless.

The man continued to analyze, his body language stating that, despite his concern for her, he was dubious.

"I think there's a dead person in the river." She threw in *'I think'* because it helped her hold on to the hope she was wrong. *Breathe in. Breathe out.*

He stared a moment, expressing his doubt before directing his gaze to the river.

Refusing to witness again what she'd already seen twice; she kept her eyes averted and pointed toward the object floating near the log.

She knew the moment his eyes settled on—her. In two long strides he stood at the river's edge, his body visibly hardening at what he saw. Maribel took the opportunity to ease herself up the bank, placing the open road behind her. Why had she taken her shoes off?

He kicked at the stand of cattails, roaring what might have been an expletive or three. Tilting his face to the sky, he closed his eyes and stilled. He stood in silence for a moment then turned back to the body.

A chance existed she could flee while his back was to her. A small, shoeless little chance. But even if he didn't catch her, the gun he carried needed consideration. Her gut said *run*, but her brain said *and die if you do*. Somehow, facing this straight on seemed the wisest choice. Unfortunately, neither her gut nor her brain specified a plan for accomplishing this, so she stood, still and silent, never taking her eyes off the stranger.

He rotated to face her like an angry drill sergeant, hands on his hips, scowl in place, putting every inch of his six-foot frame to use intimidating her—with great success.

An involuntary swallow forced the lingering taste of bile down her throat. To her ears the sound echoed between the riverbanks and she flinched.

"Who are you?" The harshness now present in his voice surprised her. Not the cool, detached inflection she expected of a murderer. Sight of the body shocked and angered him too. Her anxiety dropped a few notches.

Still she hesitated. She didn't owe him any explanations, did she? "Maribel Montgomery—and I'm not crazy, or on drugs, or whatever you think."

"I didn't say you were, but what are you doing here this time of day? You're on private property." His eyes lost their curves, replaced by wide, dark gashes below his brows.

"I work for Peg Moreland. This is her property, right?" She crossed her arms in front of her, one hand resting on her shoulder, squeezing. The tremor was trying to creep its way over her body, and she released the pressure in a gush of pointless words. "I didn't sleep much last night, and I haven't eaten anything since lunch yesterday. Then my car caught fire, and I didn't have any coffee, and I needed to go for a run this morning. And that's when I found ... her." She clamped her lips together, ending the flow of senseless chatter.

"You work for Peg Moreland? First I've heard of it. When did you get here?"

"Last night—late." Why had no one been aware she was coming, yet all thought they should have been?

"Where exactly did you stay after your arrival last night—late?" He accented the word late.

"The cabin with the blue tarp on the roof."

He received her answer with a nod and a moment of thick, pondering silence.

"Well, Maribel," he reached under his shirt, "I hate to have to do this to you."

Maribel's eyes watered as the familiar roar hit her ears, adrenaline once again shoving blood through her body with ferociousness. Afraid he planned to shoot her, she stepped back but tripped, staggering to keep herself upright.

"I don't suppose you'll want to stay here with our friend so do me a favor and go call the sheriff. His number's in here, but there won't be any signal until you get to the top of that hill across the river. Tell him it's Conner Pierce." He unclipped his cell phone, then scooped up her abandoned shoes and carried both to her. "Sheriff Griger isn't going to be excited to hear from me but tell him we found Tracy Morgan."

CHAPTER FIVE

R ock Griger threw his fishing rod into the bed of his truck, regretting it instantly. He saved up a long time to afford one that nice. That was his own stupid fault though. He could've extorted money from the drug dealers like a lot of his counterparts did. But no, he tried to be good, do things the right way.

Integrity. Definitely not a synonym for prosperity.

Neither was being born on the wrong branch of the Moreland family tree. Not that he minded that. It had kept expectations for him low. At least he slept with a clear conscience.

Most of the time.

He set his tackle box in with more care, then opened the lid to pull out the nearly empty bottle of Wild Turkey. He swirled the whiskey around in the bottle, letting the glass and amber liquid catch the morning sunlight. It still had a few good sips in it. He hated to toss it. He'd barely touched it with his breakfast today. The pain he climbed out of bed with most mornings must have taken the day off with him. Guess he couldn't complain about that.

After a moment's deliberation, he poured the last of the liquid out, then flung the empty bottle as far as he could into the field by the road. Being caught with anything that might interfere with his authority was a risk he wouldn't take. He climbed into the driver's seat and reached across to the glove compartment, retrieving a container of mouthwash. He swished some around in his mouth and then spat on the ground outside his window.

Didn't need this today.

His boat bobbed a lonely goodbye as he pulled away from the pier, putting his foot down heavy on the accelerator. Not that he was in a hurry to deal with yet another problem involving the Morelands.

This situation had gone on long enough, and the longer it continued, the messier his job was getting. He needed to end it soon. Hard to do when he wasn't sure what *it* was. Just the gut feeling something was wrong in his county.

A half hour later he rounded the bend and dropped off the hill into the river bottom. Jerking the wheel, he nosed the truck off the pavement and bounced onto the dirt and rock, sliding to a stop next to the Justice of the Peace's vehicle.

The riverbank already sported a larger crowd than it should have, but the tall woman in tight blue jeans and a white blouse that needed a few more buttons at the top was the first thing that caught his eye. Great. She was here. This day just kept getting better.

He knew the moment she saw him by the way she shifted, putting more space between her and that useless camp director, Evan Beck. A telling and troublesome piece of body language there.

Stepping out, he hitched up his pants and strode into the midst of the group without giving Ava Hardin another glance.

One of the first responders greeted him. An eager quiet settled over the crowd as they made way for him.

The JP glanced up from where he stooped over the body. He checked his watch and then scribbled something on his clipboard before addressing the sheriff. "Sorry you had to come in on your day off. Hope the fish weren't biting yet."

The fish had been biting. If he hadn't been so focused on his conversation with Ava from the night before, he might have caught one. She had blown into town like a lost but sexy cyclone. What could he say? The pickins were slim around these parts. She came on to him like he had a T-Bone tied around his neck and she was a starving Rottweiler. They had one less-than-spectacular date, then she'd given him the runaround for weeks. Until two days ago when he became interesting again. With three divorces under his belt, the one thing he understood was—he didn't understand.

"Oh, you know." An involuntary grunt escaped as he knelt beside the body. "Looks like y'all caught the trophy today though." With gloved hands, he lifted first one, and then the other, of the lifeless woman's hands, examining the body. "Any obvious cause of death—wounds, knife marks, bullet holes, syringe still stuck in her arm?"

"No, sir."

Rock angled her head to the side and probed around the back of her skull. "Looks like she may have taken a nasty blow to her head. 'Course we'll need the autopsy to know which came first—the wound or the water."

He rose slowly, pushing himself up one body part at a time. His joints grew stiffer every day. This winter would be a pain in the backside, literally. It was time to retire.

"You know her, Rock?" the JP asked.

He let out a long slow breath. "Yep. Name's Tracy Morgan. Did home health work for my momma before she passed."

Griger turned first to Conner, then Maribel. "You two the ones who found her?"

"I got their preliminary statements already." The young deputy on the scene inserted himself in their midst. He recited every detail recorded in his notebook, right down to the temperature of the water and the Toot-n-Totem logo on the plastic bag Maribel pulled from the water.

Griger lifted his hat and scratched his head. He had to get that pup onto decaf. He turned to glare at Conner. "You start work here and not long after your former girlfriend gets a job here. Now she washes up in the river—dead?" Griger shook his head.

"Yeah. I know what you're thinking, Sheriff. Ask away. I got nothing to hide." Conner spread his arms wide as if to say, bring it on.

Griger shifted to Maribel. "I find you beside a burning car in the middle of the night, and the next thing I know I'm out here talking to you because you found Tracy's body in the river. If you plan to stay around, I may need to hire more deputies."

Maribel opened her mouth to respond, but the sheriff waved her off.

"It'll keep. Just make sure you stick around so I can reach you. Both of you." His expression let them know he dared them to try otherwise.

Conner didn't worry him. He just liked to keep the boy honest by not letting him in on that fact. But he wanted to do some checking into Maribel. Never a big believer in coincidences, the timing of her arrival interested him. He also wanted to wait for the autopsy report to prove what his gut already knew—they were looking at a homicide here. He'd yet to find a jury or a judge that respected his gut feelings, although he wasn't often wrong.

Of course, in this case his gut had a little help.

The day was still early. He'd head to the station, get the ball rolling on an autopsy with the State Examiner's Office and notify the next of kin—if any of them were sober enough to hear him. Then he'd pay Peg a visit. She needed to know. And he had a few questions for her, like why she hired Maribel and why he had to find out this way. There were too many secrets in this county right now. But then, hadn't that always been the way?

Maybe he'd swing by later to harass Beck a little more. Should still be enough day left after that to get back out on the lake. He'd get Cindy to pack him a dinner. Long summer days had their perks.

That might not look good to his constituency if this turned out to be a murder, but he still had some thinking to do—the kind that's best done on the water—and he didn't intend to let a dead junkie rob him of his day off. He wasn't planning to run for re-election anyway.

Rock walked back to his truck, his feet heavier than before, as if the soles of his boots were made of lead—just like his bones. Tracy Morgan had been an incompetent mess when she cared for his mother. If he could have found anyone else willing to work for what he could afford to pay, he would have. But this was a harsh way to die.

Rolling the latex gloves off his thick, stiff fingers, he thought it mighty inconvenient of her to float up right here, right now. Because he just couldn't see her being part of whatever it was that had his peaceful county humming with menace.

He paused and spun back to glare at Evan, ignoring the attractive blonde standing beside him. "Looks like we found your missing worker, Evan. Sure hope we don't find your missing camper in a similar condition."

CHAPTER SIX

T he hot water ran out before it erased the sensation of the dead woman's body against Maribel's own unexpired and perceptive skin. She scrubbed her leg until it burned, then stood with the cold water pelting her.

She was alive, but another woman wasn't. Why? There had to be a reason for it—for her—right? She desperately wanted to believe she had a purpose other than to produce carbon dioxide.

And stumble upon dead bodies.

Growing up reading Nancy Drew mysteries and Louis L'Amour westerns, Maribel dreamed she was strength and resilience held together by courage. Once, there had been moments in her daydreaming when she believed she could stand up to evil and make justice prevail. A childish dream. Life had snubbed those notions out long ago. If she hadn't been certain of it before, Alexander's death was the proof.

She forced herself to shut the water off. Like littering, she took the possibility of aquifer depletion seriously.

Shutting off her thoughts wasn't as easy.

The morning swam in her head, a muddy jumble of images. Snippets on a highlight reel all thrown in the pot of her memory now bubbled like horror stew.

The sheriff had answered his phone from the middle of a lake where he was "busy catching fish" as he put it. He hadn't pretended to appreciate the call, and she thought she might've heard a foul word or two before she disconnected.

She watched the men lay the body carefully out on the grass. A sense of irony had chafed her conscience. So much care given to the deceased. Had anyone shown the woman that much concern while she lived?

And she remembered the stranger who had introduced himself as Conner, pacing like a caged lion at feeding time, a knot of tense energy ready to spring. When she caught him staring at her, the intensity smoldering in his eyes turned the marrow in her bones to cold slush.

Something about him reached into her chest and seized her heart, squeezing until it ached.

She didn't know him, but she recognized the storm of emotions seething in his eyes today. Anger, frustration, and a measure of self-loathing that made her tremble. Somehow it cut open her own scars. His pain was palpable in the hurt flowing from her wounds. Wounds that could never heal. There was more to his reaction than mourning the death of an ex-girlfriend. Who had this woman been to him?

She didn't require an answer to realize she wanted no part of the situation—or of this Conner and whatever turmoil he was in. Unfortunate for her since she discovered the body. Even if they hadn't said it, she made the list as a person of interest. If they ruled the death a homicide, Maribel might find herself at the top of the suspect list as well.

A slight inconvenience. She could prove she'd never been anywhere near here or the deceased woman. Of course, the usefulness of the evidence depended on the integrity of the hands that held it. No one knew her here. Unknown often equaled suspicious in small, rural towns like this. She had first-hand experience with the forces of corruption that sometimes governed.

And then there was Evan and his only slightly concealed animosity when Conner introduced them this morning. Considering the circumstances, maybe his anger wasn't directed at her. But still, weren't camp employees supposed to be friendly, or at least civil?

What had she gotten herself into here?

At least the rest of the day couldn't hold anything worse.

A half hour later, she carried a modest box of her own office supplies to the space they'd given her in the administration building. She would have preferred to work from the solitude of her private cabin, but she needed the internet connection—dial-up—only available in the main building. They didn't need help with social media. They needed help joining the twenty-first century.

The heavy box thudded onto the dusty desktop where Maribel dropped it. *So, this is what you get when you have a journalism degree and no people skills?*

Correction. I have people skills. It's just safer if I keep them to myself.

Keeping them to herself, though, made the recent interview process less than successful. That—and a not-so-stellar employment history.

Ahh ... the aroma of dust and dead bugs.

Unemployed, and a bank account with no commas. This job was a godsend in a time of desperate need. Minimal pay, but a notch above living in the back of her car.

The Pool of Siloam Camp wasn't on her short—or long—list of dream jobs. A small camp for teenage girls, which her job did not require her to interact with, the camp existed as a part of the much larger Moreland Ranch. Which one she really worked for remained somewhat unclear.

She hated summer camp, also known as the place for kids whose parents didn't know what else to do with them all summer—or didn't enjoy the near constant companionship. If it weren't for camp, she wouldn't have spent three summers gaping through the goggles of starry-eyed romanticism at a boy with a hidden, and not happily-ever-after, agenda. That should have been her first clue a career in investigative reporting might not be for her. She trusted too easily.

Or longed for love too desperately.

She closed her eyes and pressed fingertips against the growing pain in her temple. What was she really doing here?

Compiling decades of family history without anyone finding out about it. That's what they'd told her after she had accepted the job she thought was for marketing.

Most family histories were better off buried with their dead, but people wanted to be remembered, and always believed it would be for something good. Rather than doing something great themselves, it seemed to be enough if they could point to their family lineage.

Vanities of vanities, all is vanity. Aunt Rachel's voice whispered into her thoughts. Her aunt had a saying for every occasion. And for a reason she couldn't explain, those words had lodged themselves in her head to pop out at random, and often unwanted moments. It wasn't until Maribel's early adulthood, when she'd sat down to read the bible out of curiosity, that she discovered the source of her aunt's proverbial wisdom. But by then it was too late. The words were already ingrained in her subconscious with a life of their own. She had no control over when and where they popped up.

Meanwhile, she'd managed to fail Introduction to Statistical Methods three times. The brain was a strange thing.

Mack had assured her the job suited her journalism skills and was completely legal—just not something they wanted everyone knowing about. It came with a paycheck—plus free room and board—and that little necessity of life overrode enough of her other concerns.

She pulled the cord to raise the faded vinyl blinds, flinching when rewarded with a shower of dust and a view of the trash dumpster.

"I see you decided not to bolt and run?"

Maribel fanned away the floating debris before pivoting to find her doorway occupied by a familiar face best summed up as a genuine walking cliché. Faded jeans, worn out gray t-shirt one size too small, and Hollywood hero stubble smudging his lower face.

Conner—showered and smelling of Dial soap and damp skin. The fierceness of earlier replaced with lethal West Texas charm oozing from every pore.

Resilience was a quality he must possess in abundance because there was no trace of this morning's events in his demeanor.

He grinned. Add to the list of dangerous qualities dimples and blue eyes that sparkled more than they should. How had she missed that before?

"Nope. No bolting and running for me." Not yet anyway. Her brain fired a warning shot at her heart as her stomach fluttered. She hadn't forgotten the sheriff's comments about the man's sweet-talking skills, but the sheriff was right. Conner Pierce was easy on the eyes.

A benefit of taking a job at a remote camp for girls should've included no testosterone-filled temptations to distract her. She'd tried that drug to fill the holes in her heart until she woke up one morning next to someone who couldn't remember her name. It left her with the realization living that way was hollowing out the voids within her, leaving an even greater, darker abyss. One she feared she'd never fill.

Conner shuffled as if he found the moment awkward. There was nothing awkward about the smile, however. Unless the way it made her pulse race counted. No, his presence here—or perhaps within a hundred-mile radius—was not optimal.

She crossed her arms, attempting to signal her disinterest. This wasn't an attraction she felt. It was low blood sugar and lack of sufficient coffee this morning.

Conner eyed her unpacked box. "New employee, huh? Got an office in the admin building. Must be important."

"Hardly." Maribel mumbled under her breath when he didn't take the hint. She turned away from him and busied herself, attempting to open the window. If he was smart, he'd get the message and remove himself from her office.

He wasn't.

Neither the window nor the man budged.

"Not much of a talker, huh?"

"I wasn't hired to talk." She bit her lip, refocusing. There was no reason to treat him like last week's burrito wrapper, and she didn't need any more enemies. "I'm sorry. It's been a long day already and I have a lot to get done."

"And you didn't sleep good, your car caught on fire, you haven't eaten since lunch yesterday, and you're low on coffee." He tossed her words back at her, a playful bounce in his voice.

She kept her back to him, concealing her surprise. He'd not only heard her but remembered.

"So ... about this morning, I just wanted to apologize if I was a little," he paused, "aggressive."

The apology swung her head around, and she found him gazing at her, chin tucked low and looking contrite.

Not good. Focus on the aggressiveness.

"I've seen dead bodies before. I'll be fine." She shifted back to the window and continued to tug with no success.

"I thought I might have given you the wrong impression and that definitely wouldn't be a good thing. I'm really a harmless and highly likeable guy."

Silence.

"Well ... I guess I thought wrong. Need some help?"

"No on both counts." A lie on both counts.

"Are you sure?"

She glanced back to find all six feet of him leaned against the door frame, not leaving. Great. A walking, talking, loitering cliché.

Maribel moved away from the window as if it were no longer important to her and began digging things out of her box. "Yes, I'm sure. It's fine."

"But you want it open?"

No, I want you to leave. And soon. "It's fine."

"All you have to do is ask. Don't tell me you're one of those?"

"Those?" Her finger brushed against the tip of her nose as she gritted her teeth.

"Women who are offended by help from a man."

Help? No. Knight in shining armor? Well, let's say she'd fallen for that more times than the New Year's Eve ball drop at Times Square. It never ended well. Conner Pierce wasn't giving her a reason to believe him different from any of those who came before. Of course, she wasn't giving him the opportunity.

She shrugged. "I'm not. If it'll make you feel better, open the window."

"If that's what you want." The mischievous grin he wore shot needles of warning into her subconscious.

Conner walked to the window and began working to loosen it. Maribel found satisfaction in seeing it didn't open easily for him either.

After a little effort, an excellent opportunity to show off his muscles, which he seized to the fullest, the window flew up. The putrid smell of sun ripened garbage flew in.

Maribel gasped, her hand swiftly covering her nose. "Close it!"

Conner complied, a satisfied smile replacing the mischievous grin as he moved to face her.

"You knew." Maribel didn't hide the frustration in her voice.

"Yep. But you made it clear you didn't aspire to more conversation, so I figured I could either watch you waste your time and energy trying to open it, or I could help you out."

"You could have just told me."

"Not as much fun."

"Are you always this cavalier after finding a dead body—someone you knew?"

He sobered. "Hard to say. It's my, uh ... first time." He stumbled over the admission. "Unlike you, apparently. Which is why I feel pretty silly now. I stopped by to check on you and see if you needed to talk. Looks like I'm a swing and a miss all the way around."

"Maybe it's time for a new sport." Maribel offered a truce by way of the slight smile she gave him.

"Speaking of ... you haven't seen one of the campers come by, have you? Blondish hair. Kind of a little thing about this tall." He leveled his hand in the air beside him, several inches below his shoulder, about the same height as Maribel.

She straightened. Her lifelong dream had been to stretch her vertebrae to greater height. *The word is petite, mister.* "No."

"Someone said they saw her come this way, but I haven't found her."

Clearly.

Conner studied her for a long silent moment. "You sure you're okay then?"

She nodded. It was easier to lie that way.

CHAPTER SEVEN

M aribel waited until the click of the closing door leading out of the building confirmed Conner's exit. Taking no chances, she peeked out her office door before stepping out to search for cleaning supplies and air freshener. A closet next to the bathroom at the back of the building held what she needed. Rifling through the collection, she debated which air freshener to use—Pure Berry Joy or Kiss Me in the Meadow. She noted the You're Not Really Here fragrance was missing.

She mumbled to herself about the lack of environmentally friendly cleaning products as she searched, until she realized there were more voices in her ear than her own.

Muffled voices from outside. Not normal voices, but hushed voices. A conversation stitched together with the invisible thread of mutual distrust and dislike. There had been a time it would have made her fingertips tingle anticipating the story it might lead to and the career building opportunities it could bring, but the woman she was now wasn't interested in overhearing a conversation not meant to be heard. At least that's what she told herself.

"Sheriff, I know you're here about the missing girl, but you're wasting your time." Maribel recognized Evan Beck's voice.

"We found your missing worker floating in the river. What's to say we won't find your missing camper in a similar condition? You don't appear too eager to find her." It was the same gritty voice that set her nerves on edge last night and again this morning.

"You don't seriously think something connects the two, do you?" The sarcastic edge in Evan's tone expressed his opinion on the subject.

Maribel tuned in with more attention. Answering a question with a question meant there was more being spoken than the words one could hear.

"I'm as worried as everyone else, but I—we—had nothing to do with what happened to Tracy Morgan or with whatever has happened to the girl, Leah. Talk to Peg. She's the one who insisted on giving Tracy a chance since she was trying to get her life together." Evan's words were more composed this time.

"Sounds like you didn't approve of Peg's decision. You have a personal problem with Tracy Morgan?"

"We hardly had much social interaction, Sheriff, but you and I both know the kinds of stuff she was into—the kind that leads to an early death—accidental or otherwise."

"*Was* is the key word here. Tracy spent time in a rehab program, and from what I've heard so far, she'd stuck with it. Peg confirmed she'd passed the drug screen required to work here."

Evan snorted before continuing. "Sheriff, you can't come around here talking about an abduction—or a murder. Rumors will get started and they'll ruin this camp. It'd be a shame to put Peg through that now."

"Evan, I don't enjoy stirring things up. And everyone knows I'd never want to harm this camp, or Peg."

"Oh really? I thought you might feel differently about a few things now with the talk of putting in a housing development out here—and Peg's refusal. Without claiming an heir, she's going to tie the whole thing up in red tape. Then there'll be no camp and no sale to the developers. Where does that leave everyone then? All these people she claims to care so much about?"

Maribel crept to the window on the back wall where she tugged one slat of the vinyl blinds low enough to see out. The sheriff stood, angled away from her, facing the open ground that led toward the river, although the dark sunglasses he wore made it impossible to tell where his gaze went.

"I'm gonna let that comment slide for the time bein.' I don't know what we're looking at with the Morgan woman yet, but I do know we're dealing with a missing girl. And you're lucky the parents haven't set the media on us already."

"Lucky? You probably haven't even found the parents yet. They ditch their daughter here every summer and take off for their European vacations. That ought to tell you something."

"She was abducted from this camp."

"What proof do you have it was an abduction?" Evan's voice squeaked, and he coughed, clearing his throat.

"Okay then, she disappeared from here. It's a good twenty miles to the nearest town. Not likely she walked anywhere without being seen. And no cell phone service so she couldn't exactly call a ride, now could she?" The sheriff's tone made it clear he expected his to be the final word on the subject.

Evan either ignored the tone or missed it altogether. "Come on, Rock. Even you don't believe that. You didn't exactly conduct a thorough search, and it's because you know, as well as I do, she's probably another teenage runaway."

"I'll let that comment slide as well, but watch yourself, Evan. You're getting close to crossing a line you don't want to be on the other side of. Until I have solid proof one way or the other, the people of this county—and that includes these campers while they're here—are my responsibility and I'm going to cover all the bases." He leaned over and spat. "And now I've got a dead woman on my hands to boot. A dead woman who worked at your camp."

"A dead woman who had been asking for trouble all her life. Well, I guess it finally found her, but it wasn't this camp that did it. As for the girl, kids these days think they're invincible, as if they're smarter than everyone else. They don't think twice about trusting people they meet online." He let his last words fall like the banging of a judge's gavel. "And their parents don't care."

Evan's back was to her, but his prolonged sigh was heavy with subtext. "If I hear of anything, you'll be the first to know. Now, I have a new set of campers coming in later today, and I have a lot of work to do."

"That's fine. I'll mosey on. Just wanted you to know we'll be checking the background on each member of the staff, including the new girl that came in last night."

"Perhaps you should talk to Peg about that. She's the one who hired her, too."

"Oh, I've talked to Peg," the sheriff said. His speech held a hint of ... threat and accusation? "She gave me her blessing to search, starting at the top."

"Are you implying I'm a suspect?" Evan's voice pinched.

"I'm telling you there is a child that needs finding, and now a possible murder to solve, and that's the job I'm going to do." The gravel crunched beneath the sheriff's boots as he walked back to his truck.

Calling back over his shoulder, he pulled the trigger on his parting shot. "And Evan, everyone's a suspect."

Maribel eased back to the supply closet. She leaned against the wall, pressing against it for support, both eyes and fists squeezed shut. This job was supposed to be dull and completely devoid of excitement—not a future episode of *America's Most Wanted*.

She drew in a long breath, then exhaled as she opened her eyes.

Focus. Emptying the cabinet of every container, she began methodically picking them up one at a time, placing them back on the shelf in organized rows, tallest containers to shortest. She needed not to think about what she had seen or what she had heard. She needed not to think about the past. She needed not to part with the last of her sanity.

Maribel dumped the empties in the trash can as her thoughts calmed.

Whatever was going on, she could not get involved. But the thought of a missing girl, runaway or not, held onto her heart and wouldn't let go.

She headed back to the office with her arms full of cleaning supplies only to find the next surprise waiting.

"Can I help you?" Maribel asked the young girl digging through the box on her desk. She fit the description of the camper Conner sought. Turned out she was not that hard to find. Good thing he wasn't pursuing a career in search and rescue.

The girl shrugged half-heartedly, abandoning her explorations. If she was concerned about having been caught, it didn't show.

"No." She plopped into one of the guest chairs. The extra chairs needed to go before people made a habit of using them.

"Should you be here?" Maribel wanted privacy and, so far, this had not been an ideal location. She was in a repurposed storage closet, not the welcome center at Graceland.

"Where else should I be?" The girl scrutinized the box on Maribel's desk, clearly unaware of the code saying one should at least pretend not to be snooping when one got caught.

With precision—some might say anal-retentiveness, although she hated that term—Maribel set the items she carried on top of the file cabinet, taking her time. From the corner of her eye, she watched as the girl slouched in the chair, chewing on the edges of her fingertips. What was she supposed to do about this?

Maribel came around the desk to face the girl, and stood, one hand resting on the desktop, the other on her hip, trying her best to look authoritative. "I didn't think new campers were due yet."

"Yeah, well ... when you never leave that schedule doesn't really apply." The girl leaned back in the chair and drew one knee up, hugging it against her chest.

"Oh, an all-summer camper," Maribel said. "Been there, done that—"

"—got the t-shirt," they said in unison.

She settled into her chair, unable to deny the reflection of her former self she recognized sitting across from her.

"So, your parents liked to get rid of you every summer too, huh?" The girl rested her chin on her knee, studying Maribel.

Maribel shrugged. "A couple of times. It sort of stank, except being at home wasn't that great either." Understatement. Ironic that as a child she felt invisible at home and hated it. Now as an adult she pursued it.

41

She watched the girl's reaction, wondering if she struck a chord, and reminding herself not to get attached no matter how much her former self had in common with this girl. With feeling comes attachment, and with attachment comes involvement. And that would not—could not—happen again.

But keeping her heart tucked away didn't mean she didn't have one. There was already one girl in danger.

A slight nod was all she got.

"If it makes you feel better, it doesn't last forever. You do get to grow up and move on."

"Says the one unpacking her stuff at camp." The girl rolled her eyes.

Well, those words struck a chord. She stopped herself before she shot back that this was only temporary. Just long enough to find the next step.

She'd lost her first job with the newspaper after a lengthy lawsuit resulting from assumptions she'd made—and printed. Assumptions based on lies. She quit her next job to avoid being fired when she refused to wear cat ears and a tail—and purr—for the boss's birthday. Nauseous was an understatement for the feelings that boss churned inside her. She walked out those doors and into unemployment, head held high. Walking back in because her car wouldn't start had been an unfortunate and unforeseen development.

Here now, she had a roof above—albeit a plastic one—and three meals a day, along with a small amount of pay that should accumulate enough to get her to her next real job, which she needed to find posthaste.

This was a solid step forward, right? And without financial help from her marionette-loving mother. Not that she would have helped. They hardly spoke.

But the conversation she'd overheard tugged on her conscience.

"I'm Maribel." She introduced herself and reached across the desk.

"Daylee," the girl with washed out blonde hair and a swath of pale freckles across her nose said as she shook Maribel's outstretched hand. Daylee possessed the no-nonsense air of a young girl with too many adult concerns and not enough childlike innocence. Maribel knew that look well, having worn it often

42

enough when she was that age. At twenty-six, she could pass it off as serious determination, instead of a jaded disillusionment with life.

This girl wanted something. It radiated off her like the shimmer of heat waves. Her body moved with a forced indifference, but her eyes were keen to observe. She had the burden of unveiled eyes, no good for keeping secrets, no matter how hard she might try. Questions were clicking around behind those eyes—eyes that probed and tested and measured. She was lonely, yes, but she was seeking more than conversation. Maribel had no idea what that might be.

Maribel had a few questions of her own. Daylee had been here at the same time as the missing girl. She had to know her—and know something had happened.

Fiddling with a pen, Maribel stalled, trying to talk herself out of asking the questions that practically burned in her throat.

Reporters loved their hunches. But if one didn't have the gift of discernment in how far to follow them—and she certainly didn't—people could get hurt.

Leave it alone, Maribel. You heard the sheriff. He's on it. Nothing more for you to do but cause problems.

Still, picking at loose threads was what investigative journalists did.

Her conscience jabbed its bony finger in her mid-section. *But you're not a journalist anymore. And you were just a fraud anyway.*

"Want to get something to drink? Where do they keep the vending machines around here?"

Way to let it go. Maribel reached for her backpack, hoping there was enough change in it not to embarrass herself.

Daylee tilted her head as she considered the offer for a moment, then popped from her chair. "Nah. I'm good. I gotta go call someone."

"You can use my phone." Maribel pointed to the phone on her desk, not ready to let the girl slip away.

The girl rolled her eyes again. She held up her cell phone and waggled it in front of Maribel.

"I thought we didn't get a signal out here?" Conner had told her cell phone service at the camp didn't exist.

Standing in the doorway, the girl smirked. "Guess you gotta want it bad enough."

Maribel opened her mouth to ask where but, before the words were out, Daylee's gaze darted down the hallway to something Maribel couldn't see. The girl's eyes widened with a flicker of apprehension. Her unaffected manner from moments ago became skittish.

"See ya." She disappeared, sweeping out of the office like a vapor.

The sound of jangling keys carried down the hallway. Evan returning to his office, Maribel assumed. Adolescents. Was Evan's arrival what spooked the girl? She pressed fingertips against the center of her forehead. If trouble was coming, no doubt it would find her without her going in search of it.

Was it possible to get a muscle cramp in the center of one's forehead? She rubbed harder, attempting to smooth the skin back in place.

Maribel leaned back in her chair too hard, tilting it too far, and flailed as she wobbled in the unsteady seat. Expelling her frustration in a huff of air from deep within, she made a mental note to find a screwdriver. She had screws to tighten.

It didn't surprise her Daylee was clever enough to find a place where a signal existed, but who she was calling? Not a boy, Maribel hoped. Daylee was too young to know the big bad wolf was real and often disguised as everything a girl thought she could want.

Maribel didn't like how much of herself she saw in Daylee. It gave her too much insight into the girl's future.

CHAPTER EIGHT

Conner returned to the maintenance barn with more going on in his head than usual. He liked things simple. One subject at a time. But that wasn't working this morning. And his visit with Maribel hadn't helped.

For one thing, he found her too distracting to maintain his focus in her presence. That fact weighed him down with guilt. Tracy's death and Leah's safety should be the only things on his mind.

Add to that, this was the first time he'd experienced such an attraction since he'd turned his life around and he wasn't exactly sure what to do with it. Two things he was sure of. Maribel Montgomery wasn't like any female he'd known before, and he desperately wanted to know her.

Maybe he should thank the sheriff for assigning him the duty of towing her car.

He also didn't need to think about Tracy. He was sad for her. He'd believed she was past the drugs that had almost ruined her life. And there would come a time to mourn, but Leah had to be the priority now. Where had she gone and why? And was she even alive?

His anger had nearly gotten the best of him when he found out Sheriff Griger wasn't authorizing a more comprehensive search of the area around the river. Did the sheriff know something he wasn't sharing?

His thoughts flipped back to Maribel. She had avoided contact with the sheriff as much as possible this morning. Truthfully, she'd avoided contact with everyone. Even now when he'd try to engage her in conversation, she'd shut him down as fast as she could. Not exactly the sort of personality he'd expect from a person in marketing and communications.

He scowled. It was possible she was a new complication in the foul affairs intruding on the camp. It was certain she was going to be a complication for his concentration.

CHAPTER NINE

The intercom on her desk intruded Evan's voice into her office. "Miss Montgomery, may I see you in my office please?" He may have phrased it as a question, but she knew he wasn't asking. Maribel shoved the aspirin in her mouth with one hand and rubbed her temple with the other. She coughed the pills down dry, wishing for a soda.

Evan waited by his door. His mouth curved upward in a smile. The rest of his face did not. A man with a perpetually tired—or bored—expression, Evan's demeanor hinted the world was just one hangnail away from being too much.

She'd give him a chance, though. The current circumstances at the camp weren't optimal for making good impressions. And making a good impression on her shouldn't be his priority.

He pointed her to a chair across from his desk and closed the door. Something in the soft whoosh of the closing door made the pain in her head swell.

Maribel's employment contract said she didn't work for Evan, and she was thankful. She was trying to be fair and not make brash assumptions, but something about the camp director irritated her, creating a desire to be out of his company as soon as possible. He watched her as if he knew something. Or even worse, as if he wanted to know more of the wrong sort of things. Perhaps the situation with an MIA camper and the DOA employee warped his demeanor. But the way his voice tightened when the sheriff threatened checking into his background showed more than just current stress level.

He seated himself in what looked to be a rather large and expensive desk chair, genuine leather if she guessed correctly. Leaning back, he rested his ankle on the opposite knee, exposing the white crew socks he wore beneath tan slacks. His fingers ran through a thick mass of hair the color of dead grass, leaving uneven rows across the side of his head, which he then attempted to rake back into place. The grooming went on too long. The room grew smaller with each stubby fingered stroke.

Finally, he stopped dragging his fingers through the lifeless hair.

With elbows resting against the bulge below his chest, fingers steepled, Evan Beck was the poster model for a man stuck in middle management.

"I want to apologize for the way things started off on your first day here. Not a very welcoming start to your new job. In fact, I doubt anyone would blame you if you decided to leave. Most people probably would."

"I suppose so, but I won't." Choices were perks belonging to those who weren't dead broke and desperate for a job.

"Good. I didn't take you for the type. I'm relieved to hear it." His smile still didn't reach his eyes.

"Thank you."

"Well then, I guess you're getting everything in order and ready to go? Is there anything I can help you with? Anything to make you more comfortable?"

"No thanks, I'm good." *Lie.*

A humming sound came through his lips before he opened his mouth to speak. "I have not had the chance to learn much about you," he paused, adding weight to his next words, "or do a background check on you as is customary with new employees. Peg informed me she took care of it and to not worry about it."

The image of Conner throwing his arms wide and telling the sheriff he had nothing to hide this morning flickered in her thoughts. She chose less drama in her response. "You're welcome to check."

"I trust Peg and Mack, but you understand this puts me in an uncomfortable position. These girls are my responsibility and I take that responsibility very seriously. Often, they already have troubled enough backgrounds. We have to be careful in everything we say and do. Take this morning for instance. That shouldn't be discussed where these girls might overhear. You understand what would happen with a bunch of silly teenage girls if they got wind of that?"

Maribel didn't approve of the way he referred to them as silly teenage girls. It hinted at contempt. She thought of his conversation with the sheriff but couldn't recall much concern for the girls then, and none concerning the missing girl. The ache in her shoulders told her they had migrated upwards and she forced them lower, wishing the headache could take a break, at least until this meeting adjourned.

"Is there anything you want to tell me? Anything I need to know?" He lowered his hands, and leaning towards her, tapped fleshy fingertips on the desktop. "I don't enjoy receiving questions I don't have an answer for. I need to be prepared to defend your presence here at the camp—and your innocence—should the need arise."

Motionless, she held his stare. He may have attempted to sound solicitous, but there was nothing friendly in his offer. Maybe her perception of the sheriff's distrust in him caused her guardedness, but Evan inspired watchfulness. She didn't want to cause friction.

Hard to avoid friction with someone whose personality resembles wood bark more than silk. No, not wood bark. Too interesting and not abrasive enough. "Not that I can think of." Another lie.

They had cleared her of wrongdoing. But that didn't mean she hadn't done wrong. There were things she preferred everyone not know.

"Well, no offense. I know we all have things in our past we don't want others to know about or have made known to the public. Understand the sheriff will be checking into everyone's—including your—background thanks to this business of finding a body this morning."

The familiar, bitter taste of shame filled her mouth. She glanced away, unable to hold his stare, focusing instead on the model of a yacht perched in the middle of his bookshelf.

He was right, though. The sheriff would learn of her connection to Alexander's death. That alone would be enough to ignite his suspicions. When they find a person hanging in one's closet, even though the cause of death is ruled a suicide, it leaves a forever dark cloud over one's character. How could she tell the sheriff she would answer his questions all day long concerning what she'd seen this morning, but she did not want to go through the other ever again?

Evan continued to watch her as he thrummed his fingers on the desk, reminding Maribel of the tune to a popular game show, her time running out.

She shifted in the chair but stopped herself before giving him the satisfaction of seeing her lick suddenly Saharan-like lips.

After an uncomfortable moment, he moved on. "Well then, let me get a bit of housekeeping out of the way." He explained the general operations and schedule for the camp, then asked that she not interact with the girls beyond the scope of her job, which he again hinted he knew little of. The details weren't hers to share, though. That much was clear when she accepted the offer.

He told her everything that mattered, except the fact a camper was missing. And that was problematic.

The expression on Daylee's face, an emotion Maribel hadn't yet put a name to, but also couldn't forget, refused to relinquish her attention.

It was obvious Evan wasn't going to tell her more, but why?

She leaned forward when he finished, fisted hand clenched in her lap below the level of the desk, hiding the knuckles she was sure were turning white. "Is there anything else I should be aware of?"

He couldn't keep hiding the truth from her.

Evan looked thoughtful for a second, his gaze drifting to something to the left of where she sat. Maribel waited, expecting him to tell her about the missing girl now. What reason could he have for not telling her something she was bound to find out?

Was he too ashamed to admit it happened in the camp where he was responsible?

Or did he not trust her?

"No, nothing that concerns you. You're dismissed." He leaned back in his chair and steepled his fingers in front of his expressionless face as he watched her.

She stood to leave, and he spoke. "Wait, Maribel."

She paused, thinking he had decided to tell the truth.

"I'm glad to hear you're hanging around."

His remark sent chills down her back, although he couldn't know why his word choice mattered so much.

As for the missing girl, if he'd only told Maribel the truth, she might have let it rest. No matter. She could get answers for herself. She couldn't forget the unspoken need she sensed in Daylee or ignore the impression Evan chose to keep this from her on purpose. Something in his disposition stirred her resentment, awaking the tiny—albeit unarmed—rebel within.

If he didn't want her checking on things, then he shouldn't act like he was hiding something.

And he certainly shouldn't dismiss her.

CHAPTER TEN

Maribel glanced at the lower right corner of her computer screen and jolted upright. She was ten minutes late to meet Reverend Stapleton for lunch. A growl of frustration escaped, and she peered up, glad no one was around to hear.

She raced the computer mouse around on her desk, urging the device to hurry in order to log off. Afraid to take any longer, she shoved a notepad and pen in the top drawer, squared the chair under the desk, and snatched up her backpack. Late was something she never was. Charging blindly out the door, her subconscious registered something out of place, smacking her backwards like an invisible hand, saving her from a head-on collision.

Conner jerked to a stop, avoiding the same collision.

"Whoa, there! I was coming to get you. Didn't figure you for one of those, but as this morning so easily proved, it won't be the first time I've been wrong."

And probably not the last either, mister. "One of those?"

He rested his hands on his hips, smug. "Women who are always late."

"I'm not late. Your clock is wrong." It was his self-righteous air that set her off. What did he know about always? They'd only met a few hours ago.

"And did I hear you growl?"

Sweeping past him, she headed toward the front door, her steps long and quick, determined to distance herself from further conversation. She tried to rationalize her inability to admit she was late.

She was never late. Except this once.

Wait. What did he know about her schedule?

She shoved through the door before he could hold it open for her, although it was clearly his intent. She didn't have a problem with a man holding the door for a woman. In fact, she admired the chivalry. But not from him right now. There were too many other issues warring in her thoughts. She didn't have the head space left to analyze his motives or potential for friendship. And she was still irate from her meeting with Evan.

She stopped, searching around for Reverend Stapleton.

Conner walked past her and headed to the dust covered seventies model Chevy truck parked by the curb. He paused, smirking over his shoulder. "Are you coming?"

"Coming?" *Please, no.*

"Yes. Among other things, I've also been summoned to give you a ride to meet Mack."

She should have known. A heavy breath escaped her as she cut around him again and marched to the idling truck.

She pulled the handle, but the door didn't budge. Tilting her head back to peer up, she found Conner's arm extended above her, his hand pressed against the side of the truck, holding the door closed.

"What are you doing?" She spun to face him, wishing she hadn't when she realized how little space existed between them. Her heart raced up her throat for the second time today. She swallowed it down. The smell of his soap still lingered on his skin.

"Are you some sort of man-hating feminist? We don't get a lot of those around here, but then you're not from around here so enlighten me, and we'll go."

With eyes narrowed, she stared at him like he was speaking a foreign language. "What?"

"Are you a feminist, or do you just not like men being polite?"

She pressed back against the door, feeling the handle dig into her ribs. "I don't have a clue what you're talking about. I'm not a feminist, and I like men just fine." Although, not a blanket statement. There was currently an exception. Her wounds said there should have been many more exceptions. Regrets ran deep.

"Oh ... you like men just fine, do you?" He winked. "That's good to know. Now," he removed his hand from where it held the door shut and took hold of the handle, a knowing smile blooming on his face as Maribel shifted away from physical contact, "allow me to make my momma proud by using the good manners she worked so hard to teach me." He opened the door, waited for her to climb in, then winked again as he closed it.

Maribel jammed her seatbelt in place with a hostile click. She hadn't always been this way. It took a few years and the efforts of several members of the opposite sex to get her to this point. But the last one had been the Armageddon of them all. She couldn't go through that again.

Sam Latham. Dark hair, dark eyes, dark motives. He wasn't a handsome man, but what he lacked in looks he made up for in charm. Maribel had been irresistibly drawn to him from the moment he'd first spoken her name. In the weeks that followed, he'd made her laugh, made her trust, and made her do something stupid with her career, nearly ruining another man's life.

Sam Latham wasn't just charming. He was a master manipulator with a talent for forgery, and a vendetta over a business deal gone bad. Unfortunately, he also wasn't Sam Latham. Whoever he was, he vanished without leaving a single crumb to find him by. It was small consolation that ultimately his plan hadn't succeeded. Chalk her heart up as collateral damage. Not a big loss since it hadn't been in great shape anyway.

But how could a woman of her intelligence and experience have missed the warning signs that should have told her he was a fraud?

The determination to stop giving herself away piece by broken piece was strong, but she also knew her weaknesses. The need to be loved was a wound

55

for which a ready supply of worthless and temporary remedies existed. Men like Conner made attractive band-aids. And few of them minded being disposable. The truth stung her eyes. She hoped someone would prove her wrong one day.

"Thank you," Maribel said as he climbed in, not only to prove she had manners, but could use them too. She didn't plan to throw down the gauntlet of a challenge by playing hard to get.

"You're welcome." The playful lilt in his words said he had already granted forgiveness.

She leaned back, determined to look confident, despite the increasing unease about her upcoming lunch date—and the long ride to town. Although her stomach rumbled for sustenance, she couldn't say she was eager for the appointment. Until now, all her correspondence with the Reverend Mack Stapleton had been through email. A perfect system. Why ruin it?

If he started psychoanalyzing, or worse, evangelizing —well she hoped that didn't happen.

She wasn't oblivious to her awful attitude. It struck her, hard in the center of her chest, unpleasantness had become a defense against people getting too close.

Maybe that was for the best.

Conner slipped on his sunglasses and adjusted the air conditioner, flipping the vent so it aimed in her direction, before pulling out of the parking lot. "Tell me if you need more air or get too cold." He turned his head away, speaking under his breath to add, "As if that were possible."

"Heard that." Irritating one minute, considerate the next. And now back to irritating, Conner Pierce would keep her on her toes.

Besides, the irritating was safer. Considerate scared her.

His smile revealed a line of straight white teeth. From the corner of her eye, Conner looked like a person out for a Sunday drive. A guy with nothing more to worry about than traveling the backroads with his sweetheart. She twisted the silver ball earring in her right ear, then jerked her hand away. She was no one's sweetheart.

Conner slouched against the seat, one hand on the wheel, the other resting on his thigh, the classic image of a country boy at ease. His hands were brown and calloused, attesting to the work he did. She couldn't deny he was attractive.

But a hard edge about him suggested he'd seen rougher days than the life he lived right now. The undertone in his conversation with the sheriff at the river this morning was hard to ignore. There was definitely more to Conner Pierce than just a good ol' country boy.

She peered at the speedometer and noted it read fifteen miles an hour under the posted speed limit.

"I thought you didn't want me to be late. You aren't even doing the speed limit."

His lips twitched. The deep parenthesis of dimples pushed his cheeks up in round mounds of stubbly amusement. He didn't acknowledge her comment, but the truck accelerated.

Maribel caught herself before she tucked a strand of hair behind her ear like a schoolgirl. That ship had sailed—and sank—many poor choices ago.

"Well, what do you think of the camp so far? Other than finding the ... uhmm ... you know," Conner asked.

Aside from her office that used to be a storage room, the blue tarp for a roof on her cabin with a broken lock, a missing girl no one was talking about, and, oh yeah—a dead body in the river? "Not too bad. The coffee is good." Insufficient in quantity, but tolerable in taste.

"You didn't seem impressed earlier." An arched eyebrow called her bluff.

"Would you be more concerned if I had been impressed?" She faced out the window, discouraging conversation.

"Good point. So, what brings you to the Pool of Siloam?" He didn't take the hint. "Searching for healing like the blind man in the Bible? That was a different Pool of Siloam, you know, although ours has been credited with a few miracles as well."

"Just a job." Telling him of the incredibly strong need for food, clothing, and shelter seemed a touch dramatic. "And no, I'm not aware of the story or in search of magical healing." She hoped her clipped tone stopped him from filling her in.

The next few moments were silent, and she hid her smile from him. He must have caught on this time.

"Magical healing isn't the same as miracles. For one thing, magical healings aren't real." Or maybe not.

"Okay then, I'm not in search of a miracle." The words spoken aloud dug into her subconscious. Was that true? Or was a miracle exactly what she wanted?

"So, just a job then. What kind of job? You'd think they would have told the rest of us there was a new person joining the staff, but you've been kinda top secret."

"Public relations. Sort of."

"Interesting. I didn't picture you as the type for public relations, or a girls' camp."

"What does that mean?" Did he not realize she could take that as a compliment?

She squeezed her hand shut, letting the short nails gouge into her palm, punishing herself. The only place that would hire her right now—did she think she was too good for it?

He shouldered her question off.

"No really, what's wrong with me working here?" What she wanted to know was what type he took her for and how he came to such a speedy conclusion about it. "You're working here. What type are you? Wait ... you do work here, right?"

"First of all, I didn't say there was anything wrong with you working here. I'm just not sure I see you as public relations material. Secondly, I'm just a guy who needs a job, same as you. And yes, I do work at the camp—sort of. I really work for Peg on the ranch."

"And what do you do for the camp?"

"Maintenance."

"The picture on the website isn't you."

"That would be Rodgers. He fell off the roof of your cabin trying to put the tarp on and broke his leg. I guess updating the website is your job now. If you want to take some action shots of me working, I suppose I could let you." His dimples danced to the same tune that sparkled in his eyes.

She knew the song well. It was not music to her ears. She'd had a lot of time on the drive here to analyze certain things about her life that were getting her nowhere. Falling for men with ignoble intentions—always thinking this time it would be different—topped the list.

Besides, she'd need the wide-angle lens to capture the ego. The fact that he was unattractively full of himself didn't keep the heat from shooting up her neck. She couldn't see his eyes behind the sunglasses, but the devil was in those dimples.

"I'm pretty busy, actually. And what happened to the roof? It's not going to fall in on top of me, is it?"

"No, it's safe, just leaks a little. Now, I've answered your question, how about you answer mine?"

"Which is?"

"Why you're here? An office in the admin building, on site housing, and no one knows what you do. Summer is half over, and off the record, they aren't taking any bookings for the rest of the year. Odd timing to bring in PR, don't you think?" He leaned toward her, voice lowered. "And between you and me, I don't think Evan's happy to have you here."

The announcement they weren't taking any future bookings was new but lined up with what she'd heard Evan telling the sheriff. What was going to happen to the camp? "My bills don't really take a break because the season is half over. I'm just thankful for the job whatever the reason, not interested in questioning the timing." Her lips pursed. She faced away, hesitating a moment before asking, "Why don't you think Evan likes me?"

"I never said he didn't like you. And it's only a feeling."

"You do a lot of feeling and supposing for a maintenance guy."

A soft, playful laugh rolled out from deep in his chest. "And she's prejudiced too."

"I'm not prejudiced. I didn't mean it like that."

"So, you're just arrogant?"

"No-oo." The fact that it came out in two syllables didn't make it a convincing denial. "I'm sorry I said it."

"Poor ol' country boy maintenance workers have feelings too, and brains, Maribel." He made a face of mock offense as he pressed his free hand against what must be his wounded heart.

"I only meant you seem to be taking more interest in the details of the camp than I would have expected, considering your role here." She paused. "That didn't make it any better did it?"

"Not in the least." His easy-going nature was even more attractive than the dimples, but he refused to be deterred from his interrogation. "I'm thinking by his reaction, Evan isn't the one that hired you, so it must have been Peg. But why? From what I've heard and know of her, she's never been much on advertising."

"Maybe she wanted to catch up with the times, or needed some more marketing, or something." Maribel answered, keeping her eyes anywhere but on him.

"Or something," he said, his voice quiet and contemplative, as though he were plowing through her words in search of a hidden meaning.

"What's that supposed to mean?" Her head snapped in his direction.

"Nothing," he said, but the set of his jaw and the way he didn't smile said it was definitely something.

"I could ask you a few questions as well. Like what's up between you and the sheriff?"

"Oh, just the usual small-town stuff." Conner shifted, straightening a little and placing both hands on the wheel.

Apparently, he wasn't keen on sharing information either.

"How did you know her—the woman in the river?" The question weighed on Maribel until she could no longer hold it in. The sheriff had referred to Tracy as Conner's old girlfriend, but Conner's reaction—more anger than sorrow—said there was more to it than that.

He tapped his fingers on the steering wheel for a moment. "Tracy Morgan and I were ... friends at one time. A very long time ago." He added the last as if he needed to distance himself from the memory.

"I'm sorry. That must've been hard this morning."

"It was, but not for the reasons you think."

His vague comment did little to settle her curiosity. The only thing that kept her from asking more was a fear she didn't want to know. Was there no end to the secrets around here?

"So, what happened to your car?" He changed the subject but landed on one she didn't want to contemplate.

"It caught fire." She didn't need the reminder she was trapped here until the car could be fixed. Mental fatigue drained her desire to think about that or anything else at the moment.

"How?"

"Gee—let me see," she tapped her lips with her forefinger as if trying to loosen an answer. "I'm guessing something got too hot." Did she look like an auto mechanic to him? Lack of sleep, food, and normalcy were taking a toll on her already thin patience.

"No need to get snippy. I was going to offer to take a look at it."

"Did you call me snippy?" Who used that word?

"I'm trying to improve my vocabulary." The expression on his face told her it wasn't the first word that came to mind. "And you kinda are."

Chastised, she chose to appreciate his word choice.

61

An honest assessment of her disposition wouldn't prove him wrong. He wouldn't understand she had a legitimate reason. And he wouldn't understand that everything about him reminded her of the legitimate reason. Well, maybe not everything, but enough. She wasn't going to trust herself with Conner Pierce. But who was she really angry with?

"All right. I'll admit it's possible I haven't been as congenial as I should have been."

"Well, there's an understatement for you. But I believe that's the closest I'm going to get to an apology, so I'll take it. And I'll give you some grace considering how your day started out. Now, how about letting me look at the car?"

Maribel chewed on one corner of her mouth, a habit her mother told her was most unattractive in a lady. Letting him work on her car would not keep him at a distance, no matter how much she wanted it fixed. And telling him she couldn't afford to pay for repairs would be like coughing up a hairball—she supposed, never having coughed one up herself—an uncomfortable experience with an unpleasant ending. "It's not necessary."

"I don't mind. Really. No charge for looking."

"I couldn't ask you to do that." Was she desperate enough to risk giving Casanova any hooks to attach his strings to?

"You didn't ask. I offered. But all right then."

She expected him to sound offended, annoyed, upset. A bruised male ego is hard to hide, and she'd just told him she didn't trust him with her car. But all he sounded was ... nice. Could it be a genuine, no-strings-attached offer?

She crossed her arms, aware of the rise and fall of her chest. "It's a classic. Do you know anything about old cars?"

"My granddad was a mechanic. Wisest man I ever knew. I should've spent more time with him. Maybe I wouldn't have gotten in quite so much trouble. But he did teach me a lot about the old cars. I can check it out when I get it towed, which I'll be doing while you're at lunch."

"Sheriff Griger told me he'd take care of it."

"Yep. He did." Conner shook his head. "He's sending one of the deputies to help me. But he knows I'm not in a position to tell him no. Not that I would, but just so you know, Mack isn't the only one with the power to persuade me."

"So, you had to be persuaded to give me a ride to town." Knowing he hadn't outright volunteered felt better.

A flutter of a smile played over her mouth. Small towns were fertile ground for secrets, most of which were shocking, if not scandalous, when exposed. That Conner had the kind of secrets that could be used against him didn't surprise her. Her curiosity concerning his secrets was short lived, however, as a second thought materialized.

"Wait. You aren't joining us?" He wasn't much—and he might be dangerous—but he was still the most familiar thing in her life right now. She needed something constant, even if not entirely dependable. She'd lowered the definition enough even Conner's presence at lunch qualified.

"No, wasn't invited. And I have a car to tow. Besides, sounds like you and Mack have business to discuss. He said I'd have plenty of time to get the car moved."

The closer they got to town, the less Maribel heard of Conner's conversation. She didn't like the unease beginning to ferment on her insides. Just a job, no different from any other.

Only not. And she needed it.

At least until she had the money to repair her car.

CHAPTER ELEVEN

M aribel realized she was holding her breath as Conner pulled into a spot in front of the Buffalo Nickel Dime Store, where a sign in the window said Everything's a Dollar.

Small Town America in all its seductive simplicity.

A stately two-story limestone building stood across the street, the trim around the doors and windows painted in flashy but fading turquoise with a matching sign across the top that read, "Momma Mae's Café" and writing in the front window proclaiming, "God Bless America," both in vintage Americana font.

He handed her a slip of paper with his cell phone number. "Just text me when you're ready, Miss Daisy."

She shot him a glare before hopping out that said she didn't find his reference amusing. There was no traffic as she crossed the street made of red brick, a Civilian Conservation Corps project that had endured, reminding those who saw it life could be much harder than most people experienced these days. She squeezed the handle of a door latch and a shopkeeper's bell greeted her as the heavy door opened.

The place was almost empty. The lunch crowd had come and gone— although what constituted a crowd around here, she didn't know. A chalkboard sign at the front announced today's special—chicken fried steak. She suspected it was the special every day. Her stomach growled.

Momma Mae's occupied an old building, recycled from its earlier life as something Maribel was sure she would learn about in the pictures lining the walls. She liked when old buildings held onto their original character while surviving in modern economy.

Behold, I am doing a new thing. Aunt Rachel again.

Easier for buildings than for humans. Maribel wasn't sure about her aunt's words but appreciated the feeling her aunt was always with her.

A mismatched collection of old kitchen tables, all sporting plastic squirt bottles of ketchup and napkin holders made of horseshoes, gave the restaurant a homey feel. Overhead, ceiling fans made lethargic circles. As expected, bare brick walls displayed an assortment of black and white photos. The discordance of it all beckoned to something nostalgic within her, but she could never enter into that kind of chaos. Methodical order was the only thing holding her sanity together.

She tugged on the hem of her shirt while her eyes adjusted to the dim lighting. A booth in the far corner invited her, a place where she could enjoy her chicken fried steak alone. But alone wasn't on the menu today.

A couple of old cowhands, faded jeans and tan work shirts covered in several layers of dust, sat at the counter, hunkered over the remains of their dinners, and swabbing thick pieces of Texas toast through the last of their gravy. There was no hurry in them.

Momma Mae's Café—a place where time stood still.

A lone gentleman sat at a table near the back. The shiny silver laptop in front of him looked out of place here. The sleeves of his crisp black shirt were rolled up. His shirt hung untucked from his faded, definitely-not-Wrangler jeans. His salt and pepper hair, groomed but a tad long for a country preacher, rested against the collar of his shirt. The computer wasn't the only thing looking out of place here.

"Reverend Stapleton?" Maribel hesitated. Whatever he was doing had his full attention, and he hadn't noticed her.

"Yes! Miss Montgomery, I assume." He jumped up, gave her hand an enthusiastic shake, and held a chair for her, easing her back to the table as she sat. "And please, call me Mack."

"I'm sorry I'm late." She took pride in her punctuality and considered tardiness an unredeemable character flaw.

But the slow internet connection and unsuccessful search for information on the missing girl distracted her. And for nothing. Without access to the camp database, and with only a first name to go on, she had nothing to work with. Figuring out how to ask around without getting on the wrong side of Evan was a plan she needed to cultivate.

Peg hired her, through Mack, and dictated her job description, but she suspected Evan, as the facility director, could make her life miserable and her employment status tenuous. It was a boat she wasn't willing to rock.

And how would it look to find a dead body and start asking questions about a missing girl all before lunch on her first day?

"No problem at all." He motioned toward the open laptop. "I'm going over some thoughts for next week's sermon. I like to come here to bounce ideas off Cindy, although she seems to have disappeared. Maybe not the best idea to get ahead of myself, since I haven't given this week's yet, but when the Spirit moves, right?"

Her lips thinned, stretching across her face like a rubber band. She hoped it passed for a smile. The Holy Spirit visited her aunt, and now it seemed Mack too. But she'd never received a visit. She was fine with that, wasn't she?

"I see my substitute got you here safe and sound. No doubt you found his company more enjoyable anyway." He grinned and pulled the plastic covered menus from their place, handing one to Maribel. "Let's order."

As if on cue, a waitress with spikey brown hair and blond highlights popped through the kitchen door and approached their table, reaching behind her to tie on a black waist apron as she walked.

67

"Hey, Mack. Just got back from running some food over to the sheriff's office. He thought he'd get back to fishing this evening, but something must have come up because he is in a mood now. You just don't mess with that man's fishing time. How's Peg doing?"

"Well, I had to make my own decisions on some sermon material so if anyone complains, I'm sending them to you. Glad you're taking care of Rock, though. He needs someone to do that." Mack sighed. "As for Peg, the news this morning hit her pretty hard. She believed Tracy was going to come out all right this time. She is more committed now than ever to complete her ... uh, project."

"Peg ... always seeing more in people than they see in themselves and always more concerned about others than herself. How'd her last round of chemo go?"

"Not good." Mack let the statement hang between them for a moment. "I don't think we'll talk her into another one, but she's got a great deal of peace about it. She always has."

"Bless her heart. I think everyone's about figured it out. She still trying to keep it a secret?"

"I'm pretty sure everyone knows. But you know Peg, she can't stand a fuss."

The woman peered around and lowered her voice. "More like she don't want any more aggravation." She swiveled to face Maribel, shifting conversational gears so fast Maribel almost had whiplash. "Hi! My name's Cindy."

"I'm Mar—"

"Oh, I know who you are, hon." Her French-tipped fingers waved Maribel's introduction aside. "Mack's been telling me all about you. We're glad to have ya here. You met Peg yet?"

Maribel shook her head.

"I love that woman to pieces, and you will too." She pulled her notepad from her back pocket. "Now, what'll it be?"

Cindy's 'and you will too' hit Maribel more like an order than an encouragement. She avoided eye contact as she placed her order—chicken fried steak with fries instead of mashed potatoes, and extra gravy. Yes, today was an extra gravy day. Closing the menu, she placed it back in the slot with Mack's, tapping the edges so they lined up square and even together. Order and control eliminated chaos. Order and control took away the anxiety-laden sleepless nights. Order and control equaled safe right?

CHAPTER TWELVE

W hen Cindy left, Mack leaned back in his chair and smiled, warm like the lights of home on a dreary winter night. His ease drifted over to Maribel, loosening the tension that squeezed her together. Her aunt was the only other person capable of having that effect on her.

The dead woman in the river and the conversation Maribel overheard between Evan and the sheriff had thrown her. But in the easy-going atmosphere of the café, she could believe those things belonged in someone else's story.

Cindy returned with a Dr. Pepper fizzing in a red plastic glass so large Maribel needed both hands to hold it. She tore the end of the paper wrapper covering her straw, dropping her straw in the glass. She folded the wrapper into a small, symmetrical square and laid it next to the napkin holder, aware that Mack watched her as she did, but unable to stop herself.

"What do you think of Turnaround?" he said.

"I haven't really had the chance to explore much. It was dark when I came through last night and since my car is ..."

"Oh, yeah, I guess that would be a problem. Well, it's a pretty simple place to live. More cows and horses than people. And more chickens and stray cats than cows and horses. Most folks are from families that have been here for generations. It takes a bit to learn your way around the local family trees, so you have to be careful who you talk about." He winked as if they were conspiring to graffiti the local water tower.

71

Maribel didn't tell him she wouldn't be here long enough to need to know how to swim in the local gene pool.

She surveyed the pictures on the wall. "Looks like a place with a lot of history."

"All the way back to the days of the Republic of Texas. We even have a legend of some buried Spanish treasure located somewhere in the county. Of course, in Texas who doesn't?" He scanned the walls. "There's a picture of Peg's great-great-great-grandfather and his brother here somewhere. He was the town's first sheriff, and ... his brother was the town's first outlaw. Are you interested in history?"

"One of my favorite subjects in school. I enjoy it when I have time." Who was she kidding? Time was almost all she had for a few weeks, and she'd been so self-absorbed in her problems she hadn't given anything else a second thought. It occurred to her in this moment that she wasted an indecent amount of time for what? Self-pity.

"You should meet a lady who just moved in. Said she's here for the quiet so she can finish writing a book. Some sort of historical something I'm ashamed to say I can't remember at the moment."

"I'll do that. Might be nice to make friends with another newcomer as well."

Mack laughed. "That's understandable. How's your Aunt Rachel?" he asked. "When Peg asked me to contact you about a job, I couldn't believe I actually knew your aunt from a mission trip we took to Guatemala a few years back. Small world—or big God."

"She's doing well. She travels more and more every year doing mission work." Maribel frowned. "But I thought you found me through my aunt?"

Maribel tried to recall the exact wording of the email she had received. It had given her the clear impression Mack had found out she was available through her aunt. How did Peg come to know beforehand?

"No. Peg contacted me about what she wanted to do and said Becca found your listing through a job search site. She believed you were the one. Peg has pretty strong feelings about those sorts of things sometimes. She's usually right."

He slid his glass to the side, making room for the platter of salad Cindy brought. "Although I'm certain this is far below your capabilities."

Maribel shifted in her seat, uncomfortable with the thoughts bumping around in her head. Hunger, exhaustion, paranoia—her recall of the details brought confusion, not clarity.

The steamy aroma of her favorite southern comfort food took over as Cindy deposited the heaping plate in front of her. Maribel dumped the extra gravy onto the already smothered steak until it was well hidden beneath the excess of creamy sauce. If only she could do the same with the details of her life.

Mack poured a small amount of oil and vinegar on his salad, then added a generous sprinkle of pepper. He glanced around, searching the cafe, then gave the salt shaker a generous joggle over his leafy greens. "Let's pray."

Maribel lowered a French fry back to her plate.

Her stomach growled again in perfect timing with his "Amen."

Mack's gaze flickered in her direction. "Your aunt mentioned a little trouble with one of your past jobs. I got the impression she's worried about how you're handling it."

The moment she'd been dreading. Maribel swirled her French fry in the puddle of ketchup she squirted onto her plate, careful not to let it intermingle with the gravy. She believed in equality of condiments, but ketchup and cream gravy had no business running together. Kind of like dinner and emotions.

Not something she wanted to think about. And certainly not something she wanted to talk about. She was not the victim, but she knew all too well if she shared the story, everyone who heard would be eager to treat her as if she were. She didn't deserve their sympathy, their expression of comfort, their attempts to convince her it wasn't her fault. There was a real victim who deserved those things. "I'm good. Aunt Rachel worries too much."

"Sometimes it helps to talk, especially after the rough start you had this morning." His gaze settled softly on her and she lowered her eyes to the plate where her fork pushed the food in random circles.

If she said anything at all, the entire story would come out in one ugly gushing tidal wave, and she wasn't ready for that.

When she didn't respond, he added, "Well, I'm not going to push you, but if you ever want to talk, I'm a pretty good listener. In fact, if you ask around, a lot of folks will tell you I'm a much better listener than preacher. I hope you'll catch a sermon sometime, and you can decide for yourself." His good nature and easy manner flowed over the conversation like the gravy on her plate, abundant and warm. Try as she might, she couldn't find a way to take offense at his offer.

How much had her aunt told him, though? Did he know how small a part of her life God occupied—when she even acknowledged Him at all?

Mack took a bite of salad, keeping any further thoughts to himself, leaving Maribel to wonder if this entire thing was arranged by her aunt to draw her back to church.

"About the job?" No harm in getting that discussion started the sooner the—well, maybe not so bad.

He chuckled, a low amused sound, as he nudged pieces of lettuce around with his fork. "Yes. I apologize for making the job sound a little secretive by not telling you everything right at first. Peg's wishes. I hope you'll forgive us. That's one of the reasons I wanted to meet with you as soon as I could." He set his fork down, pushed back from the table, and clasped his hands in his lap. "Mrs. Moreland—Peg—is a very intelligent, fascinating, sweet lady. But a bit eccentric at times." His eyes bounced around, observing nothing, and giving the impression he had to search for the words he wanted.

Maribel crossed her ankles, drawing them up under her chair.

"Maybe eccentric's not the right word. Let me just tell you she is a fifth generation Texan, and every one of those generations has been lived out right here."

Maribel may not have as many Texas generations behind her name, but it only took one to understand the character of those who did. A character she admired and respected. She wasn't naïve, though. Mack's statement let her know this job would take humility, finesse, and a sturdy backbone.

He seemed to be considering his next words while he held her gaze. She knew the look from years of honing her interview skills. He was weighing how much he trusted her, how much he wanted to risk telling her. She laid her fork aside and rested her hands in her lap, trying to let the mirroring technique build his trust. Holding his stare, she attempted to look trustworthy, afraid she more resembled a puppy waiting for a treat. She was out of practice—or confidence.

He paused, giving her the impression he was protecting something. Or someone.

Cindy walked up with a pitcher of Dr. Pepper, interrupting the moment as she refilled Maribel's glass. She narrowed her eyes and glared at Mack. "You didn't put salt on that salad, did you?"

Mack tried to look innocent, but Cindy didn't buy it.

"I can tell you moved the salt shaker. You're supposed to be watching your sodium intake."

"I did watch—right out of the shaker and onto the salad. Salt is biblical."

"Yeah, well it says to be the salt, not to eat the salt. Did he tell you he had a heart attack last month?" Cindy put her hand on her hip and spoke to Maribel.

"No."

"I go back for a checkup in a few days, and I am confident the doctor will tell me my heart is doing perfectly fine. Should I get him to write you a note too?"

The front door opened, and the new customer caught Cindy's eye. Maribel glanced over to see a tall, thin woman heading to the cash register. The same woman she'd seen at the river this morning hovering near Evan.

Cindy rolled her eyes at Mack as she spun and headed to the kitchen.

"Afternoon, Ava. We were just talking about you." Mack greeted the woman who now stood in front of the cash register, arms crossed.

Ava's eyes flashed with surprise before expressing wariness. "I can't imagine what about."

"We were just discussing an interest in local history and I was telling Maribel about your book. I'm afraid I did a poor job though."

Ava waved a coy, dismissive hand in his direction. "I find it's bad luck if I reveal too much of the details too soon." She ran her tongue over glossed lips.

"Terrible news this morning. I hope this isn't too hard on Peg." One eyebrow flicked up a fraction.

"Oh, she's a strong woman. Besides that, she knows where to go when she needs backup." He glanced toward the ceiling, but Maribel knew he saw beyond. "How about you? Writing that book got you eating a late lunch today?"

"It's not for me. Thanks to all this drama, Rock is back in his office on his day off, so I thought I'd take him something to eat. Goodness knows when he'll ever take a break for himself."

Drama wasn't the word Maribel would have chosen to describe the discovery of a dead woman or the disappearance of a teenage girl. She took in the details of Ava's appearance: blonde highlights, manicured fingers, a too-even-to-be-natural tan, and wrinkles around her neck that said the absence of them on her face might not be completely honest. And yet all the unnatural embellishments to her appearance didn't displace the bitter edge in the angles of her smile. It would be easy to label the woman, but Maribel didn't. She had too many of her own shortcomings to cast stones right now.

"Well that's very good of you, Ava. Tell Sheriff Griger to give me a call if there's anything I can do to help."

Cindy set a brown paper to-go bag and a large Styrofoam cup on the counter and punched the order into the cash register. "I wish I'd known who this was for when you called it in. I could have saved you the trouble, seein' as I just took him his dinner. Oh, well, I guess he can save yours for later. Or share it with a deputy. You didn't order any, but when you said it was for him, I put some extra Ranch dressing in there to dip his fries in. He likes 'em that way, but you probably don't know that."

Maribel couldn't tell if Ava heard anything Cindy said as she handed the waitress her credit card. Instead, the woman's eyes kept making furtive hops in Maribel's direction and then away again.

"Where are my manners? I didn't introduce you to Maribel yet, did I?" Mack realized his omission and hopped out of his chair.

Ava smiled in a way that made Maribel think it might be painful and came toward them, extending her hand enthusiastically. Or should Maribel say, aggressively? "I'm Ava Hardin. I saw you this morning at the river. So, you're the one who discovered the dead body?"

No surprise the hand felt cold. "Pleased to meet you. And unfortunately, yes, I am."

"That must have been quite a shock. I'm curious, did you see her from the bridge?"

Maribel shook her head, then shifted her focus to the paper placemat beneath her plate, hopeful Ava had no more questions on that subject.

"Oh, I'm sorry if I upset you. I guess you never forget the first dead person you see. Was she your first?"

The questions people asked no longer surprised Maribel. "Uh ... no."

"Well, my goodness. You must lead a much more interesting life than I do. Evan said he thought she might have been hit on the head. What do you think? Did you see anything that made you think she might have been—you know—a victim of something criminal?"

Ava stared, unblinking. Maribel shifted in her chair. If this woman had ever had to stare at the body of a dead person, she'd have enough empathy and respect not to ask for the details of an image no one ever wants to remember. Especially over lunch. Were all writers this curiously insensitive?

Awareness finally came to Ava. "Oh, no. I'm so sorry. You're trying to get on with your lives—after all, you still have one—and I'm just going on about dead bodies. Life is for the living, right? But it's so hard to enjoy life when you have to be reminded of the suffering of others, don't you agree?"

Her odd speech rattled Maribel's nerves. Something about the woman felt familiar. Maribel shook it off. Probably just her brain stereotyping the woman based on her appearance and Maribel's experiences. Relief came in the form of Cindy's arrival.

The waitress shoved the bag containing the sheriff's meal into Ava's hands. "Better get this to Sheriff Griger before it gets cold, although he probably won't be hungry since he just ate. And remind him to be taking his calcium pills before he breaks a bone, and his fish oil so he don't wind up like Mack with a bad heart."

"Yes, I should get this on over to Rock. Maybe we'll run into each other again soon, Maribel." Ava walked away as if she carried an organ donation and not a paper bag filled with a greasy hamburger and soggy fries.

"That woman." Cindy snapped a kitchen towel attached to her apron, making it pop in the air as the door closed behind Ava. "And Rock Griger ought to know better than to be taken in by a flouncy little tart half his age."

"Now, Cindy, she's new here—and perhaps a little different. She's a writer after all. But try to keep an open mind. God bless the good folks of Turnaround, but we aren't the easiest bunch of people to get used to." Mack reseated himself and started to eat another bite of his salad, but added, "And I'm really not sure I'd say she was half his age."

"Mm-hmm. Making a fuss about taking the sheriff his lunch. Well, did you know she bought Evan a desk chair? Berg delivered it himself and had to put it together. He came in for breakfast the next day and told me all about it. Real leather—from Italy. Like we don't have enough cows covered in leather right here. Seriously—what's wrong with good ol' Texas leather? And what kind of woman gives a man a desk chair? And one made of real leather from Italy at that. Now she's over here taking the sheriff food. I don't like … it."

Maribel guessed it was Cindy's Christian roots stopping her just before saying *her*.

Mack opened his mouth to reply, then closed it when Cindy continued.

"I do feel sorry for the sheriff though. I tell you, this missing girl case has got him in a stew and now he's got Tracy's death to deal with too. He's going to work himself to death trying to take care of you people." She glanced at Mack's bemused face. "What?"

Mack promptly composed himself. "Nothing. I was just going to say I'm also not sure you should be telling people your preacher has a bad heart."

"You know what I mean." She socked her fists down on her hips.

A bell dinged from the kitchen and Cindy steamed back through the swinging double doors.

"Missing girl case?" Maribel wasted no time in asking.

Mack gave her a funny look. "You don't know? I'm surprised Evan didn't tell you." He rubbed his chin, his hand against the slight growth of bristles making a soft scratching sound.

"A girl—one of the campers—disappeared from the camp sometime last Thursday. The sheriff's got all the bases covered there. I have faith she'll show up soon." His level of emotion fell short of what she anticipated. Equally puzzling was the swift change of subject that followed. "I also guess you picked up on the fact that Peg has cancer?"

She nodded.

Sadness pulled down on Mack's face, aging him. "It's the world we live in, diseased and broken and an ugly mess. Knowing that doesn't take the pain away. But ... 'I would have lost heart, unless I had believed that I would see the goodness of the Lord in the land of the living.' That verse carries me through—always. It wasn't easy, but I have learned to see—to really look for—the goodness of Lord all around me."

Maribel lowered her eyes. Life wasn't fair, and it certainly wasn't always good. She thought of a boy who didn't live long enough to even think about getting cancer. She swallowed the bitter twang that always crept up her throat at his memory. Her stupidity for trusting the man she thought would be "The One," her irresponsibility for writing the newspaper article—her first and last exposé—without properly vetting all the facts. Her shame the boy received what she deserved. The fact he did it to himself gave her no comfort. Her carelessness set the ball in motion, but she bounced free. Where was the goodness of the Lord in that?

No longer hungry, Maribel stared at the half-eaten steak on her plate and the pile of fries growing limp as they cooled. She reached for the soda to rinse the ugly taste from her mouth but set it back without drinking. She didn't deserve the relief.

But what if the ball had already been in motion?

Mack inhaled and let out a long breath, as if purging himself of pain.

"Peg's prognosis isn't good. I'm afraid she won't be with us much longer. But she won't stand for pity. Leave it to Peg to remind us all the pot has no right to ask the potter why he made it that way."

Mack opened up and relaxed as he went on to talk about Peg. She'd had a baby out of wedlock but had never married. His voice tightened, and he stumbled over words that came a little faster as he told Maribel how she lost her only child when he was killed by a drunk driver.

"Peg loves with her whole heart, but in this small town her family helped found, there are some false beliefs and grudges that have gone on for generations. Peg doesn't trust blindly." He leaned forward, hands folded on the table in front of him. "Peg specifically wanted an outsider to do this job, although I wasn't confident we could find one to come here. You, Maribel, were the answer to our prayers."

Maribel wanted to laugh at his misguided comment, but the earnestness in his expression stifled the impulse. Still, if God was as good as everyone said He was, there was no way He'd make her an answer to anyone's prayer.

"Peg will fill you in on the details, but for the most part your job is just to organize and record the Moreland family history, every detail—without drawing unnecessary attention to the project. Surprisingly, no one has ever set out to do that before. But then, the Morelands have always been a private people."

She bit her lip. Hadn't she already failed at the low-profile thing? Discovering a dead body drew more attention than a pig in a tutu walking through the front door.

"She is the last of the Moreland family. Every bit of their history and so much of the history of this county will die with her. I'm glad Becca was able to talk her into doing this."

Becca was the receptionist at the camp and, from what Maribel had seen so far, the keeper of all information worth knowing and a great deal that wasn't.

Mack cleared his throat. "There are some things you'll discover that, well let's say, need to stay within the family a little longer. Peg will tell you what you need to know there. I want to ask you to be … careful. For Peg's safety and for yours, let's keep this quiet."

Sorrow clouded his eyes by the time he finished. Mack wasn't only working for the woman. He was protecting her, and if Maribel read the signs right, he was doing it out of a deep affection. But protecting her from what?

"Sounds like I'm supposed to be digging up a family treasure." She tried to elevate the mood, then recoiled at the unnatural sound of her voice.

Mack sighed. "More like keeping it buried."

CHAPTER THIRTEEN

A dead woman, a missing girl, and a family secret. All connected by way of the Pool of Siloam Camp. Maribel's need-to-know nature throbbed with concern—and a no small measure of alarm.

She squinted as she stepped from the ease of the café into the furnace of midday, a hermit crab leaving the safety of its shell. The heat from the sun blasted her, but the questions generated over lunch added their own brand of fuel to the proverbial fire. Could there be a secret in the Moreland family history so dangerous it called for a warning?

Conner pulled his truck to a stop by the curb in front of her. She hesitated, not wanting a repeat of their earlier encounter. Only so much conflict could be tolerated at this temperature after the meal she'd eaten.

He came around to open the passenger door.

Silence settled in the cab as they drove out of town, Conner's mood reflecting her own, quiet and introspective. He didn't ask any of the questions she expected, no nosy inquiries about why she met with Mack or what they discussed. In fact, his pensive demeanor had her wanting to ask the questions.

Conner was probably a nice guy, maybe even the real deal. But she wasn't willing to trust her gut feeling when it came to men, especially ones pretending to be nice guys. She wasn't convinced of their existence any more than she believed in unicorns or Sasquatch.

After a few minutes of silence, he handed her a folded piece of paper. "I hope you don't mind. I towed your car out to the camp. It was closer and it'll be more convenient for me to work on there. I can borrow any extra tools if I need them."

She took the paper, brow furrowed. Unfolded, she saw a list of numbers—dollar amounts. Surprisingly small ones.

"By the way, the Falcon is a really nice car. Needs a paint job. I'm thinking something like Candy Apple Red would suit the car—and you. If you ever want to sell it, I'd be interested."

Maribel stared at him, eyes unblinking, trying to process a piece of too-good-to-be-true fortune. And that he thought red suited her. She pressed her lips between her teeth to keep them from giving her away with the flattered grin.

Freedom—or at least the illusion of—might be within the reach of her bank account. She considered his other offer, to buy the car, but she couldn't imagine ever parting with it.

"My dad gave me the car." Her voice resonated low and soft, the memory catching in her throat, as if the recollection of her dad's kindness was a skittish fawn she didn't want to scare off. Her father's death six years ago had left the gaping wound of his abandonment as raw today as it was the day he left them. She held on to the car as if it were the only thing keeping the pain from engulfing her. They'd planned to restore it together.

Actually, she had planned, and he gave in to her incessant pleading. It was as close to being a son as she could get. They'd been down to choosing the paint color. She'd come home that day excited to tell him she'd chosen baby blue, but he was gone. No explanation, no goodbye.

No I'm-sorry-you're-not-enough-to-make-me-stay.

The baby blue paint job never happened. The car, like the relationship, remained unfinished.

Why did she hang on to it when it reminded her of the one person who had the power to give her what she needed most, but never did? Instead of love, she'd gotten a car—and not even all of that.

"All right, then." The subtle flicker of understanding in Conner's eyes, tender and respectful, connected with something inside her, resonating with the hurt she tried to deny. But he saw.

His dimples hopped back into place, changing the atmosphere and steering them away from the melancholy that tried to creep in. "Well, good news, it shouldn't take much to fix it. A mouse built a rather large nest under the hood and got into the wiring. I think most of the fire was from the burning nest. Damage to the car is actually pretty minimal. Those are the repairs I think you'll need, and the prices for the parts. All estimates, of course."

Maribel opened her mouth to protest, but he stopped her.

"Don't worry about the money. I'm not going to charge anything to do it, and you can pay me back for the parts whenever you're ready."

She studied the numbers written on the paper. And free labor? "What's the catch?"

"Catch?"

"Yes. There's always a catch. Why are you doing this?"

"Just trying to be nice and help you out. I've been on the receiving end of someone else's compassion before and I want the chance to do the same for you."

It sounded like charity, which she did not want. But somehow, he also made it sound like she'd be doing him a favor to let him.

"How long do you think it will take?" She tried not to sound skeptical of his motives, or desperate because of hers.

"I'll have to do it in my free time, so it may be a few days. It'll take longer to get the parts shipped in than to do the actual work. So, is that a yes?"

She fidgeted under his scrutiny—a look that dared her to say no.

"All right. But I promise I'll pay you back." She meant it, even though the words always sounded worthless.

"Great." The dimples deepened. He flipped his sunglasses up and leaned toward her, arresting her with blue-sky-in-the-morning eyes—eyes full of warmth and promise. "But don't take this as a hint you need to hurry up and leave us here because I promise that is not the case."

Yep. Promises—often made, rarely kept.

The drive to Peg's house was both taking too long and going too fast. Maribel crossed then uncrossed her legs for the hundredth time. She adjusted the air vent again. Her conversation with Mack perplexed her, but the only danger she really worried about was losing this job if the woman didn't like her. She'd handled tough interviews with peculiar and intimidating people, but the thought of sitting down to talk with Peg Moreland had her stomach swimming around inside her for a reason she couldn't explain.

Maribel didn't believe in premonitions, but an unjustified amount of anxiety was unsettling her insides.

She tapped her fingertips on the armrest, wishing she'd eaten a salad for lunch. Had she become so insecure she expected failure at every corner?

No, she had not. She stopped drumming and crossed her arms.

She knew Conner noticed her odd behavior, but his thoughts stayed in his head where they were best appreciated. A plus one in the nice guy category. He might earn her respect if he kept up this behavior.

Massive oak trees stood guard over the two-story rock house, the quintessential image of an 1800s Texas ranch house. Thick cedar posts lined the porch stretching across the front of the home. A still gleaming state historical marker hung by the front door, declaring the house's past held enough historical significance the future would want to know.

The bright blooms of antique roses dotted the hedge growing along the front.

Beyond the house stood a wooden barn almost as big, with overgrown weeds filling pens made of weathered wood and sagging, rusted wire. Originally red, the paint on the barn had begun to fade and peel.

An antique tractor sat beneath the awning of another barn made of tin. The sheets of once shiny gray metal were now dull under years' worth of oxidation.

Other than the colorful roses bordering the house, the place looked as if it had drifted into a long slumber, resting from decades of activity while wondering when life would resume.

The grand old ranch was passing away.

"Want me to go with you?" Conner asked.

"No." Maribel unbuckled her seatbelt but didn't move.

"Peg's awesome. You really don't have to be nervous."

"I'm not nervous."

His eyebrows went up and stuck mid forehead as he nodded. "I see." He tapped his fingers on the steering wheel and scanned around as if indifferent to the delay. And her dishonesty.

Maribel ignored him. She stared at the house nestled in the shaded embrace of the oaks and the blanket of roses. Her heart squeezed in recognition. She knew this place, and yet she didn't. It was nothing like any dwelling she'd ever occupied. And yet the feeling she'd come home was as real as the jug of sweet tea sitting on the floorboard between her feet.

Ridiculous. She picked up the jug of tea Cindy sent for Peg, shoved the door open with her shoulder, and swung out.

"Want me to wait?" Conner called to her through the door she'd already slammed shut.

"No. I'll walk back." Two miles in the convection oven of a Texas summer afternoon wasn't her ideal stroll, but she had a critical need to be alone with her thoughts.

CHAPTER FOURTEEN

◆

Maribel crossed the yard and stepped onto the porch. A worn trail cut a
path to the front door. She could imagine the musical jingle of spurs
as visitors of the past made their way to this same door.

She knocked, then took in her surroundings while she waited. A wind
chime missing two of its silver tubes hung from one side of the porch and two
colorful hummingbird feeders dangled, one on each side, empty and still.

The door opened, and a petite woman smiled up at her from a once tanned
face now whitewashed by disease. Dressed in faded denim jeans and a long-
sleeved purple work shirt—the kind with pearl snaps instead of buttons—the
woman was a living replica of a past fading from memory. A simple red bandana
covered the top of her head, accentuating the broad smile she wore. And then
there were the house shoes—fuzzy brown puppies wearing Santa hats.

"Welcome." Peg's eyes sparkled as she ushered Maribel inside.

Across the threshold, Maribel stepped back in time.

"I used to love sitting on the porch for visiting. That's how we used to do it,
you know. But now days I can't take the heat. I think it's some of this blamed
medication they have me taking. I take so many pills, it's a wonder I don't rattle
when I walk. Or do I?" She shimmied a little and unexpected laughter erupted
from Maribel.

Peg noticed Maribel studying her slippers. "You like these?"

She wiggled her feet, modeling her footwear. "I can't keep my toes warm
these days, despite the heat that keeps me shut inside." She swung her arms in

the air, dismissing the lack of logic. "Mack gave me these last Christmas. Seein' I'm probably not going to need them this Christmas I figured I might as well wear them now. Don't want them to go to waste."

Everything inside Maribel fell to her ankles and puddled around her feet. It rose up again as conviction for the self-pity she allowed herself to indulge in.

Slightly bowed legs and a measure of arthritis caused Peg to walk with a wide, swinging gait as if her hip joints weren't exactly where they should be. She was a short woman, shorter than Maribel even, and squarely built. Her fingers, resting at odd crooked angles, spoke of the arthritis and years of hard work. It wasn't difficult to imagine the woman in her younger days working alongside the men, keeping up with some and outdoing most.

The house itself smelled of a home inhabited by a life in its final days—decades worth of lemon scented furniture polish and bacon grease, intermingling with the odd scent of a human body being manipulated by copious quantities of medications. Maribel knew from experience the smell of a house revealed a lot about the life within it. She grew up in a house that smelled of bourbon and Coke chasing Chanel No. 5 perfume out the door.

She remembered the jug in her hand. "This is for you, from Cindy."

"Oh, bless her heart. She takes care of me." Peg leaned towards Maribel and whispered even though they were the only ones around. "She adds extra sugar for me."

Peg eased herself into a worn leather recliner.

"Would you like a glass of iced tea? You'll have to be a sweetheart and get it yourself. And if you don't mind, I'll take one too." She winked, her mischievous face beaming.

Maribel laughed again, any remaining anxiety vanished.

"Help yourself to some pie while you're in there."

A freshly baked pecan pie presided atop a glass stand on the kitchen counter, filling the kitchen with a caramelly sweet aroma. The rest of the kitchen stood in disarray. For a woman who lived alone, she dirtied an abundance of dishes.

The first cabinet Maribel opened contained two gaping boxes of Little Debbie's snack cakes, a half-eaten bag of Spicy Nacho Doritos, a jar of peanut butter, and some Pop-Tarts. And she thought her diet was bad. This woman ate like a teenager.

She opened another door to find shelves jammed with every spice and seasoning she could imagine. The labels indicated many of them were far past their expiration dates. Another opened door revealed neat rows of glass mason jars filled with a variety of dried beans and rice. Better. But the empty pizza box in the trash can made her think this might not be the go-to cabinet.

She located two clean glasses, filled them with ice and tea as thick as syrup, and carried them to Peg. The woman waited patiently, hands clasped loosely in her lap, a level of inactivity that didn't look natural for her.

Thanking her, Peg took the glass with both hands. "That pie is the first thing I've cooked in a while. But someone special asked, and I couldn't say no. I've always been a sucker for blue eyes and dimples. I don't want him to know I was too tired afterwards to clean the kitchen. Besides, those dirty dishes won't go anywhere before I get back to them."

Blue eyes and dimples? Maribel frowned at Conner's selfishness and insensitivity—asking Peg to bake for him when she wasn't well.

"Now my great grandmother used to cook huge meals for all the ranch hands—we used to have a lot of men working for us—and she kept the cleanest kitchen I ever saw. I did not inherit that quality from her." Peg laughed.

"Don't need to do much cooking nowadays. My appetite isn't what it used to be, and folks are always bringing me too much food, pretending they have extra and want to share. Like everyone in this town suddenly lost their appetite." She took a drink before setting it on the stack of TV Guides and crossword puzzles resting on the table by her chair. "I don't want to rob them of the blessing, so I just play along."

Peg gazed down, as if forcing her thoughts to trace the curves of the cowhide rug covering the center of the floor.

Maribel sipped her tea and waited, using the moment of quiet to observe the room.

The furnishings of the house had no style or theme. Just an odd assortment of things accumulated over many lives. It was nothing like the houses she'd lived in growing up where everything matched to perfection for exactly two years before being replaced. Yet the feeling of home swept over her again.

It took little effort to imagine wrapping up in a thick quilt and falling asleep on the sofa, dreaming deep peaceful dreams. Then, waking up much later, slack bodied and groggy, unwilling to move while the aroma of supper cooking—fried chicken and vegetables from the garden simmering with salt pork and fresh loaves of yeasty bread browning in the oven—wafted over her. The low hum of murmured voices as family gathered together at the end of the day lent a peace the hurry of early day didn't have. It felt safe.

But so had the camp just a few hours earlier.

Was that what Peg was thinking about now? Her home once filled with love, with peace. A safe place where the outside world couldn't enter.

"I've been praying for you ever since Mack told me you agreed to come. But more so after this morning. I'm sorry you had to be a part of that. Even sorrier for Tracy. I try to live without regrets, but it's not easy when you think someone might have missed out on something because you didn't act in time."

Maribel squeezed her hands around the glass she held. That was a sentiment she recognized all too well.

"Well, we have business to tend to, don't we?" Peg sat up, shoulders and spine straightening. "Mack's worried I'm not ready yet. He thought I should reschedule, but there isn't much room for rescheduling in my calendar." Peg chuckled. "And I know what I need to do. What did you think of our preacher?"

"He's very nice. I enjoyed our lunch." Part of it anyway. Mack had an unexpected effect on her, and she needed more time to figure out whatever it was stirring around inside her. "You have a beautiful place."

"I was born in this house, and my daddy before me, and his before him. I don't guess too many people do that anymore." Pride resonated in Peg's voice, eliminating physical traces of her illness if only for a moment.

How would it feel to have that strong a connection to something, roots running that deep? A simpler, purer life perhaps. A life without regrets.

That option wasn't open to Maribel anymore, was it? Good lives were for people who did good things.

"My great, great grandfather built this house in 1894. Lots of memories. Lots of memories for this whole place." Despite the cheer with which Peg spoke, Maribel detected a touch of sadness lingering in her words as though she felt she were betraying her ancestors by not leaving an heir.

Would it be sad to leave a world where one was all alone? The thought jarred her. Wasn't that what she was trying to do? Keep people out of her heart so they couldn't bring her any more pain, or more truthfully, she couldn't bring them any more pain? If she succeeded with this plan, she'd be alone.

"I opened the camp after my son died, and it was beautiful. I'm sorry to say I've let things slip as I've gotten older thanks to this blasted arthritis—and now the other. Mack told you, right?" The expression she wore said she accepted the truth without resentment or self-pity.

Maribel nodded.

"Cancer." She folded her hands. "I've tried to not let on how bad it is. Don't want folks running around like they're in mourning already. Or circling around like vultures hoping for an easy meal of my dead carcass." She shook her head. "Did you know vultures don't wait for newborn calves to die before they start eating them? Peck their eyes out first. Well I don't plan to go down like a newborn calf."

Maribel pressed back in her chair and snapped her startled, gaping mouth closed, thankful Peg didn't notice her reaction to the unexpected—and unpleasant—animal science lesson.

"Mack does what he can to help," Peg continued without pause. "I think he still struggles with what happened. He's always taken responsibility for me." She paused and drew in a few breaths. "It hurts to watch him go through this again, after all he went through with his wife."

She sank back. "I don't want anyone feeling sorry for me. I'm ready to trade this worn out, arthritic, old temple for a new and glorious one."

She gave Maribel an inquisitive look, as if something more interesting popped into her head. "Tell me about yourself. From what I've heard you're a smart young woman. Why are you so desperate for a job you took one you are unarguably overqualified for?" Peg stared at Maribel, no judgment, just curiosity. A straightforward, honest question with no subtext. And an unhidden flicker of humor brightening her eyes.

Maribel squeezed the arms of the chair, shifting her hips against the soft leather cushion. Revealing the real reasons, much less any of her feelings, was not on the agenda. But the genuineness in Peg's open expression caused a bit to slip out before she could stop it. "Just trying to figure out what it is I'm supposed to be doing."

The words—the idea—felt new to Maribel. Something she hadn't before been able to express. Yes, she wanted to know she had a purpose. A place. A reason for existing. But there was something more, something that lived even deeper in her well of longings—and needed to stay there.

Emotions from this morning created a growing pressure that might burst through the wall she tried to maintain, though.

Peg reached over and placed her cold fingers, birdlike bones covered in loose, paper thin skin, on Maribel's knee. The touch of the winter-like hand held the warmth of the sun on a fresh spring day. "One perk of old age is always speaking your mind—hold it against me for the rest of my life if you'd like—but there's a difference in searching for and running from. Dear, I can't help but wonder if running isn't what you're doing here."

Maribel stared at the hand—so frail, yet strong and certain where it rested on her leg. She dared not meet Peg's eyes, but the woman's words shot like an arrow through her heart, making her eyes sting.

"Well, I'm glad you're here." Peg gave her a quick pat and withdrew her hand. A soft laugh rolled out from her lips, but soon turned into a cough, and the cough turned into several minutes of something that sounded like a handful of gravel grinding around in her chest.

Maribel took Peg's glass and refilled it, then brought it and a cool, damp kitchen towel to the woman. She patted the older woman's brow and cheeks with the cloth. When the fit passed, Peg sat for a minute, regaining her breath before she continued. A canister of oxygen sat ignored by her side. "Thank you, dear. I've never been good at accepting help from others. I think God brought me to this point to teach me there is still good to be had in one's vulnerability. Perhaps we'd better get started while I still can."

Peg took a slow drink of tea before applying a generous layer of lip balm. Then she brought her hands down on her legs matter-of-factly, calling the meeting to order.

"Maribel, I will trust you because God tells me I should. The secret is I'm giving this land, camp and all, to the church to become a home—not just a camp—a haven for girls in need." She took another drink, her countenance saying the images in her head were as sweet as the concoction in her glass.

"There's a bunch of narrow minded, self-righteous, judgmental folks that won't like this idea. They think it'll bring something unsavory to Turnaround. Hogwash! Besides, this town already has plenty of unsavory and nobody seems to get too worked up about that. The issue really is nearly everybody in this county has some Moreland blood in them. They know there's a land developer wanting to purchase this ranch and they all think it'll make them rich somehow."

"The prospect of easy money brings out the worst in people." Another truth Maribel knew all too well.

"Mack and I agree, it's best to keep my decision quiet until the paperwork is finished. I have attorneys going through all the deeds dating back to the Land Grant, so we can avoid any surprises. But there are quite a few personal papers they won't bother with. That's where you come in. Becca just thinks you're here to collect the family history. Other than the attorneys, only you and Mack know about the girls' home and the need to have everything recorded correctly."

Her lungs labored to catch a breath causing her chest to struggle up and down.

Maribel scooted to the edge of her seat, ready to offer whatever Peg needed. Unexpected emotions crept in. She didn't want to get attached, but she was learning that compassion is stronger than fear.

"I'm a stubborn, tough ol' bird, some might say. I should have taken care of this a long time ago, but I guess no one ever really believes they're dying. I love this place. It's part of my family, not just a hunk of dirt or a piece of paper with a deed on it. As long as this land has been owned, Morelands have owned it. I don't want to see it torn apart, especially not for greed."

Peg's hand shook as she lifted her glass for another drink. Small beads of perspiration dotted her forehead and above her lip.

Maribel rose and reached for the cloth lying beside Peg's glass, but the woman waved her back to her seat.

"I'm too old and too blasted tired to put up with the nonsense." She rested again. "I just want to spend my last days in whatever peace I can find. Your job is getting our history together. Mack and Becca also want the house made into a museum. Mack says it will help people to see that the past doesn't have to determine the future. It took a little talking, but I've come 'round to the idea."

"I like the idea," Maribel said, meaning it. It appealed to her sense of order, her yearning to safe-guard something good.

"The Morelands weren't perfect people—far from it, but we tried. Same as most folks, I believe."

Her hand trembled as she reached up to swipe away a tear forming in the corner of her eye. "Pardon me, the medication makes me a mite weepy sometimes."

The urge to wrap her arms around the elderly woman tore through Maribel's heart, but she held still. Another moment she didn't wish to shatter by doing the wrong thing.

"Sometimes I've wondered what the difference was. Why our family survived things that tore others apart."

"And have you found the answer?" Maribel leaned forward.

"The Lord is my Rock, the solid rock on which I stand."

Maribel sank back into her chair. She wasn't sure she understood, but Peg's words resonated somewhere inside her making it impossible to dismiss them.

Everything about the woman picked at the stitching holding Maribel's heart together. Eventually she might find a loose thread and Maribel would be unraveled.

"I wish to make this home for girls become a reality before I die. And therein lies the real reason I'm asking you to keep this quiet. Real Estate developers could tie this mess up for years if they can find anything to question my right to do with it as I see fit. I want to get this done before they have a chance."

Her voice now whispering out of a dry throat, Peg reached for her oxygen. With the clear plastic mask pressed to her face, she inhaled and closed her eyes, her body relaxing as she gave it what it craved.

Maribel sat still, unwilling to intrude on the silence. A loss she couldn't define welled up from deep within. Like an anchor tossed into the sea, whizzing the line from the deck to vanish in the dark depths of the unknown, her desire to keep her heart in solitude sliding itself into a bottomless ocean of longing.

Peg wasn't picking at the loose strings of Maribel's heart. She had simply cut her anchor line and tossed it overboard. Instead of being anchored in place, Maribel sensed release.

CHAPTER FIFTEEN

eg's thoughts flowed freely, filling Maribel with knowledge and a sense of purpose. The conversation also brought an undefinable feeling of kinship. An hour later Peg's head began to sink, her speech trailing off. The faint but steady rise and fall of Peg's shoulders comforted Maribel as she watched the woman sleep.

Peg had talked, her speech broken by the occasional need to regain her breath, giving Maribel the details of the Moreland family from beginning to end. The entire spectrum of emotions came forth with the memories.

The weight of Maribel's responsibility rested heavily on her conscience. Yes, she needed to help preserve a valuable family history, but she needed to get it done soon without giving away any of the purpose. A home for girls would be a beautiful legacy, and she was as determined as Peg to see it happen.

Maribel rose and, picking up their glasses, carried them to the kitchen.

She searched in vain for a dishwasher but found only a sink overflowing with dirty dishes.

Emptying the sink, she then filled it with warm water and soap, surveying the pile of dishes beside her. After washing each one, she found a towel, dried them, and replaced them in the cabinets. The simple act of service gave Maribel a sense of completeness.

Another thought occurred to her. She found an old pitcher and measured sugar into it. Adding water, she stirred until the sugar dissolved, then carried the mixture out the back door, careful to avoid knocking over the shotgun leaning against the wall. On the front porch she refilled the hummingbird feeders and returned them to their hooks in view of the windows.

Back in the kitchen she cleaned and dried the pitcher, then wiped down the counters as well.

Peeking in the living room, she found Peg awake, staring out the window where one of the feeders hung.

"Thank you." Peg gazed at Maribel, merriment in her eyes. "The little mooches will be back by dinner time. I do enjoy watching them. I just can't keep up with them anymore. They're going to have to find their sugar water dealer somewhere else soon."

Maribel held up a glass casserole dish. "I wasn't sure where this one went."

"Oh, horseradish, girl! What have you done? You aren't here to be my maid." But Peg's grateful smile told Maribel she'd done a good thing. "And, uh—that thing goes in the linen closet at the end of the hallway. You can put it back in there behind the stack of towels."

Puzzled, Maribel hesitated, thinking Peg would tell her she was kidding, but the woman had gone back to staring out the window. Curiosity propelled Maribel to the linen closet to investigate. Three other casserole dishes sat stacked at the back. She added the fourth and closed the closet door.

A soft rustle, so faint she questioned having heard it, sounded from the room at the end of the hall. Old houses had a life of their own. Or maybe Peg had a cat she had forgotten about.

"Let's leave off for today. I think I'd better get some rest. Plus, it's almost time for *Wheel of Fortune*. Gotta keep my mind sharp." Fatigue weighed her voice into a slow drawl. "Are you planning to walk back? I thought for sure Conner would be here to pick you up."

"He offered but I told him I needed a walk."

Peg asked if Maribel minded taking Conner his pie, and Maribel couldn't say no.

"I'll have Conner bring over the trunk tomorrow. Start there. He'll wonder what we're up to, but let's keep him guessing. Men like a woman full of mystery." The twinkle in Peg's eye glimmered a little less than earlier.

The only problem with that is I don't want to be liked. Maribel nodded.

With the pie in reluctant hands, she headed to the front door and started to close it behind her when Peg spoke again.

"They'll come to take the last of my cows to the sale soon. Some of those gals have spent their whole lives here. I raised 'em myself. First time in nearly two hundred years there won't be any cattle on these hills." She blew out a sharp breath. "Then it'll be just me out here for a little while longer. But can you imagine the sounds of girls laughing and happy, feeling this place is a safe home for them? It's a new beginning."

The expression on Peg's face as she shifted made it impossible for Maribel to look away. "And Maribel, dear, don't lie there letting the vultures—whatever they are—blind you. Stand up and fight."

Maribel left with a plate of pie and a tangle of unexpected emotions, not the least of which was a heavy dose of conviction.

Stand up and fight. Easier said than done when the ground beneath one's feet quaked like anything but terra firma.

The Lord is my Rock. It was a strange mix of Aunt Rachels and Peg's voices that spoke into her thoughts this time. Great, they've joined forces.

She stood on the porch after the door closed behind her, soaking in the peacefulness surrounding the old house at the end of the road. It struck her how literally it had become the end of the road. But there was change coming and this would one day be a place to show teenage girls what safe and loving really was. Maybe it was also the beginning of a new road.

Would it be it a road she could travel?

CHAPTER SIXTEEN

———◆———

Sweat trickled down the low places in ticklish streams, matting Maribel's hair against the back of her neck and making her shirt stick to her body. She lifted her hair and enjoyed the cool relief of dry air brushing against her damp skin. Despite the heat, she felt herself unwinding, stress seeping from her body in the steady flow of perspiration. Soon she'd go for another run, just not anywhere near the river.

A melancholy mood hung over her. It carried the almost paralyzing awareness that something had to change. Both Mack and Peg had spoken things Maribel didn't know she wanted—or needed—to hear. Coupled with Conner's act of unsolicited generosity, the effect threw her off balance. She shoved those things aside to focus on something more tangible—the plight of a missing camper. Did Peg know about the girl? Maribel hoped not, and she hadn't brought it up.

As the tension left, a new determination, mingled with faint traces of a long-forgotten confidence, worked its way through her. For the girl and for Peg, this had to be investigated until there were satisfying answers—and a teenager was safe from harm.

Having stared death in its bloated, waterlogged face this morning, she didn't want to imagine a similar fate for a teenage girl who should be making new friends and happy memories within the safe confines of summer camp.

She didn't believe either Leah's disappearance or whatever happened to Tracy Morgan had anything to do with the work Peg had her doing. Peg and Mack were paranoid about the need for secrecy. Who would object to Peg leaving the property to the church as a home for young girls in need? And even if somebody objected, no one would resort to physical violence—murder—over it. Had Mack meant to imply they would? Or did the prospect of a housing development—a potential financial bonanza for the community—mean there was more to this than Maribel realized?

Surely, a possible murder and a missing girl related to a proposed housing development were too big of an intrigue for this rustic little community.

Conner presented his own sort of mystery as well. Maribel cringed. She didn't know what to do with her feelings about him. She didn't know what her feelings about him even were. They hadn't exactly had a normal day. And for the most part, he'd been nothing but helpful. Well, he might not have a danger sign around his neck, but she couldn't ignore the "proceed with caution" sign that flashed in his eyes.

Whatever he turned out to be, he might at least be able to answer some of her questions.

She headed to the maintenance barn, planning to rid herself of the pie and the chance he'd come foraging for it at her cabin.

The Falcon sat beneath a tree near the barn. She gave it a brief inspection as she passed, unwilling to observe the extent of the damage. With the hood lowered, the mess inside stayed hidden. It worked that way for people too. At least it had for her so far.

The overhead barn door was up, but it was dark inside. She called his name. No answer.

She tugged at her damp shirt and fluttered it to stir the air against her skin as she eyed the stairs that led to his quarters. She huffed up the steps and knocked, then called again. Still no answer. Hesitantly, she put her hand on the knob and turned, not sure she wanted it to open. Locked. Must be nice.

She considered leaving the entire pie for him in the shop below, but the idea of a stray cat—or worse, a rat—enjoying something Peg had worked to make made that option unacceptable. Giving up, she left the barn and headed to her cabin, pie still in hand. She might eat it all herself and tell him she dropped it on the long walk home.

The unexpected opening of her front door made her stumble. She froze as Conner stepped into view. He paused, fiddling with her doorknob, then pulled the door closed and started down the porch steps. Maribel slid over to the wall of the maintenance building, hoping the narrow slice of shadow hid her presence.

As she stood there, he circled the house, prying at each window until he disappeared on the other side.

It was his responsibility to maintain the property. But was it acceptable for him to enter her private space without telling her? She might have had unmentionables lying about, for Pete's sake.

She didn't. They were all folded and stacked in the dresser by color and fabric type. But that didn't lessen the niggling sensation of offense prickling through her veins.

If he decided to poke through her belongings, he'd discover details she didn't want him to know. And ask questions she preferred not to answer. She shouldn't have been so careless in leaving things where they would be easy to find. Maybe her intuition was telling her not to trust him. Or maybe she didn't wish to know he'd found something that made him not trust her. He wouldn't be so nice to her once he knew the truth. The old familiar paranoia rose up, reminding her there was no one to trust.

He reappeared, rounding the far corner of the cabin, walking in her direction. Maribel slipped back into the maintenance barn, hoping he hadn't seen her.

Maribel was mature enough to understand her own jaded emotions contributed more to her distrust than anything he had done so far.

The urge to throw the plate of pie against the wall assailed her thoughts. Maintaining the level of distrust it took to make everyone sound suspicious had become second nature, but it was also exhausting. That wasn't the way she wanted to live.

She also wasn't one prone to impetuous acts of anger and didn't want to clean up the mess a thrown pie would make.

Neatly arranging some tools left on the workbench into a perfect row, she made room to set the pie. In need of looking more purposeful than perturbed, she searched for a screwdriver. A plausible excuse since she did need one.

Even though she anticipated him coming, she jumped when he came through the door.

"I see you made it back. I would have come and got you, ya know." He spoke like a person with a completely clear conscience. He stopped and stared, hands on his hips. "Mind if I ask what you're doing?"

He had the boldness to ask what she was doing?

Why did people think only dogs had hackles? She felt hers rising. *Yes, I do mind.*

"Peg sent you a pie." She pointed to the plate. Her voice sounded tight even to her. "And while I was here, I thought I'd borrow a screwdriver."

"Pecan?" The word practically dripped with saliva. He lifted the foil and devoured the pie with his eyes. "I suppose I should share since you went through the trouble of getting it here without dropping it."

"As a matter of fact, Peg did say you were supposed to share. Want me to leave yours in your room upstairs?"

"We could share some now. I actually have some forks right here." He flipped open a toolbox sitting on top of the workbench and produced a container of plastic forks. The skepticism on her face must have prompted his explanation. "The cafeteria got tired of me losing theirs, so they gave me a package of disposable forks."

"Which you plan to recycle when you're done with, right?" Maribel's eyebrow arched, daring him to deny his obligation to environmental stewardship.

"Of course." He nodded his head and studied her as if she'd just turned purple.

106

"It's too hot to eat pie right now." Maybe it was the heat or maybe it was having her private space invaded, but a growing hostility made the inside of the barn seem even hotter. She fanned herself with her hand, debating how much she even wanted pie. It was less that she wanted pie, but more like she didn't want him to have it all. "Do you have a plate I can borrow?"

"Sure." He tossed the package of forks on the workbench next to the pie and headed to the stairs. Maribel picked up the pie to follow him, and Conner spun to a stop. His hand shot up to block her. "Just ... just wait here. I'll be right back." His tone had more of a not-wanted quality to it than a let-me-save-you-the-trouble feel.

He watched to make sure she complied, adding, "I'm a bachelor. You don't want to see what's up there." He jogged up the stairs, leaving her wondering what he meant by the last statement. Disappointment brushed over her the same horrid way the corpse had touched her this morning. If he didn't want her to see his private space, it was because the truth about who he really was lived there.

Trust no one.

She watched him slip a key from the top of his door frame, returning it to its perch after opening the door. What was the point? His only hope—a really short thief.

The weight of his steps had shaken the wooden staircase, causing a movement in the space underneath. Something swayed in the shadow and caught her attention. A rope dangled in the open void. The memory overtook her before she could look away. Her hand shot to her throat and her chest ached as if every breath she took were filled with evil.

Any thoughts of peace, any hope of new life she experienced today, were ripped away. Nothing could ever take away the past, and with it clinging to her she could never have a future.

The sound of Conner's steps trotting down the stairs pulled her back into the present.

He carried a bottle of water and handed it to her. "You okay? You're white as Evan's crew socks, at least the new ones."

She swallowed before attempting to reply. "I'm fine. Just the heat."

"You should drink that then." He nodded at the bottle of water in her hand.

"Oh, yeah, good idea." She clenched and unclenched her muscles, hoping he couldn't see the tremor as she lifted the bottle to her lips.

Conner was making a pretense of not watching her as he cut into the pie and slid most of it onto his plate, but she wasn't fooled.

The questions she thought she could ask hung in her throat. Even the ones about the missing girl froze and stuck as he handed over the plate with her share of the pie.

Trust no one, not even yourself. The voice whispered in her ear again. Her brow wrinkled. For the first time she was aware the voices were predictably different. It wasn't always Aunt Rachel she heard. Sometimes, like now, it was her father. One always encouraged. One condemned. The realization made her head reel.

Conner cocked his head to the side, eyes narrowing. "Is there something you wanted to say?"

"No. Thanks for the water." She had almost forgotten he was there.

"Ah, then there *was* something you wanted to say."

"What?" Confusion melded itself to her vocal cords, and the word came out in uncertainty. Could he read her mind?

"Obviously, you wanted to say thanks for the water."

The cool water must have restored her equilibrium because she laughed. An awkward laugh, not a bold, confident one. "That's right—thanks for the water. I should probably be going now." Shifting so she only half faced him, she stepped away.

"Aren't you forgetting something?"

She paused, puzzled.

"The screwdriver you were looking for when I got here? What do you need it for, anyway?"

"Yes. I need a screwdriver to fix my desk chair."

"You could ask me to do it. I am officially the maintenance guy until Rodgers gets back." He dragged the word just enough to emphasize he thought it was an obvious solution.

"It's no big deal. I was going to take care of it myself."

"You know, some guys might assume you were just fabricating a reason to hang around and see them. Lucky for you I'm not one of those guys, but looking for a screwdriver is a pretty weak excuse for loitering in my shop." He ran his bottom lip between his teeth and grinned with eyes that flashed like sparklers on the Fourth of July.

"And they'd be wrong." Her statement sounded cold, even to her ears. Judging by how quickly he dropped the dalliance, he heard it too. But she couldn't stop the rest from spilling out. "Contrary to what *they* believe, everything is not all about *them*. What *they* want, think, like, even what *they* hate isn't all there is. There is so much more, but you never see it because you think it's all about you."

She stopped, clamping her mouth shut, the venom in her outburst solidifying the words until they hung like shrapnel between the two of them. How had *they* become *you*?

The thick silence that followed seemed to hold her rant in place, suspended and exposed. It wasn't the summer heat that burned her skin.

She should say something—anything—to ease the tension, but she didn't trust what might come out of her mouth right now.

Conner went to the tool chest. "Phillips or flathead?"

"I don't know."

His stoic expression told her that was the answer he expected but nothing else.

He pulled one of each out and handed them to her.

The drawer made a raspy, grating metallic sound that sent chills down her arms as he shut it back. "Be careful you don't tighten the screws too hard. It could create more problems than you started with."

CHAPTER SEVENTEEN

C onner had delivered the boxes Peg sent while Maribel was at breakfast the next day. Whether he had intended to avoid her or not, she was thankful to not risk another encounter just yet.

Or for the next two days as she sat in the cabin poring over and organizing the papers.

She'd ventured away for one visit to Peg, only to come home with yet another box. Curiosity made her itch to open it, but Peg had insisted she save it for later. It felt like Peg was playing a game with her when she handed Maribel a chain from around her neck with a key dangling from it and told her not to open it until it was time.

Maribel had asked the obvious question. How she would know? She received a less than helpful answer. She just would. Even more puzzling was Peg's suggestion that Maribel keep the box and key someplace safe.

Out of respect for Peg she played along. Respect and the inexplicable belief that Peg would somehow know if Maribel cheated. Since her cabin door didn't lock, she'd hidden the locked box in the one place she judged safe: the trunk of her car.

The lack of physical activity caught up with her, making her restless tonight. She hadn't been able to forget the missing girl, but every time the thought surfaced, she forced her attention back to the documents in front of her. Just get this job done and move on. There was nothing she could do that wasn't already being done.

If only she believed that. She'd made one trip to the office for another unsuccessful search of the internet on her way to dinner last night, concluding the only real source she had was the girl named Daylee. And she couldn't just pop into their midst and ask to speak to the girl.

Her cabin sat about two hundred yards up the hill from the rest of the camp. She liked the vantage point. From the steps of her porch, Maribel saw Conner light the bonfire she'd watched him construct this afternoon. The flames rose in ribbons of red, yellow, and orange. The faint breeze carried the scent of the wood fire toward her, as the wispy gray smoke rose, vanishing into the night sky.

The nocturnal sounds of summer wafted through the dusky evening. A symphony of whippoorwills, frogs, and locusts lifted through the twilight, to be punctuated by the high-pitched laughter of teenage girls enjoying new friendships as the fire drew them together.

The warmth of the day clung to the night, refusing to let go. Maribel drew her hair into a ponytail and slid her bare feet into worn-out tennis shoes. Evan's warning to stay away from the campers still sounded in her head, but he'd driven away promptly at five o'clock.

Fabricating a reason to be there, she took her camera. Peg might enjoy seeing the photos. If Evan caught her that would be her story.

She snapped pictures of the girls posing with new best friends, sweaty, flushed faces with hair pulled back in scraggly ponytails that would make their mothers cringe. These girls hadn't been here when Leah had gone missing. They didn't know.

Safe. These girls believed they were safe. And nothing around Maribel told her otherwise. How did one of them just vanish?

Even amid the carefree spirit and merriment, Maribel knew to watch for the ones hovering in the narrow strip of safety at the farthest edge of the light, just close enough to be out of the dark and the frights that lurked there. Not close enough they'd be expected to take part in the camaraderie and antics of the more exuberant campers. These were the girls who didn't feel they fit in— or didn't want to.

She was familiar that particular piece of real estate.

No surprise the precocious girl from her office was there, her dark eyes darker, looking as if she were somewhere else in spirit.

Maribel crossed over to Daylee and took a seat on the log next to her. She watched the counselors performing a skit at the front of the crowd for a moment before attempting conversation. "I guess you've seen this before, huh?"

"Yep." The girl leaned forward, hands clasped, forearms squeezed between her knees, as if she were folding in on herself. She reminded Maribel of a giant metal clip trying to hold her pieces together. What hidden hurts lay buried in this child? A child ... barely ten years younger than Maribel. Had she looked the same at that age?

"Definitely a low-budget production judging by their acting skills."

"Totally."

"Does it get any better? I may head back and turn in for the night." *Come on Daylee, talk to me.*

Talking to teenagers took a different approach than conversation with adults. She had no experience with teens, but that much she comprehended. Trust was essential, but sometimes harder to come by. Perhaps rightfully so.

Daylee shrugged, then rolled her head to the side just enough to see Maribel. "The next part is kinda interesting."

"And what is the next part?"

One of the counselors ambled into the circle. Her hair tucked into a cowboy hat and a fake mustache stuck beneath her nose, producing a poor attempt at disguising the fact she was a female.

Maribel shot Daylee a you-can't-be-serious look.

The girl gave her an impish grin. "Have you heard the story of the lost treasure?"

Maribel shook her head, although she did recall Mack mentioning a legend about a lost Spanish treasure.

"Then listen. There's supposed to be a whole treasure hidden around here somewhere, and no one's ever found it."

Daylee focused her attention on the fake cowpuncher. Maribel did the same with significantly less intrigue.

The girl's interest surprised her. Maribel didn't see her as the type given to believing far-fetched fairy tales.

She listened closer to the presentation, trying to figure out what captivated the girl. When the fake cowboy—Bud was his name—began telling the tale of the legendary lost treasure, an invisible string tugged even harder at Daylee.

As expected, the tale soon morphed into a ghost story, extracting happily frightened squeals from the girls, causing them to huddle together and hold on to people they just met. Everyone except Daylee. She stared at the fire, once again deep in her own thoughts.

Exhaustion won out and Maribel rose to say goodbye. "I think I'll head back now."

"Do you think ..." Daylee paused, then shook her head.

"Do I think what?" Maribel waited, hopeful this would lead somewhere useful. Instinct told her it was too soon to push the girl for information.

"Do you want an ice cream sandwich? Mr. Beck promised to bring us some tonight." A veil slipped over the girl's face but not before Maribel understood. What Daylee asked and what she wanted to ask were two different things.

Maribel recognized Evan walking toward the group carrying an ice chest, no doubt filled with ice cream sandwiches.

"No, thanks. I'd better go." Maribel hesitated, "But if you ever want to talk about anything, you know where to find me."

She scanned the distance to her cabin. The porch light she'd left on did not shine back at her. Grand time for the bulb to burn out.

Halfway up the hill, she froze. A faint lifting of the hair on the back of her neck came simultaneously with the chill bumps racing down her arms. Someone somewhere was watching.

She glanced back at the bonfire. Had Evan spotted her? But he was still there, engaged in passing out the ice cream with no sign he was aware of her presence. She listened to the night noises for anything out of place. Nothing unusual. And nothing to justify the sensation. Her paranoia had been silent for the past few days, but here it came again.

She inspected her house and its surroundings more closely. Nothing but a burned-out bulb. Right?

She walked on, determined to stomp out the fear, until she reached her porch. Her cabin gave her a measure of security she didn't feel in the open.

Like a schoolyard game of tag, she made it to base. Safe.

Only not.

She opened the door and flipped on the interior light, even though it blinded her to the darkness behind her. She examined the inside from the doorway but saw nothing amiss. After flipping the exterior switch up and down with no results, she checked the filaments in the bulb. Not burned out but somehow loosened. Odd, but these things happened sometimes, right?

Embarrassment shimmied over her that she let herself get spooked by nothing. *Stupid ghost stories.*

A half hour later Maribel, showered and ready for bed, pulled back the covers and climbed in between the threadbare sheets, her still wet hair dampening the pillow. Unable to close her eyes despite the fatigue, she picked up the camera to scan through the pictures she had taken. She didn't know what she might find, but the faint tingle in her fingertips needed something to do.

Her breath caught. She fumbled to hit the zoom button, focusing on the upper corner of the picture. She checked through several of the photos that followed and found the same.

Reporter training taught her when one sifted through what was there, sometimes the payoff was seeing what wasn't. But not this time.

The image of a man skulked in the background, his pale colored shirt reflecting enough of the light to make him visible although he never left the shadows. Always following the girls.

Scrolling back to the beginning, she went through the photos with a new perspective. She stopped when she recognized Conner stepping out of one of the girls' cabins. The same man that appeared in the shadows. What was he up to?

She clicked through the pictures but found nothing else unusual.

Annoying. That's what she'd felt about him when they'd met, but nothing sinister. Someone her track record told her she needed to avoid. She plowed her fingers through her hair, shoving it back from her face, then covered her mouth with her hand. It wouldn't be the first time she misread a man.

She should tell someone, but what could she say? All she had were pictures of him in the shadows and the sensation someone had been watching as she walked home alone.

She rubbed her arms, trying to rid herself of the ominous chill creeping over her, thousands of icy ants marching over her skin. Had he been watching her walk back tonight?

He knew she was alone. He knew the lock on her door was broken. What else did he know?

She got up, checking the windows, making sure she latched them, and pulling the curtains completely closed. She doubled checked the chair wedged under the doorknob. Then she searched the kitchen, finding only a small paring knife with a blade so dull it would do more damage with the plastic handle.

She returned to bed, placing the knife on the bedside table. The girls gathered together in the safety of their cabins with their counselors tonight.

She was all alone. And he knew it.

CHAPTER EIGHTTEEN

C onner rolled over and stared at the clock.

3:17 a.m.

And no way to stop the parade of thoughts marching through his brain like the Russian Army through Moscow's Red Square.

How did Tracy die? With her history, drug overdose remained a possibility. Or her habit of associating with the wrong crowd. But she was trying to get her life straightened out, and he didn't need to dwell on her past. Fear there was more to it troubled him. Guilt that he escaped that life, but Tracy hadn't, could cripple him if he let it. What had he done right that his life changed, and what had she done wrong that hers hadn't? The question had eaten at him until one day Mack pointed out the obvious.

Conner accepted the mercy offered, never looking back but applying himself to the path set before him.

Maybe Tracy had too. In the end that was what mattered, right?

He exhaled. Where was the missing girl, Leah? Was she still alive? Was her disappearance connected to Tracy? His gut told him the two were linked. With no logical explanation, he still sensed it. What made no sense was how little concern anyone else exhibited regarding the girl's disappearance. The sheriff, Mack—they knew something he didn't and, while their reassurances to be patient didn't put out the burn in his veins to find and protect the girl, somehow it kept it contained. He trusted Mack, and that would have to be enough for now.

Completing his community service hours—he was thankful for whatever Mack did to get him here instead of picking up trash on the side of the road in an orange jumpsuit for the next decade of his life—brought him here. But did Mack suspect something was about to happen? He'd told Conner to keep his eyes open. To watch. No mention of what he was watching for. He felt like a creep slinking around spying in the dark tonight.

He exhaled again, harder this time, trying to purge the frustration that fogged his mind. If Mack suspected something, Conner had been too late. He threw his arm up over his eyes, trying to block the thoughts.

And the new girl, Maribel, what brought her here? And why did she have to be so hot?

Correction. Not hot. Magnetic, his thoughts drawn to her like the tiny metal shavings on the Wooly Willy game he played as a kid. He spent hours using a tiny plastic stick with a magnet in the end to coax the metal shavings into every absurd hairstyle and facial hair anomaly he could imagine. He experienced a new sympathy for those metal shards, having to be dragged around against their will by a force they couldn't resist.

The unsettling mixture of vulnerability and guardedness in Maribel's eyes sent him scrambling to—to what? Rescue her? She was clear on how she would feel about that.

No, he told himself. He only wanted to show her. Show her *what* was a question he needed to avoid other than to say kindness.

Maribel Montgomery. Just like the chocolate candy that shared her initials, she wasn't melting in his hands either.

But he couldn't let that interfere with his purpose. Besides, he didn't know for sure she wasn't part of the problem, a suspect. He felt like a criminal for searching her room, especially since he'd found nothing suspicious about her, but the timing of her arrival raised suspicions. He watched her hovering around the fire tonight, noting she focused more on Daylee than anything else. If so, her interest in the girl made him uneasy.

Trust no one.

He growled in frustration and socked the pillow over his head, replacing the arm that didn't do any good.

He spent the next hour tossing in a labyrinth of thoughts before giving up on any more sleep. Dressed for a run, he hoped to sweat out the meditations plaguing his brain.

By the time he finished the run, he should have a plan for the day. A solid idea of what to do next besides unstop a shower drain in cabin number four and mow the entryway again because the grass might have grown a fraction of an inch. He had poked around the camp and come up with nothing. Nothing except a thin thread of hope in the girl named Daylee. She and Leah seemed close before all this began. But if he couldn't gain her trust, get her to talk to him, that wouldn't help either.

He dug his tennis shoes out from under a pile of dirty athletic wear, noting he needed to do something soon, or the smell would chase him out of his own room. He'd almost had to suffer self-inflicted humiliation if he hadn't stopped Maribel from coming up. After strapping on the running belt that held his cell phone he paused before reaching for the Glock he carried when he ran. Somehow, he'd concealed the weapon in the grass far enough away the crime scene techs didn't find it the morning they found Tracy. He didn't want to think about what that would do to his record if the sheriff caught him with a gun right now. Whether or not the sheriff trusted him he couldn't tell, but Conner was aware he'd brought that on himself.

He strapped on his knife sheath instead. At this time of day, one never knew what might crop up out there. Monday morning was proof enough of that.

CHAPTER NINETEEN

Conner. What did she know about him?

He really did seem to be a nice guy. In the light of day, her thoughts from last night felt surreal. A tad melodramatic. Didn't everyone think they lived in a B-rated horror movie when the lights went out?

Something about him made her feel like the city of Jericho, walls preparing to crumble. That story had always sounded ridiculous when her Sunday school teachers read it to her as a child, but she was feeling a little more open to it at the moment—in a metaphorical way, at least. Conner wasn't the only one marching around her walls, trumpet in hand. Mack, Peg, and even Daylee were all shaking her foundations, weakening the walls that protected her heart. Vulnerable—a feeling she loathed.

The gun Conner wore strapped beneath his t-shirt the morning they met had not gone unnoticed. Neither had the fact he snuck off before law enforcement arrived and came back without it. A maintenance worker that repaired old cars, ran, wore a gun he felt compelled to hide, and stalked around a girls' camp in the night. Certainly not the norm. And until she had good answers to her questions, she couldn't trust herself to trust him.

What had she discovered so far? Not much. She had learned Tracy worked here before her death. Leah went missing about the same time. Given what Maribel had heard pertaining to Tracy's character, the timing of Leah's disappearance was doubly concerning.

Both were less than a week after Conner took over maintenance for the camp.

The thought soured in her stomach.

Questions outnumbering answers drew her like cat hair to a favorite pair of black slacks. She could pick at them as much as she wanted, but it would go on being an aggravation until she did something with the cat. The problem was, how did she find the cat?

Following the same line of investigation everyone else took would only bring her to the same place they were. She needed new information. She needed to find out what Daylee knew.

Splashing cold water on her face, she reached for the towel, realizing it wasn't renewal she felt, but new. Not a refreshing of the old, but something altogether different. A whisper of a purpose, even if only temporary. And she needed to locate the girl for a talk.

She dried her face and dressed in a pair of lightweight hiking pants, pulling on a t-shirt before collecting her hair in a ponytail.

A rustle from her bed made her freeze, hand suspended midair as she reached for the light switch. She wasn't alone.

Ducking back into the bathroom, she grabbed the only thing she could find—her hairbrush. Why wasn't there a window to escape through when she needed one?

She eased out again, armed with the bargain bin grooming tool, and switched on the light, prepared to swing.

The girl wasn't going to be a challenge to find. Daylee sat curled up on Maribel's bed, pale and wide eyed.

"Was it her?" She whispered, as if the volume of the question influenced the answer.

"Who?" Maribel suspected she knew, but she wanted to hear it in Daylee's own words. She walked over and sat beside her.

"The girl they found in the river. Was it Leah?"

"No." It had taken longer than Maribel expected for the news to spread at camp, but it had made it nonetheless.

"Then was it Tracy? How did she die? Did someone kill her?" Daylee's eyes were windows without curtains, the fear behind them visible.

"I don't know how she died. They have to do an autopsy." Why was murder the girl's first assumption? Maribel hedged her answer. No good could come from telling Daylee about evidence of the head injury. Not until they had real answers.

"Do you think Leah is dead too?"

Maribel put her arm around Daylee's shoulders and hugged her close, surprised at how natural the action felt. She did it to comfort the girl, but she was also stalling while she pressed together an answer.

Daylee shivered.

What the girl needed was reassurance and hope. And the source of that had eluded Maribel for a long time. She didn't know if she could go there. She understood the words, but without belief they were awkward and unpleasant, like a mouthful of under-cooked rice. Not exactly wrong, but not exactly right either. And hard to get out.

"Tell me what you know about Leah." She brushed Daylee's hair back from her face, keeping her touch soft, tentative.

Daylee sniffed. "We just met here. We were in the same cabin. She cried at night sometimes. Her parents were getting a divorce. She said they fought over money all the time, and she didn't want to go home. And she was afraid of her dad when he was mad."

"Do you think she ran away?" The girl's shoulders rose and fell in answer.

"Do you know where she might have gone? Did she have any money or a place to go?"

Daylee pulled away. She stared at the bedspread, not making eye contact. "I think she was doing something with Tracy, the woman who worked in the cafeteria."

"Doing something?"

"Right before she disappeared, she asked me to do her a favor. She needed me to be a lookout so she could get in the maintenance barn and steal a shovel. Well, she didn't say steal, but I kinda figured it was stealing if she had to sneak to get it."

"Did she say why?" There could be any number of silly reasons for a girl to swipe a shovel. Maribel wouldn't be hasty in her conclusions.

"She said Tracy asked her to, but the rest was a secret. She wouldn't tell me why. She said that soon she'd have enough money to get far away from her parents. But I overheard her and Tracy talking about a treasure. Tracy thought it was buried near the river." She angled her head to study Maribel. "I think she was talking about the lost treasure from the story they tell at the bonfire."

Maribel stared at the far wall, thankful Daylee couldn't see the thoughts in her head. She needed to control her alarm, conceal it from Daylee. And to remind herself the correct explanation was most often the simplest one. Tracy was high and drowned in the river, and Leah ran away from a bad home life.

Only not. Because those two events had landed in the middle of something starting to hint at a much more complicated problem.

Her reporter instinct should have had her snapping to ask questions, but instead she flailed. Her unexpected compassion for Daylee made this a lot messier.

She sat still, absorbing Daylee's sobs in her heart as her shirt absorbed the tears. She rested her cheek against the top of the girl's head, feeling the soft hair and sticky nervous heat of her body.

"When did this happen?" Maribel asked. She ran her hand over the smooth hair. "Daylee?"

"The day before she ... before she was missing. The next day after breakfast she was gone."

A feverish cold filled her body. "Did you tell anyone?"

Daylee shook her head.

"Why not?" She whispered, trying not to let the rising panic bleed into her voice.

Daylee swung her face to Maribel, her eyes even wider than before and more liquid, resembling rainwater pooling over blue gray marble. "She was really scared. She didn't say why, but she told me not to say anything to anyone. She said I totally couldn't trust anyone."

"Tell me what happened and what she said."

"Her bunk was next to mine, and I woke up when she snuck in after curfew. It was late, and she looked so freaked out. She wanted to climb in my bunk with me, but I didn't want her to because she was sweaty and muddy. She said something bad happened and that we couldn't trust anyone. That's all she said. But she made me promise not to tell. She was still in bed when I went to break-fast the next morning and when I came back, she was gone." The girl's body sank as she spoke, and she disintegrated into Maribel's hug again, sobbing. "I'm sorry I didn't say anything. I didn't know who I could tell. But you're here, and I thought maybe you didn't count since you weren't even here at the time."

She let the girl cry for a moment, unaccustomed to the role of comforter, stroking her hair as she leaned against Maribel's shoulder. Then Daylee stiff-ened, withdrawing from Maribel's embrace as she seemed to pull her vulnerable pieces back together.

Maribel stood and walked across the tiny floor space, her steps smooth and measured. "You didn't tell anyone else about this?"

"No. I promised Leah I wouldn't tell anyone. And I kept thinking about the look on her face, and she scared me too."

Ten paces and back again.

Rubbing the now completely taut muscles in her neck, Maribel tried to think. "How did Leah and Tracy know each other?"

Daylee shrank. "Tracy let her smoke with her behind the cafeteria."

"Did anyone see Leah taking the shovel?" The shovel niggled at her brain, but she couldn't pinpoint why.

125

"I don't think so. I was the lookout, and I didn't see anyone."

She came across the room to Maribel. "I'm scared."

"I know, but we'll find her." She gripped the girl's thin shoulders and stared into her eyes. "Do you have any idea where Tracy thought this treasure might be, or if she found it?"

A hesitation, slight, a fraction off beat. Daylee shook her head.

"We need to tell the sheriff."

"No! Please." Daylee jerked away.

"But Daylee, he might be able to help. He wants to find her too, and he needs to know everything."

"No. I'll say you're lying, that you made it up. Please." The girl begged. "I don't want to talk to anyone else."

"Why?"

The girl wrapped herself up in her arms, avoiding eye contact.

"Daylee?" A growing unease caused a sternness her voice didn't usually have.

"I saw him." Daylee's eyes darted up to Maribel, then back down. "When Leah didn't come back that day, I went to look for her. I thought she might be hiding by the dock. She did that sometimes when she wanted to smoke. And I ... I saw the sheriff carrying a shovel down by the river. The same one Leah had taken."

"Are you sure you saw the sheriff? And how do you know it was the same shovel? Aren't they all pretty much the same?"

"The one from the camp had yellow and green spray paint on it. It was the same one. And yes, I'm sure it was the sheriff. I mean, I'm almost sure. It was a long way off and it was hard to see in the trees." Daylee's words came fast, her speech defensive. "But Leah did say not to trust anyone. She didn't say why, but she meant it. Maybe she knew he killed Tracy. Anyway, I couldn't keep it in after I heard about a body being found in the river. I had to tell someone, and I hoped maybe I could trust you."

Could Daylee believe the sheriff had something to do with this, that he might have been the one to kill Tracy? What did this mean for Leah?

But could Maribel afford to assume it was only an overactive teenage imagination?

The covertness with her job, the missing girl, and now the dead woman. She could understand Daylee's fear. Nothing around here fit in a logical way. But it did have the impression of a thread slowly pulling the odd and misshapen pieces together.

"Do you think she might have told Conner? Or that he noticed the missing shovel?"

Daylee's eyebrows knit together as she considered the possibility. "I don't know. Why?"

"No reason. Only wondering." Maribel fumbled around trying to sound indifferent. No need to stir up suspicions.

"You think he has something to do with her being missing? Do you think he was the one I saw with the shovel?"

"No. I just wondered if he might have seen her taking the shovel—oh, I don't know what I thought. I was hoping there might be someone else she told as well." Conner and the sheriff looked nothing alike. If Daylee thought it could have been either of them, then odds were just as good it was someone else altogether.

"You aren't going to tell anyone, are you?"

"I'm not sure. I need to think. But it would be best if you don't tell anyone else. Not yet anyway." While she didn't wish to look like a lunatic presenting this questionable story to others—placing her only source of income in jeopardy, not to mention the last trace of any professional competency—the truth was she had no idea who she could trust.

She peered at the girl now sitting on her bed, tracing the patterns on the bedspread with her finger. Could Maribel figure out what happened to Leah without exposing Daylee to harm?

The possibility she could put Daylee in danger filled her thoughts with doubt. She bit her lip, fighting off the reminders of past failures and mistakes knotting her stomach.

Had she been a praying person, her prayer would have been, *Please, Lord, don't make me responsible for another person's life.*

CHAPTER TWENTY

The familiar smells of bacon and industrial strength sterilization greeted Maribel when she stepped into the cafeteria. And just like that she was a lonely, misfit thirteen-year-old at camp. The gravity of her conversation with Daylee dragged the memories of isolation and loneliness from the well of insecurities she denied holding onto.

You are fearfully and wonderfully made. Aunt Rachel's favorite pep talk. The words had stuck far better than the message had. Maribel gave her aunt credit for faithfully trying to build her up after her father deserted them.

Maribel headed straight for the coffee, thankful to find the urn still plugged in and dispensing liquid life even though breakfast had ended. She filled the Styrofoam cup and added a hefty measure of creamer and sugar. She stirred it, disliking the sound of the plastic spoon scraping against the Styrofoam, instead of the comforting sound of her favorite mug, a gift from her aunt.

Perfect love casts out fear—another of her aunt's favorite sayings—had been painted in elaborate gold lettering on the side of the pale green porcelain. The cup always felt just right in her hand even though she never thought about those words. Despite Aunt Rachel's efforts to pour the Good News into Maribel through the medium of strong, dark coffee, she missed her aunt. But sometimes she missed the coffee more. There were just some truths she didn't know if she could face.

Something powerful enough to cast out fear right now would be handy. But she doubted love was the thing. She needed something Herculean, something resembling Sherlock Holmes and the Green Berets. Inquiring about a missing girl was one thing. Putting a girl in danger by reckless actions was another.

But which action exposed her to more danger? Keeping Daylee's information secret or revealing it to someone who might not be trustworthy?

"That stuff is bad for you." Conner walked past her carrying a handful of what must have been his breakfast—a bottle of water, a granola bar and two bananas. The dark swath down the middle of his shirt and the way his hair hung in dark spikes told her he'd been running. That and the fact he still wore his running clothes, not work clothes. She suddenly felt too warm to want a sip of hot coffee.

"Is that so?" It was the first time she'd seen him since her melt down in his shop, if she didn't count the pictures from last night.

"All that caffeine in coffee ... not good."

Maribel took a long sip from the cup, forcing herself not to flinch when the still-too-hot liquid burned her tongue. "What if it's decaf?"

"Is it?"

"No."

"So why the lack of concern for your health?"

"YOLO, right?" The word surprised her coming from her own mouth. She had never liked the *you only live once* mantra popular among the younger crowd—as if she were old. She somehow knew it would annoy him, though, and that made it acceptable at the moment.

"Not if you do it right, babe. God's got a better plan." He grinned, saluting her with a banana and left. "Gotta go, but we'll talk more later. Until then, consider drinking a little more water."

We'll talk more later ... great. Now he was an evangelist. She should find a helmet in case he wanted to clobber her on her already addled skull with his bible—if he even actually had one. But at least he'd been gracious enough not to bring up the incident in his shop.

Topping off her cup with more coffee, she found a seat near a window and let the caffeine take hold.

Sounds like you're running. Peg's words rang in her ears. A different running. And maybe she was, but she wasn't sure she knew how to stop. Or what might happen if she did. Like a cartoon character racing across the ground as it crumbled away behind her.

Yeah. Let's talk later, Conner. You can explain what you were doing in my cabin without telling me and even better, what you were doing in the pictures I took last night.

Where were the warning signals that should go off in her brain? The knot in her stomach that said, "Get out while you can." Had she ignored them so long they'd gone silent? A "use them or lose them" deal?

Maybe there was nothing sinister regarding what Conner did last night. Maybe he was a nice guy, if one was into that kind of thing, which she wasn't.

But where did Daylee's new information fit?

She sighed. Just a nice guy.

Like Ted Bundy.

CHAPTER TWENTY-ONE

Maribel tucked her notebook into her backpack with a bottle of water and set off on the path to the river. It seemed possible Leah might have witnessed Tracy's murder. That would account for the girl's fear. Did it account for her disappearance as well?

Checking around the river had to be the logical next step if there was something more Maribel could learn. It was the only step she could take at the moment.

Her notebook made a plausible pretext if anyone asked what she was doing. She would find a quiet place to do some journaling. Writing helped untangle the things in her head.

Scattered fine, wispy white lines of clouds known as mares' tails brushed across the blue sky in delicate strokes, bright against the perfect blue. She inhaled, letting a breath of peace seep in, expelling the tension.

As she passed by the open field behind the maintenance barn, she saw Conner and stopped to watch, curious. He didn't notice her as he maneuvered a sizable round cross section of wood onto square bales of hay stacked together to make a wall. He paced back from them and Maribel saw the target rings painted on the wood. With practiced movements, he pulled the knife from the sheath on his belt, took aim and threw it. The blade spun end over end in a silvery whirl until landing in the target with a thud, second ring from the center.

A small exclamation escaped Maribel's lips, alerting him to her presence.

"I didn't know I had an audience, but thanks for the enthusiasm. You want to try?"

"It was just a muscle spasm. And no thanks. I don't think your target is big enough."

He laughed as he walked over to pull the blade from the wood. "I just started practicing a few weeks ago and thought it might be something to teach the girls. I'm not terribly accurate with it myself yet, though. That red circle in the middle is still in pristine condition. But it is stress relieving and helps me think. You should try it. I'm told it helps relieve muscle spasms too."

"You should be careful what you ask for or you might end up worse off than Rogers." She would need a new hobby for relieving her stress if she couldn't bring herself to go running again soon. But there'd be no stress relief in anything that brought her into contact with Conner.

"Where you headed?"

"I thought I'd walk to the river and look around."

"Want some company? The river wasn't all that fun for you, as I recall."

"True, but I think I can handle it myself today."

"Suit yourself." He tossed the knife at the target again with deadly accuracy, sinking the blade into the red center. "You must be good luck but be careful wandering off alone. You know to watch out for snakes, right? And take some water."

"I can take care of myself." Refraining from shuddering at the mention of snakes, she walked away without waiting for his response.

It took less than five minutes to be out of sight of the camp and standing on a ridge overlooking the river. A dock ran out from the bank below and a rope swing dangled from a pole at the opposite end. A handful of scratched and dented aluminum canoes rested on the slope, far from the water's edge, an emergency safety pole draped in faded orange life jackets standing guard.

It brought back memories of her childhood. She recalled the little girl she had once been, fearless, imaginary sword in hand, with the unwavering ability to be ever victorious in the battle of good versus evil. How swiftly reality had ripped the sword from her hand and used it to cut her heart in two. Little girl fantasies were not real life.

But would she always be the girl who couldn't, or was she just the girl who wouldn't?

She let the trail take her over the slope to the river. She didn't know what she expected to find. The only thing she had was a notion the search for answers started near the river. The image of Tracy Morgan's dead face stared at her. For Tracy, it ended here as well.

Tracy involved Leah in an idiotic scheme to find a treasure, the removal of which required a shovel taken from the camp maintenance barn. The river brought them Tracy. Leah was missing. Who had the shovel?

Daylee thought she'd seen someone carrying it away the day after Leah was gone, but Maribel had doubts about her story. For one, she couldn't be sure if it was a man fitting the sheriff's description or Conner's.

She left the dock and continued on the trail leading along the bank to the bluffs lining the river bend.

She veered from the well-worn trail and found a narrow path made by the wildlife. It led to a stone shelf jutting out above the water before receding into the thick growth of vegetation. A bluff rose behind her. Refrigerator-sized slabs of gray and yellow limestone rested at varying intervals on their slide to the river bottom. In front of her the jade-green ribbon of river persevered as it flowed past, smooth and quiet and determined. It moved forward with a purpose.

Maribel rubbed her arms, chilled despite the intense summer sun. She had no purpose. She was going nowhere. She only existed day by day, tucked away in her safe little shell. But a restless dissatisfaction with this way of life was causing a rockslide of a different kind. A dissatisfaction that had been there from the beginning but now grew too strong to stop.

A second ledge stuck out farther above her. The need to conquer something she feared, even something as inconsequential as inanimate rocks, urged her upwards. She worked her way over the scree using the scattered boulders as steps for her obstacle course higher up the bluff. Atop the uppermost shelf, she allowed the moment to wash her in boldness. Not so much she didn't still exercise caution. She seated herself and scooted to the edge. One small accomplishment at a time.

She dangled her feet over the ledge in a moment of innocent childlike pleasure, once again enjoying the triumph of her elevated position. Her fear of heights was second only to her fear of snakes. But for the moment, she was a conqueror.

Once settled, she took out her notepad and pencil. If she chose to, she could flip back through the pages and reread things from the past.

But she didn't want to look back. Not now. Something else stirred in her damaged soul.

The smell of juniper in the warm air stimulated her senses. Something—or Someone—spoke to her in the soft rustle of the breeze, like a breath whispering truth in her ear.

You are enough.

She sat unmoving, memories of the past unspooling in her mind, memories of the girl she used to be, or at least used to think she was, a mirage-like shimmer in her mind's eye. She wanted to be angry for how her life had turned out, but angry at whom?

When had she accepted the belief she wasn't enough?

He set my feet on a rock and gave me a firm place to stand.

She closed her eyes, aware she knew the words, but not the one to whom they belonged. The sun shone against her face, making the insides of her eyelids like a pool of molten lava, fiery and red. Even if she found such a place, did she have the courage to stand?

She wanted the peace Peg had in the face of death, and Peg had said knowing God as her rock got her through. If only it could be that simple.

The air hummed with the chattering crescendo of cicadas in the trees. A constant buzz that reminded Maribel of water sizzling on a hot surface. A proper analogy for the heat today.

With her eyes still shut, she let the warmth work on her tight muscles and aching psyche.

A tingle of apprehension skittered over her body and made her scalp prickle. The all-too-familiar feeling of being watched unsettled her once again. She sat transfixed, absorbing the sudden silence of the cicadas and aware of the slightest stirring around her as a butterfly bounced among the wildflowers. She considered each motion of her body, trying not to give away her suspicion and making no abrupt movements.

She scanned in front of her, paying close attention to the far side of the river, listening. Cautiously, she glanced over her shoulder. Thoughts of a mountain lion crouched in her imagination, causing her pulse to quicken. But there was nothing. Only blue-sky hovering above the chalky outcropping of rock fringed in shaggy green cedar branches.

She released a slow, deep breath and wiped the excessive moisture from her eyes with unsteady fingers. Her paranoia was getting out of hand.

Not wanting to hang around any longer, she rose too fast. The second foot did not find a solid landing as rocks loosened by the recent rains crumbled and gave way beneath her. Off balance, her arms flung wide, scraping her palms over the jagged edges of rock as she tried in vain to hold on. Her shoulder raked hard against the ledge, a biting pain followed by her skin grinding against the rough stone. Then nothing. Maribel fell through harmless air, no pain, only anticipation of impact. A shard of time to tell herself the distance to the ground below was not great enough to kill her unless she landed headfirst.

Probably.

The impact knocked the air from her chest and arrested her lungs as she landed on her back.

Relax. Her survival instinct took control, urging her body to respond with a calmness that didn't suit the fears stampeding through her thoughts. Air flowed back into her lungs.

She mentally checked each body part for pain before allowing herself to move. A sharp pain on her head where it hit, a pulsating ache where her shoulder landed, and the burn of peeled skin, but other than that she seemed undamaged. She wasn't ready to move yet just in case. Without opening her eyes, she rested in the gratitude she was still alive

The cicadas had paused their noise, perhaps waiting to see if she lived. Then, she heard it.

The distinct scratching of briers against thick material. Someone walking through the brush above her. Her heart beat against her ear drum, drowning out the surrounding sounds. She swallowed, forcing her heart back into her chest so she could hear.

Someone else was out here. She ran her tongue over her lips, registering the metallic taste of blood where her teeth cut into her lip when she fell.

She didn't move. Her eyes closed, ears keen to hear. She flexed her fingers, slow discreet movements, searching for something. A rock not much bigger than her fist was all she found. She clutched it, pulling it to her side.

Time became unmeasurable. Flying or crawling away from her, she couldn't tell. The cicadas resumed their song. She didn't know how much time passed before she felt confident it—whatever or whoever—was gone. If they wanted to harm her, they'd had their chance. She couldn't lie around like this all day with the sun roasting her until she resembled beef jerky.

She rolled slowly to her side, pushing herself up with the arm that wasn't hurt.

Taking her time to stand, she felt like a china doll, fractured and sore, but not shattered. Still gripping the rock in one hand, she felt around and found the lump on her head protruding. Good news. The lump protruded. Painfully so, but at least she didn't think she had a concussion.

New knowledge, molten steel hardening in the shape of determination, came over her, and she recognized in herself the will to fight.

She located her pack and her notebook, counting the pencil a loss, and headed away from the river and into the open. The pencil had been a small gift of encouragement from her aunt. At least Maribel assumed the *If not now, when* message written on it was supposed to encourage her. It didn't, and she couldn't say she was sorry to see it go.

A half hour later she stood in her cabin, water stinging the scrapes on her palms as she worked to wash away evidence of her fall.

A search of the cabin had failed to locate a first aid kit. Maybe she should find the camp nurse for some antibiotic ointment.

She changed into the loosest shirt she could find, limped to the Rec Hall vending machine for a candy bar, then hobbled to the office hoping no one saw her.

Easing into her chair, she noted the missing wobble and a need to thank Conner for taking care of it. She still had his screwdrivers, but the task had not crossed her mind since she acquired them. She pressed the intercom button and waited for Becca to answer.

A high-pitched voice responded, causing Maribel to shrink back from the phone. Audio feedback at a heavy metal concert was less brutal. How many had they interviewed before they found a receptionist that sounded like Minnie Mouse on helium?

"Becca, I'm sorry to bother you, but I have a minor problem I didn't want everyone to know about."

"Is it that time? I keep an extra stash in the restroom at the back, behind the stack of toilet paper in the corner."

"No." Maribel silenced her before she could say more. She pressed two fingers against the middle of her forehead. "No. I fell and scraped my shoulder. Do we have a first aid kit handy?"

Long pause. "Ohhh. I'll get with the nurse. I'm sure she has something."

Maribel didn't want the nurse. She just wanted the ointment, but not long after, she sat ointmented and lectured on wound care, and the necessity of accident-prone people not wandering off alone.

Unable to concentrate on anything else, she picked up the camera and connected it to the computer. Might as well apply some scrutiny to those pictures from last night. She downloaded them from the camera, then enlarged and reexamined each one. Would she see something to justify her suspicions concerning Conner? The realization she hoped she was wrong paralyzed her fingers. Journalists couldn't think that way. Impartiality wasn't a suggestion. It was a requirement.

She'd been down this road before—ignoring the facts because a man seemed nice—and now a boy was dead.

A wave of hot nausea rolled through her. Another one of her mistakes could put Daylee, and possibly Leah, in jeopardy.

The only person who knew she had gone to the river this morning was Conner. If someone had been watching her, the odds of it being him were worthy of a trip to Vegas.

Her fingers tapped harder than necessary against the keys as she saved the incriminating pictures in an unnamed file.

She'd decide what to do with them later.

CHAPTER TWENTY-TWO

M aribel settled on the steps of her cabin as evening crept close. It was
becoming her habit. She listened as the night sounds lulled the day to
sleep. A breeze fluttered her hair, tickling it across her cheek, a soft caress. She
had developed a few aches in her body as a result of her fall. But for the moment
her soul was quiet, and that was enough.

The bonfire burned again tonight. The girls gathered around it, at ease
in their unawareness, tucked into their confidence they had nothing to fear.
Chattering, laughing, and squealing, they let their marshmallows catch fire,
waving them around like sugar torches. Happy. Carefree. An innocence that
couldn't last.

No such thing as a broken world.

What would it feel like to have that much innocence again? When had
she lost it?

She scanned the cluster of girls for Daylee, spotting her when the girl
glanced Maribel's direction. Daylee's nervous body language beckoned Maribel.

Maribel rose and trekked down the hill to the fire.

She started across the circle to where Daylee sat when Conner stepped into
the ring of light, guitar in hand. Great, a talent for every occasion. He seated
himself on the stump near Daylee and leaned over to speak to the girl.

There was too much noise for Maribel to hear the conversation, but whatever he said drew a fleeting smile from the teenager. Right before she shot
Maribel an anxious look. She turned back to Conner, leaning away from him,

shaking her head no. Maribel didn't know if it was his attention or the warmth of the campfire that darkened the girl's cheeks. He held the guitar out for her, then shrugged, grinning as she shook her head again. Surely he wasn't flirting with Daylee. Maribel hurried to seat herself beside the girl, shooting Conner a glare she hoped communicated he was crossing the line.

And telling herself that wasn't disappointment bubbling up inside her like soda fizz. Junk food induced indigestion more likely.

She frowned, unable to interpret the unfazed expression on his face. He stood and ambled around the perimeter of the fire, strumming chords as he went.

The other girls assembled in a circle, the thrill of the flaming marshmallows replaced by the opportunity to watch Conner play his guitar. Maribel was confident if they didn't already have a crush on him, they would now—counselors included. She rolled her eyes at their naivete.

He moved around the circle and settled in a spot across from Daylee. Maribel watched, not liking the path her thoughts took. His actions implied a keener interest in Daylee than his interest in the others.

"Hey, girls, let's get Conner to do his bird imitations for us." A cute, perky counselor bobbed herself into the space next to Conner, placing her hands on his shoulders.

"Which one do you want to hear?" he asked, a pleased smile on his face.

Maribel bristled and rolled her eyes again. Typical male ego, a little flattery was all that was ever needed.

Conner took his time taking requests imitating different birds—owls, hawks, cardinals, blue jays—asking the girls to guess. Maribel could admit he did an impressive job.

"How about you, Maribel? You haven't asked for anything yet." He rubbed his chin, mimicking serious contemplation of what her choice might be.

"How about a whippoorwill?" Maribel asked, instantly regretting it. The look he gave reached out to her like moonbeams. The lonesome call of the whippoorwill—which he imitated with uncanny accuracy—made a foolish choice for her heart.

Perhaps he thought so too. He was quick to turn away, clearing his throat. He plucked at his guitar a few times then began crooning camp songs.

Maribel leaned closer to Daylee. "Do you play the guitar?"

"I'm trying to learn, but no way am I going to play in front of Conner yet," the girl replied. They tried talking about musical preferences but had too little in common to sustain a conversation centered on music.

She didn't miss the way Daylee watched Conner, wary, but intrigued, maybe even hopeful.

"There ought to be some sort of child abuse law against the stuff they make us do at camp," Daylee said.

Maribel laughed. These were the same songs they'd endured when she went to camp years ago, and they were still just as silly.

Conner kept going, counselors and campers following along in a tuneless disaster that came together beautifully harmonic around a campfire. After several rounds of the traditional tunes, he began to serenade them with other melodies. Beautiful songs that spoke of greater things.

Talk between Maribel and Daylee ceased. Maribel stilled as the notes floated over her, captivating her. Taking her hostage against her will was more like it. The crack of the fire, the warm night wind caressing her skin, combined with the resonate timbre of Conner and his guitar, soft, soul-soothing sounds. The notes didn't just silence the night. They silenced the noise in her head and the chaos in her heart, demanding she be still.

Then the words of an old hymn—*I'll strengthen thee, help thee, and cause thee to stand*—floated up from his soul as if he had written them himself. They flowed into her heart as if he'd written them for her.

When through the deep waters I call thee to go—Maribel couldn't recall the name of the hymn, but she recognized the words. Or maybe they recognized her.

The song took her back to childhood days at church with her aunt. Although it was her mother who always insisted she go, never once had she seen her mother or father pass through the doors. Church was where she learned not all families were like hers. In those old wooden pews, she came to see the discrepancy in what she heard on Sunday mornings and what she lived with the rest of the week.

Church lost its relevance to her life when it lost her trust. The surface beneath her feet became increasingly slippery. But she continued to play the part, sitting next to her aunt in the pew, pretending she knew who Jesus was. Pretending she belonged.

She shifted, drawing a glance from Conner. A delicate longing stirred deep within her, a breeze through the ashes. And then she knew when she had lost the innocence of her childhood.

She wanted to push the tender feelings away. These were not feelings she wanted to explore. She sat up straighter, spine rigid and arms crossed.

Daylee stared at the fire, her eyes glazed and unfocused, her thoughts, too, dwelled in deeper places.

The need to slip away to her cabin, to get away from the strange mix of emotions stewing within her, urged Maribel to leave. But she couldn't tear herself away from Daylee, not when she didn't understand the teenager's state of mind at this moment. The unknown thoughts of teenagers were scary things. The memory of Alexander was enough to keep her from leaving the girl.

Alexander, the boy who died because Maribel hadn't paid attention. She wouldn't make that mistake again.

CHAPTER TWENTY-THREE

A streak of lightning sliced through the dark, a sky-wrenching clap of thunder only a second behind.

The storm exploded quickly.

"Party's over. Time to head inside." The counselors hopped up and rushed the girls to shelter. A chorus of groans replaced the music as the girls complained and trudged with much-voiced disappointment to their cabins. The counselors prodded them on, not wanting to call a parent because a camper under their watch got zapped in an electrical storm. More lightning sizzled through the atmosphere adding an exclamation point to the counselor's request they hurry.

Daylee stood, spat out a half-hearted goodnight to Maribel, and joined the procession of disgruntled campers heading for cover. The slump of her shoulders said Daylee thought herself alone even in the crowd of other girls.

Maribel watched her walk away, unaware that the only one left besides her was Conner.

He had set his guitar aside and began cleaning up the leftover supplies.

"Want to help out?" he asked. Not waiting for a response, he handed her a basket, then told her he'd be right back.

He trotted to the cafeteria with his guitar in hand. While they sent everyone else to shelter, he left her standing here alone, a human lightning rod.

She redirected her attention to the pile of marshmallows, graham crackers, and chocolate bars scattered across a folding table and stacked them in the basket. Unable to resist, she grabbed a skewer and slid a marshmallow onto the end. A flash of lightning suggested she make it quick.

Hurrying to the fire, she positioned the marshmallow near the flames, making sure not to get it too close. She concentrated on rotating it at the proper speed, letting the heat reach all around until the inside became so soft it spun around on the hot utensil, much the same way she felt as she watched Conner returning.

"I think the goal here is to get all this picked up and get ourselves safely back inside before the storm arrives." Conner picked up the metal roasters and stuck the ends in the fire to burn off the residue.

"It's bad luck not to roast a marshmallow over the fire at camp," she lied.

"Uh-huh. It'll be worse luck to get fried by lightning. One dead body this week is sufficient."

Maribel glanced across the fire to where Conner stared back at her, acknowledging with annoyance the fire light illuminated and accented everything rugged and handsome about him. And that they now had an odd connection because of their shared experience at the river. Like it or not, a dead body was binding.

"I'm almost done."

"Impressive how you're not content just to destroy yourself with unhealthy food choices, but you're willing to risk your life to do it." He took the skewer, marshmallow and all, from her hand. He smashed it between the graham crackers and chocolate and shoved it back to her. "Let's go."

"It wasn't ready yet." Maribel argued, indignant that she had lost control of her own creation.

Another streak of lightning ripped across the sky. Large, icy drops of rain splatted against the ground.

Conner grabbed the basket and skewers in one hand and snatched her empty hand in the other, giving her no choice but to go with him. He headed to the nearest building—the cafeteria—increasing his pace to a jog as the drops intensified, then a run as the torrent came down full throttle.

Maribel raced beside him, laughing, the aggravation of an imperfect s'more forgotten. Running in the rain always had that effect on her. She still had her doubts about Conner, but the rain settled a surreal quality over the evening. Nothing that happened tonight would exist tomorrow. YOLO, right?

Conner held the door open for her, water cascading from his amused face.

The security light from the kitchen gave a soft, unflattering glow. The building felt sticky warm to her drenched body, but still she shivered. She ran an empty hand through her hair, pushing back the wet mass of waves she knew would be forming. Small puddles of water gathered at their feet.

Conner shook his head, sending droplets in all directions, leaving his hair mussed.

"What's so funny?"

"Nothing." She refused to meet his eyes as she tried to swipe the water from her bare arms. Nothing other than the childish delight brought on by running in the rain. Maybe that little girl she had been still existed in there somewhere. "I like the rain, that's all."

"Nearly getting electrocuted is fun to you?"

"No. Not the lightning—the rain."

"Getting soaked in a downpour makes you laugh? Interesting. But I am glad to see you can laugh. I wasn't sure you had it in you." He crossed his arms and stared at her, chin lifted, playfully inviting an argument.

She tossed her ruined snack into the nearest trash can, refusing to play his game.

"What's that supposed to mean?" Okay maybe she would play, but just a little.

"It means you're so serious, and well, un-fun."

"Un-fun? Is that even a real word?"

"That's your question? I call you a stick in the mud, and all you can worry about is my grammar?" He lifted the hem of his t-shirt and swiped at his wet face.

Maribel averted her eyes because that was better than spontaneous human combustion. They must not bother running the air conditioner here at night.

"So how'd I do?" he asked. "On the whippoorwill?"

She cleared the scratch that caught in her throat. "Not bad. It was almost believable."

"Almost, huh?" He rubbed his jaw, giving her a scowl that said he didn't agree.

"Yes. If the conditions were right, it might fool me. That is the goal, right? To deceive other birds, or people, into thinking you're the real thing."

He looked dumbfounded. "You know, I enjoy making the sounds. It's fun—that's pretty much the only reason I do them." A roguish grin that matched the devilish merriment in his eyes sent a different kind of shiver through her body. "But you know what they say about the call of a whippoorwill, don't you?"

"No, but I have no doubt you're going to tell me." She pretended to be busy squeezing excess water out of her shirt.

"Nah, it's probably too late for you anyway."

"Too late for what?"

"If you must know, when a single woman hears the first whippoorwill of the season, but he only calls once, she will stay single for at least a year."

"And if he calls twice?"

"Then odds are much better in her favor for an end to her singleness. But he'd want to make real sure before he made that second call."

She couldn't stop a hasty glance in his direction and burned when he winked back.

"Speaking of fun, I didn't see you singing along tonight."

"I don't sing."

"Everyone sings."

"Not me." She used to. But then she grew up and recognized she wasn't musically inclined.

A slide projector in her brain clicked images through her thoughts. Images of her ten-year-old self, dressed in a dark green satin dress, on her way to the church Christmas pageant. Standing on the stage searching for a father who never came. And one last effort to please him by singing her song for him when she got home.

Only he hadn't wanted to hear. "Stop that racket. The game's on." Maribel knew why she didn't sing. And she knew when she'd started believing she wasn't enough.

"God loves a joyful noise."

Maribel lowered her eyes, fussing with the dripping hem of her shirt. What did he know about what God loved?

And why was it so hot in here? She twisted the fabric in her hands, then regretted the action as water streamed to the tile floor. That could be a fall hazard. She spun to go find something to dry the mess and slipped.

Conner's hands claimed her as soon as she began to fall. She was happy to avoid another fall today. The problem was, he didn't at once right her on her feet. He left her off balance and leaning on him.

A ripple of fear shot through her because in this moment she didn't know what she wanted to happen next.

"I think I'd better get this cleaned up, though." The words came out louder than she had intended.

He continued to stare at her, but Maribel refused to contemplate his thoughts or what the look he gave her meant.

"Why don't you sit? I'll get the mop." Ignoring her protest, he maneuvered her to the nearest chair, handling her as though she were fragile.

He disappeared in the back, returned to mop up the puddle, then disappeared again, staying gone for a long time before returning with two cups of hot tea.

Maribel eyed him with suspicion. This was not behavior she was accustomed to with the previous men in her life. He wasn't playing the game correctly. How could she keep her defenses up if he kept coming at her with the unexpected? "What's this for?"

He blinked, a mixture of surprise and confusion on his face. "Well ... drinking."

An amused sound skipped through her lips. "You are something else."

"I try to be."

This time her laugh echoed in the empty dining hall.

"Oh, now she gets a sense of humor." He rolled his eyes as he took a seat across from her. "What's funny now?"

"Nothing. You've definitely got your act down good." Enough of the double jeopardy she had put herself in. She arched an eyebrow, holding her hands in front of her, palms out. "It's even better than your whippoorwill impersonation."

"Act?" His eyes narrowed as he leaned back, folding his arms over his chest. He rolled his shoulders back, accentuating his broad, and now defiant looking chest.

"You're genuinely just a nice and helpful guy?" Her tone said *yeah right*.

"Yes. That is exactly what I try to be. Why does that bother you?"

"I didn't say it bothered me."

"But it does. You can't stand for anyone to be nice to you. How messed up is that, Maribel?"

Her mouth pinched. Her wet clothes felt even chillier against her now hot skin.

Outside the thunder pounded, its rumble vibrating through the air. "You're one to talk. Singing praise songs like you're God's right-hand man."

"Technically that would be Jesus."

"What?"

"God's right-hand man. It's Jesus. I mean, there's the whole Trinity thing, but—"

150

"You know what I mean."

"Nope. I don't think I do." He shook his head, his face a perfect mask of mock seriousness. "And about that whole YOLO thing ..."

"I'm not really into the whole God-loves-me-and-has-a-plan thing." Another conversation she didn't want to have. There was no point in trying to convince a hypocrite he was a hypocrite.

"Are you saying you don't believe in God?"

"It's more like I'm saying I don't believe he believes in me."

Her ears felt hot enough to singe her hair. She hadn't meant to say that. It was between her and God—as if God even cared. She picked up the cup and sipped the hot tea. She set it down, tracing an unseen pattern with her fingertip, avoiding eye contact. *Do not let your guard go AWOL. And whatever you do, do not notice the way he is looking at you. How had the conversation turned into this? And why was it so hot in here?*

"What were you doing in my cabin the other day?" She changed the subject.

He cocked his head to the side, the wrinkles around his eyes deepening. Would he deny it?

"I am in charge of maintenance, so it's kinda my job to take care of the buildings. If you need me to make that clearer for you, I was checking on the roof since there was rain in the forecast. And Sheriff Griger mentioned the broken lock."

Of course, he had a reason. She should have learned by now not to jump to conclusions. If her ears got any hotter, he might smell burning hair. "Oh— then thank you."

Her fury burned out too soon. She desperately wanted to stay angry and hoped he'd give her more fuel for that fire.

She eyed the exits but, from the sound, the rain was still falling in a torrent.

Conner rubbed his chin, then reached for his cup, spilling a few drops when he set it down. He cleared his throat.

"About what you said—"

"I don't want to talk about it." She cut him off with finality. The problem was, she wanted to talk about it, but not enough to go the places it would force her to go. And not with him.

His movements were slow, cautious as he gave a slight nod.

"Doesn't appear we're going anywhere for a while. What shall we discuss then?" Conner shifted gears, speaking with an ease she was starting to envy.

She inhaled the faint scent of rain and wood smoke, mixed with the earthy smell of the tea and the fruity essence of her shampoo. She wanted to ask him about the song she had never heard before, or the one about strength, standing, and deep waters, but that was a doorway right back into the conversation she wanted to avoid. "Tell me about Tracy Morgan?"

He bit the corner of his mouth and looked away. "An odd conversation to have, especially since we've already had it. But Tracy was an old, old girlfriend from a previous life. There's really not much more to say."

From what Maribel heard by the river, Tracy Morgan was no angel. She never even rose high enough to be a fallen angel. She had been born into low and unfortunate circumstances and stayed right there.

Conner had a lot of nerve to lecture her on her relationship with God. If Tracy had been his girlfriend, his life couldn't have been much different. And that was trouble she didn't need.

He brought his palms down on the table and patted twice, then drummed his fingers in a slow rhythm on the wood laminate tabletop.

Silence didn't bother Maribel, but this one buzzed like a swarm of yellow jackets, making her anxious. But not enough to make her ask any more of the questions stinging her insides.

"Sounds like the rain is letting up." He walked to the door to check while she picked up their empty cups and returned them to the kitchen.

"Now's as good a time as any to get out of here. I'll walk you to your cabin." He stood at the door but didn't move to open it, as if his statement had been a question and he waited for her to answer. Did he hope she'd suggest they not go just yet?

"That's not necessary. I can see it from here." She protested but knew he would ignore it. She froze, arrested by the sudden realization she trusted Conner to do certain things. That's what this was, right? Trust. When had she believed in him, expecting trustworthy behavior? For a moment she wished the rain hadn't let up, and she could stay here in his presence a little longer, despite the sensation of swarming yellow jackets in the air.

The thought terrified her. She shot out the door as if lightning had suddenly struck her. This was not what she wanted.

She couldn't remember ever being this conflicted in her thoughts before. She'd been flat out wrong in the past, but she had never had a moment of doubt until the dust settled, and the evidence lay in rubble at her feet. This double-mindedness frightened her.

She couldn't trust him. She needed to remind herself of that.

CHAPTER TWENTY-FOUR

M aribel stomped across the open ground. She could hear Conner splashing behind her as he tried to keep up.

She didn't slow down. Not even when she reached her cabin.

Not until the idea hit her. How to get the proof she needed to guard her heart. He was attractive. He was virile. He was a single man who had desires. And he had a past with a woman everyone was eager to speak poorly of. If she offered, he would stay. He'd show her he wasn't the altar boy he pretended to be.

She bit her lip. Or would he? She stopped before opening the door and whirled to face him, tipping her chin so she peered up through her lashes to see the puzzled, suspicious expression on his face.

"Thanks ... for everything. You're different, you know that?" She would have gagged on the coquettish tone of her words if she wasn't aware of how unattractive that would be. "So, am I really that 'unfun'?"

"You have your moments." His eyes darkened, as if he were reading her, as if he understood where this was leading. Or thought he did. Maybe this was working.

She tucked her hair behind her ear, positive he was well versed enough in flirtation to recognize the gesture. That was a gesture, right? At some point he needed to step up and take charge of the advance so she could reject him. That was the goal. Nothing more. She didn't have a subconscious desire to know Conner found her attractive, did she? Of course not. But hadn't that been the real motive in every relationship she'd entered?

Fear of being forever unwanted had led her to seek confirmation she was desirable, that she deserved to be pursued. What she was now coming to understand was the desire and pursuit were never for her but for what she could offer a man, primarily in the physical realm.

This new knowledge rocked her for a moment, but she could explore that later. She had to see this moment through first.

But this felt like Satan's dirty work. And she was an idiot who should have thought this out a little better. *Just do it.* Then she could think clearly about the real issues at hand. Unfortunately, what she suspected with her heart went against what she expected with her brain. It scared her to know she hoped her heart was right.

"Maybe we should talk about the YOLO thing. It's hard for me to talk to others, but not you. I truly believe I could tell you anything." *Oh, for the salvation of any minuscule shred of dignity you have left, stop talking.*

Conner nodded, but remained silent. A muscle in his jaw twitched.

"Do you want to ..." she cleared her throat, shifting her eyes to the porch as she ran her tongue over her lips. "Do you want to come inside? You know, to talk some more."

He stood like a granite statue, hard and unmoving. The look he gave her as hot as a solar flare. Then he walked toward her with slow, measured steps.

She swallowed. *Bad idea. Very bad idea.*

He came so close she had to tilt her head back to see his face. The scent of the tea lingered on his breath. He leaned down, his lips within inches of hers. Her brain froze as her body betrayed her, and her heart hopped out and ran toward him at full speed. What was she supposed to be doing, because this certainly wasn't the plan?

His warm breath fluttered against her cheek in a deep, husky drawl. "No, Maribel. I do not."

He pulled back, searching her eyes in a way that shot pain deep into her soul, then turned and walked away.

He'd been kind to her, and she had betrayed him.

Did anyone else smell burning hair? She felt an intense kind of heat reserved for the especially mortified. She spiraled around, flinging the cabin door open. That something was wrong registered a second too late. Her feet slipped, flying up in the air while the rest of her smacked onto the wet concrete floor of her cabin.

She didn't know if it was the sound of all the air leaving her lungs, or the thud of her body hitting the floor that caught Conner's attention, but when she opened her eyes again, there he stood, staring down at her.

"Well, I guess I will come in." He flipped on the light and knelt beside her. "Anything broken?"

"Does pride count?"

She appreciated the smile she received, considerate and warm, not the disgusted and disappointed look she deserved.

"I can't imagine you'd have any left after that painful attempt at seduction."

"That obvious, huh?" She moaned as she tried to sit. "And for the record, it was flirting, not an attempt to seduce you."

"Whatever you tell yourself to feel better. But I found it encouraging too." He slid his arm beneath her shoulder and scooped her up like a child. "So, did I pass?" The row of white teeth exposed by his smile showed how much he was enjoying her humiliation.

"You knew?"

"Well, let's just say your poker face needs work. So, did I pass?"

"You passed." Like a kidney stone. How long did it take self-respect to regenerate?

She started to protest being transported in this manner, but his expression silenced her. He carried her to the bed and deposited her with more tenderness than she deserved. Then he retrieved a towel from the bathroom and brought it to her. "You're wet."

"Thank you. And for what it's worth, I'm sorry." Avoiding eye contact, she brushed imaginary dirt from her shirt.

"At least now I know it's something you can't have had much experience—or success—with." He sat on the edge of the bed and cupped her chin in his hand, stealing her breath and causing her heart to thump. He squinted into her eyes, then wiggled her head from side to side. "Anything hurting?"

Other than the immense pain exploding in her heart, no. Physical attraction she understood. But tender care, this was new to her.

She closed her eyes as he ran his fingers through her hair, feeling the back of her head for a lump. She winced.

"Ah, there it is. Good news, I don't think you have a concussion." He stood. "Stay put. I'll be right back."

Ah, there it is—bad news. I think I broke my own heart. She didn't bother telling him he'd found the lump she acquired in an earlier fall. She opened her eyes, thankful his back was to her as he headed out the door so he didn't see the tears clinging just above her lashes.

An hour later he had the floor dried and buckets placed under all the leaks. Fortunately, the end where her bed and belongings were remained dry. And they said unlevel foundations were a bad thing. This one sloped to the middle, creating a wading pool in what had been the dining area.

He refused to let her help, or even get up from the bed. Maribel watched him discreetly, unsettled by her own feelings. Was he as genuine as he claimed to be?

"Are you sure you're not hurt?" he asked as he adjusted the position of a bucket. "I can take you to the emergency room if you want."

"I'm fine."

He stared at her with doubt. "Okay, call me if you change your mind. I checked the forecast and there's more rain coming. Let me know if the buckets get full, and I'll come empty them for you." He surveyed the ceiling then adjusted the placement of the bucket again.

"I'm sure I can empty them myself."

"Only offering." He rotated to leave, then paused and stared back at her. "And just so you know, I'm not a hypocrite, but I'm still a long way from perfect. The next time you play with fire, we're both going to get burned."

CHAPTER TWENTY-FIVE

It was Conner's turn to stomp across the wet ground. Was he a hypocrite? His past was certainly not spotless. He knew he wasn't the person he had been but couldn't deny that keeping his thoughts—his actions—in check tonight required everything he had. Now and then old feelings still pestered and tempted him.

For what I want to do I do not do, but what I hate, I do.

It was growing less true. Mack said it. Progress, not perfection. One degree of glory to the next.

But the feel of her hair in his fingers, the sweet smell of her shampoo mingled with the freshness of rainwater—he growled and swung his thoughts in another direction.

How could he tell Maribel those songs spoke to his heart when he didn't know what to say? Despite his skepticism at first, there were words so powerful they would keep him anchored in the roughest storms. He'd uttered more than one silent prayer tonight, thanks to her.

He'd seen it in her tonight too. Something deep within her resonated with the words of the songs, even if she didn't recognize it. She held herself so far away, almost unreachable. It bothered him in a way he wasn't prepared for. She kept herself—her heart—in a hard shell. But when he watched her talking with Daylee tonight, she had come out. There had been unguarded compassion on her face.

And when she ran laughing through the rain, he had received a precious and rare glimpse into her soul. Then she drew back, hiding in her protective shell, determined to destroy the will of anyone who dared to try entering.

Not bothering to hit the switch, he climbed the stairs to his loft by the glow of the security light outside, the heavy cloud cover reflecting the beam into the barn. He tossed his still damp clothes on the floor and stepped into a cold shower.

With enough of his own problems, he couldn't let himself get distracted by the need to throw a lifeline to someone who didn't care if they were drowning. But how could he not?

Tilting his head back, he let the icy water spray his face.

Her presence generated so many questions. He'd seen her resumé when he'd gone through her things. With her credentials and talent, why a job here of all places? Did she have something to hide? Or was she here for a story to get her foot back in the door as a journalist?

How different was that from what he was doing? His choice to be here was out of his control. But it was still just a means to an end.

He pulled on dry clothes and lay back on his unmade bed. He reached for his bible and flipped it open. What would it take for him to trust her?

What would it take to rescue her from herself?

CHAPTER TWENTY-SIX

Maribel awoke with a body that refused to move and a mind already in overdrive. Sleeplessness had been her companion for months now and last night was no different. Every time her eyelids slipped closed, the slide projector in her brain turned on, determined to replay every defeating moment of her life.

Now she had new slides to add. The one of Conner, when he told her he wasn't a hypocrite, haunted her the most last night. Even in her memory, he reached forward, seeing her truth and touching her soul. His words weren't accusing her. They were asking a question. Will you trust me?

She sat up and ran her fingers through pillow-pressed hair, wincing when they brushed against the bump from her fall.

At the mirror, she studied her reflection. Daylee needed help. Comfort for certain, but protection if the wrong person found out she might know something. And the girl, Leah, she needed someone to keep searching for her. To understand the seriousness of a missing teenage girl.

But could Maribel be the one any of them needed? Could she handle whatever was going on? Or would she make it worse?

Her ill-conceived plan to out Conner as a hypocrite last night came to mind.

Showered, dressed, and headed for coffee, she stepped out in time to see Conner driving away. Their conversation from last night still rang in her ears.

As she watched his truck disappear down the road, a solution to her dilemma with the man presented itself. Just this once she thought, coffee could wait.

From her porch she took a circuitous route around a few buildings as if she were getting some exercise. The path brought her to the backside of the barn, out of sight from everyone else at the camp. Just to be safe, she'd brought the screwdrivers Conner had loaned her. If caught she could say she was returning them.

She snuck through the backdoor, unnoticed. The morning sun shone through two windows on the east wall, illuminating the interior so she didn't need the overhead lights.

She poked around, snooping in corners and through carts and toolboxes. Other than the shovel, she had no idea what she hoped to find. She did know stalling here helped her work up the courage to go upstairs.

She ran her hands down her jeans and gave herself a you-can-do-it pep talk while wanting to find he'd moved the key.

Yes, it was morally wrong to snoop through someone's private space. But wasn't it more morally wrong not do everything she could to help Daylee?

Okay, to be honest with herself, she didn't think she'd find anything criminal in his room, much less anything that could help Daylee. This was about needing to prove to herself one way or the other who Conner really was. And it was completely wrong.

The fear of being caught came out in a thin wet sheen soon covering her entire body as she climbed the stairs. Even as far up on her toes as she could go, she couldn't reach the top of the door frame for the key. A short thief indeed.

She tested the wooden railing, then used it as a step ladder, reaching until her fingertips touched the key. Careful to return the key to its exact spot above the frame when she was done, she filled her lungs with a slow breath and held it. Releasing the air, she gripped the knob and turned.

The window air conditioning unit kicked on as she stepped in the room, and she jumped. She hoped it was only a small scream that escaped, but her heart pounded in her ears with such vigor, she couldn't say.

Closing the door, she leaned against it and did a quick survey of the room. He had a door that locked and apparently wasn't as concerned by what he left lying out. He could leave his unmentionables scattered about—and did. She tried not to notice. And to resist the urge to tidy up. The smell alone was enough to deter her from digging around too much.

The first thing that greeted her, after the general messiness of the place, was the open bible on his bed. Numerous sticky notes in a variety of colors poked out of the pages. Maybe she was wrong. Hope surged, until her brain stepped in. She couldn't forget the boy from camp all those years ago. He sang in the church band and quoted scripture like Billy Graham. It had been a nifty tool he used to gain a girl's trust.

But she saw her name scrawled on one of the notes and scrutinized it closer. It was attached just below a scripture on the open page. She read the words he'd underlined, letting her fingers trace along the page beneath them.

Now may the God of hope fill you with all joy and peace in believing, that you may abound in hope by the power of the Holy Spirit.

Hope. The word resonated deep inside her. She wanted hope. And Conner must have wanted it for her too. Conviction for what she was doing weighed on her with increased heaviness, tempting her to abandon the search.

Forcing herself to focus on her reason for doing this, she turned her back on the nightstand and moved to the battered wooden desk sitting against the far wall. Emotions weren't allowed to interfere with the work of a good reporter. The rule no doubt applied even if she wasn't a good reporter.

The top drawer was filled with an assortment of instruction manuals and a few invoices for purchased materials. The receipts for the parts for her Falcon were clipped together separate from the others. She removed the paperclip and flipped through them until the window unit kicked on again, snatching them from her hand and fluttering them to the floor. She dropped to her knees and hurried to retrieve them, scurrying as she got them back in the correct order.

The second drawer held more of the same. But not the third drawer.

She pulled out the manila folders and opened the first one. She froze. Clipped inside the file was a picture of her from her days at the newspaper, her name written in blocky letters on the opposite page, along with details from her life that needed more than a random search of the internet to find. A sob shook her body as she recognized the details of Alexander's death, the pain flooding her again. It sucked the air from her lungs.

This wasn't right.

She sat for a minute, calming herself. Whatever she had hoped to find, this wasn't it. She reread the notes, each time hoping they had changed. Handwritten details of her former addresses and past employers. The places she shopped and names of friends—although that was a short list.

He had been searching her cabin.

With her cell phone, she took pictures of each page.

The door to the shop below her opened, a faint squeak of the hinges followed by the hissing drag of the rubber flap across the concrete floor. Her hands shook as she hurried the file back to its hiding place. The drawer jammed. Why wouldn't it close?

The stairs squeaked under the weight of footsteps. She shoved harder against the drawer and finally it gave way. But the sound of it slamming sounded loud enough to have been heard in the admin building. She searched for a hiding place. No room under the bed and she couldn't bring herself to open the closet door—ever. A camo covered recliner sat near the wall. The sparsely furnished, one-room residence was not a mecca of hide-n-seek opportunities. Especially when one didn't want to be sought.

Another thought punched up her panic. Had she locked the door back when she'd entered?

She lunged behind the recliner, curling into a ball with her feet pressed against the wall and her back pressed into the fabric, for once appreciative of her small stature. Too late she realized her phone wasn't on silent. Not that anyone ever called her, but now would be an excellent time not to have a signal.

The door opened, but no footsteps followed. Instead there was the clicking of the doorknob twisting back and forth, jiggling. He must've noticed it wasn't how he left it. When he moved away, his steps were slow. She imagined him rotating around in the middle of the floor, scanning for anything out of place. She could practically feel his suspicions burning through the upholstery between them.

He had to be able to hear her heart beating. The bass drum in a marching band didn't make this much noise. What would he do if he found her?

Apparently, she did believe in the power of prayer because she was doing a hefty amount of praying—and hoping.

Long minutes passed before she heard him set a plastic bag on the counter, pull something—maybe a bottle of water—from the refrigerator and leave. The clicking sound announced he had locked the door this time and double checked.

Maribel didn't move, waiting for her pulse to slow. She realized she held her breath and forced herself to release it. The outer wall of the building vibrated against the soles of her feet when he closed the door below her.

Climbing from behind the chair, she hurried to the window to confirm he had left.

Then she locked the door behind her when she fled.

CHAPTER TWENTY-SEVEN

C onner sat across from Mack in the comfort of Momma Mae's, fidgeting like an anxious prom date.

"You nervous about something, Conner?" Mack sipped his coffee, although how he could manage that in the middle of a July day in Texas Conner didn't know.

He folded his hands on the table in front of him, interlocking his fingers and avoiding Mack's stare. "No."

Mack nodded and took another sip, his eyes saying *oh really.*

"Just frustrated, I guess. Tracy's death and Leah's disappearance. It's been a week. I should have found something by now. Do you know what the odds are of finding her alive now?"

"I do. But God isn't limited by statistics. He makes the odds, he doesn't play them."

"There has to be a connection to the camp, or evidence from her time there that points to something, anything." Conner smacked the table with his fisted hand. The salt and pepper shakers jumped, causing heads to spin their direction.

"You don't believe it was a random abduction," Mack tilted his head, "or that she ran away?"

"No, it's just a gut feeling, but I don't. There must be something I'm missing. Something right in front of me and I can't grasp it." He stared at the placemat in front of him as if reading a map. "And there's Tracy. I should have tried harder."

"I don't know that there's anything more you could have done. As humans we don't possess that kind of power. We plant the seeds God gives us. But when and how they grow is his business."

"There must have been something I could have said, something I could have told her."

"What could anyone have said to you before you were ready to listen?"

Conner leaned against the red vinyl bench. He scratched the top of his head. "I tried to talk to her once, but she definitely wasn't ready to listen."

Was this how it would be with Maribel too? The possibility knotted his insides.

Mack leaned forward, forearms on the table. "And you blame yourself? You believe if you had said the right thing it would have made a difference?"

"Yeah. I keep going over our last conversation, but I don't know. I keep thinking she never had much of a chance, and the way I treated her back then didn't help."

"But you changed and you're not that person anymore. There's only one with the power to change a person—and it's not you. What you feel is normal. You've received a beautiful gift—one freely given and undeserved—and now you want to share it. You want everyone to experience the freedom you found. But you can't make someone choose to accept the gift. You can love them. You can speak to them in truth. And you can pray for them. But you cannot decide for them. If you don't accept that, you'll make yourself crazy with doubt and grief. Or you'll give up. Then what will happen to the next person who needs you?"

Mack sat back and took another drink of coffee. He didn't intrude on the silence as Conner processed Mack's words.

"What about you? Have you changed your mind about Leah?" Conner came back to a problem he might still be able to solve.

"No, I haven't." For a moment it looked as if Mack wanted to say something else, but if he did, he kept it to himself.

"Daylee's afraid of something, but I can't figure out what, and she won't say much to me. She might be opening up a little more to Maribel. Maybe that's an angle I can work." He peered up, his eyes drifting to Mack's, reluctant to ask his next question. "Do you think any of this has to do with that stupid story about the treasure?"

"You don't believe in the mysterious lost treasure?"

"We are missing a shovel from the maintenance barn, but no. If there was a treasure, someone would have found it long ago."

"I agree it seems likely. Well, keep your eyes open. You're in the best place for figuring out if there's anything going on there. A little history research might help. Try talking to Peg. Or Maribel. I hear she likes history."

"That's something else too. How much do you know about Maribel? She told me some stuff last night, but I can't help feeling there's something else she's hiding."

"What makes you say that?"

"I can't put my finger on it, but she's very guarded. That's usually a sign of something."

"Or maybe someone hurt her, and she doesn't trust easily." Mack arched an eyebrow and gave Conner an accusing stare. "Have you told her everything there is to know about you?"

Conner sank in his seat as if Mack had slugged him.

Mack laid his money on top of the ticket the waitress left and rose. "I gotta go, but Conner, don't give up or get discouraged. Remember who you serve and what he can do."

He took a few steps, paused, and glanced back. "And don't get too worried about that pretty little brunette at the camp." Mack grinned and walked away. "I have it on good authority she's not a murderer or a kidnapper."

CHAPTER TWENTY-EIGHT

Maribel slumped on the leather sofa in the cool, dark sanctuary of Peg's living room. She sipped tea with enough sugar in it to give a hummingbird diabetes and listened to Peg as her mind wandered in no particular direction. Most days Maribel would have enjoyed the meander through Moreland Memory town, but her head—no, her entire body—was numb.

She hoped coming here would submerse her mind in something other than what she'd discovered in Conner's room.

Peg's voice was soothing, like a quilt Maribel could wrap up in and fall asleep. She knew she would awake rested, safe in the dusky light of the old house, a shelter insulating her from all the things troubling her life.

The ringing of the phone shattered the moment. Peg picked up the cordless handset on the end table and spoke into it as if it were a dirty sock.

"Oh, horseradish!" Peg smacked the phone down after only a few broken sentences of conversation.

"Reporters." She spat the word out like a mouthful of vinegar. "Don't they know I'm a sick old woman?" The sauciness in her voice made her self-assessment sound a bit overstated.

"What really upsets me is that I can't think straight with all this dad-burned medicine I'm taking. It makes everything so muddled. I know the answer, but I can't quite get to it." Peg leaned back in her chair and closed her eyes, wilting like a morning glory in the heat of day.

When she opened her eyes again, they were glossier than before. "I wasn't always this way. I've run this ranch by myself since my son died. And it darn sure wasn't easy. Droughts have stretched us thin and cattle markets so low you'd make more money giving the calves away."

Maribel picked up her notebook and opened to a blank page.

"But that's not what upsets me." Peg continued. "It's these greedy reporters. Don't care about nothing but the next big story. They don't care about Tracy Morgan. They just want to find dirt. There was a day when I could have set them straight. But all I do now is make myself look like an addled old woman."

Maribel dug her thumb into the opposite palm and squeezed, letting it cut into her flesh the way Peg's words cut into her conscience. She stared at the floor. Yes, she had wanted a story back then, but never at the expense of someone's life. But that was the price paid for her carelessness, her striving to impress. How was she supposed to live with that?

"Are you all right, dear?" Maribel's eyes met Peg's. The genuine concern she saw there was more than she could handle now.

She wasn't all right. And she didn't know if she ever could be.

"I'm fine. I'm going to get another glass of tea."

She surged from her seat with her glass in hand and headed to the kitchen. She sat the glass on the counter and stared out the window, hands gripping the edge of the smooth tile until her knuckles turned white. Everything inside pushed against her carefully constructed dam. If it cracked, she would drown.

No, she wasn't all right.

She poured out the remaining tea from her glass, watching the mink brown liquid swirl down the drain, then refilled the glass with tap water.

And he would have given you living water.

Her aunt had doused her in scripture, but Maribel never purposefully memorized any of it. Why were words she'd never believed coming so often to mind lately?

When the Spirit moves, right? Mack's words entered her thoughts. She had discarded them, but was it possible she was being guided by something beyond her own reasoning?

Your ears will hear a voice behind you, saying, "This is the way; walk in it."

"Are you sure you feel okay?"

Maribel startled, not the voice she expected.

Peg stood in the doorway, hand pressed on the frame for support. Peg seemed smaller today, as if she were shrinking from existence.

"Too much excitement this week, I guess." Maribel tried to smile.

"I've always been a good judge of character, and I like you. But this load you're carrying on your shoulders, are you keeping it there on purpose?"

Peg's voice and her question were an invitation, a lifeline if Maribel would take hold. Somehow, Peg knew and understood Maribel was slipping under.

"Oh, horseradish!" Peg squinted out the front window. "Speaking of being a good judge of character, I can't stand that writer woman. And unfortunately, she is parking her fancy car in front of my house at this very moment."

Maribel walked over and peeked her head around the door, watching through the front window as Ava headed toward the house carrying a foil-covered casserole dish.

"Should I ask?"

"Oh, it's nothing big. She says she's researching history for a book she's writing. Research or not, she's just plain nosey. And between you and me, she's as phony as a three-dollar bill. I haven't figured out a phony what, but I will. Anyway, those aren't likeable characteristics in a person." Peg's shoulders rose, a you-can't-blame-me-for-not-liking-a-person-like-that expression masking her face.

"I suppose people who write about history have a lot of questions about history and such." Maribel said. Peg was the second person she'd met who hadn't taken a liking to Ava. Maribel watched the woman cross the yard. She carried herself like a soldier preparing for battle. From Peg's reaction, that might not be too far from the truth.

"Uh-huh, well her questions are pretty well limited to one topic. I guess she didn't get the message the last time. I'm not interested in discussing it with her."

Peg put her hands on her hips and stood for a moment, a five-star general formulating battle strategy against the approaching enemy. "Oh, double horse-radish! She's got another blasted casserole. That woman absolutely CAN NOT COOK. Apparently, she's not content to let the cancer get me."

"Do you want me to send her away? Tell her you're resting?"

"No. Tormenting her keeps me going these days." Peg crossed the room, covertly peering out the corner of the window so she could time opening the door to the exact moment her visitor raised her hand to knock.

Maribel didn't miss the backdraft of anger that flashed in Ava's eyes as the door swung open.

"Hello, Mrs. Moreland." She spoke more loudly than necessary.

"It's Ms. Moreland, and hello yourself." Peg matched her chirpy syllable for chirpy syllable.

"I thought I'd stop by and check on you. May I come in? I made you a Frito casserole."

"Well, thank you. I'm sure it will be just as good as the tuna Jell-O mold you brought last week." Peg moved aside the exact amount needed to have not moved enough, and Ava wiggled herself inside sideways.

"Let me take that for you," Maribel offered.

"And if you don't mind, while you're in the kitchen, see if any of my other casserole dishes are sitting around? I need them back. I'm running out of pans."

Maribel smiled, confident she wouldn't find any of the missing dishes in the kitchen. She cut her eyes to Peg, who gave her an I-don't-know-what-you-are-talking-about look, and then a wink. There was at least one mystery solved.

Searching for a place to fit the dish into the refrigerator, she moved a six pack of sodas, a squirt can of Cheez Whiz, and a cardboard pizza box with half a cheese pizza. Shouldn't someone be monitoring Peg's diet?

Maribel winced. Her own diet was in self-destructive mode. What was she trying to do to herself?

Do you not know that your body is a temple?

She didn't feel like a temple—unless the Temple of Doom counted. But Conner had cared enough to comment on her eating habits. Why? Or did she want to know? After all, he'd also cared enough to stalk her—at least on paper, anyway.

She returned to the living room and found Peg and Ava exactly where she'd left them.

Ava wheeled to face her, hand extended and eyes wide, so the whites matched the slip of teeth showing between lips smeared with pink lip gloss. "Maribel. I didn't expect to see you here.. I understood you worked for the camp. Taking a break?"

"Something like that, I guess. I didn't see any other casserole dishes in the kitchen." Not a lie.

"Oh my, this medicine gets me all confused sometimes. There's no telling what happened to them. Must have thrown them away. I would completely understand if you never brought me another." Not a convincing act by Peg, but Maribel had the distinct impression it wasn't meant to be.

"Well, Maribel, I'm so glad to run into you here. I've been hoping we could get to know each other better, especially if you're going to be hanging around for a while." Ava chose not to pursue the casserole dish mystery. "So, now I'm curious, what is it that you do?"

"Hospice care." Peg blurted the words.

Surprise left Maribel's jaw sagging, her mouth agape, an open train tunnel expecting the enlightenment locomotive to chug on in.

A sharp laugh escaped Ava, but she was quick to regain her composure. "Hospice? What an interesting career choice—helping people die. You seem like someone who'd be good at that. But I was told you were working at the camp. Surely, hospice isn't necessary yet." With what must be a delayed afterthought, she pressed a hand to her heart as if she had a nasty case of heartburn.

"Yes. Weren't we fortunate to find such a jack-of-all-trades in our hour of greatest need?"

Maybe the medication was befuddling Peg's thinking. It was certainly befuddling her speaking.

"Besides, it's never too early to start preparing. How about you, Ava? From the looks of it, we're about the same age. Are you starting to contemplate the end? You shouldn't wait too long to prepare, you know." Peg took Ava's hand in hers. "My, your hands are cold, and your skin is pale and maybe a little blotchy. Are you sure you feel all right?"

Maribel managed to get her mouth closed while she listened to Peg antagonizing the woman.

With effort, Ava pulled her hand from Peg's grasp. "We are nowhere near the—" she exhaled and straightened. "Yes, I'm just fine. Thank you for asking."

Ava's eyes hopped from Maribel to Peg back to Maribel. Her expression said she was pretty sure she was being played. "I just didn't get the impression from Evan that she was here as a hospice worker."

Maribel remained silent, trying to imagine how a hospice worker might look standing here. She was sure she missed the mark, achieving more of an unhinged lady-in-waiting thing.

"He's in denial," Peg said.

"Well, not knowing things can get one in trouble," Ava said. "Perhaps with Maribel here to help you, we can go ahead with an interview for the book I'm going to write."

"Nope. Not interested." Peg crossed her arms, planting her feet square with her shoulders. It would have been a more intimidating stance without the slight wobble.

"That makes no sense. This is a great honor." Ava was a woman unaccustomed to being denied.

"James Michener asking to write a book about our family would be a great honor. I don't know you."

"But you know James Michener?" Ava's voice was heavy with sarcasm. "And you do realize he's dead, right?"

"And I'm looking forward to meeting him soon."

Maribel noticed the pronounced rising and falling of Peg's chest and the slight tremble in her hands. The little color she had was fading. Maybe now was a good time for hospice to step in. What had Conner said? One dead body this week was enough. And it wasn't looking good for Ava.

"I think it's time for your afternoon rest." She placed a gentle guiding arm around the older woman's shoulders.

"Yes. Yes, I believe it is." Peg played her role as a hospice patient well, her voice uncharacteristically submissive.

"Thank you for stopping to visit, Ava. I should help Ms. Moreland get settled now."

The three of them stood and stared for a span of time that bordered on painfully awkward. Then Ava about-faced and marched across the yard to her silver Lexus.

"I don't want to rush you with your work, but it might be best if we get this business finished as soon as possible." Peg watched out the window until the car was out of sight, then moved to a second window to spy even longer. "Now, I think I will take that nap."

Maribel gave her a questioning look, as Peg moved to yet another window to further monitor the car as it drove away.

"What? That woman snoops. I almost had to pepper her with buckshot to get her to leave last time."

CHAPTER TWENTY-NINE

Maribel opened the lock and caught the chain in her hand as it slid from the handle. Pulling open the barn door, she was met with the thick, stale smell of dirt saturated with oil and vermin refuse, aged and undisturbed for years. She dropped Peg's keys into her pocket. Laying the chain on the ground inside, out of the scorching sunlight, she stared into the black interior.

When Peg mentioned cataloging everything in the barn that might be of value, either monetarily or historically, Maribel volunteered. Anything to keep her away from the cabin and her thoughts away from Conner.

But she may have jumped in too soon. Several decades' worth of tools and equipment filled the barn. Implements used to carve out a corner of civilization and plant a place for generations of a family to grow. Antiques now, these items had once been the instruments of survival needed in the untamed ruggedness of West Texas. The hands that held them, used them, created, and cared for them knew hardship, pain, satisfaction, and joy. These tools chiseled a life from the hardships, and love grew. And yet, now they were just things.

Maribel ran her fingers along the curved wooden handle of an old hand plow, smooth as glass from years and miles of use.

She waved her hand, fanning air against her face. The heat of midday was not the time to tackle this project inside the metal building doing an imitation of a bar-b-que pit. But it was easy to get lost in the work at hand. Everywhere she observed, the dents and scratches, rust and peeling paint, waited to tell her their story.

She tugged a washtub filled with empty glass bottles to the side, then edged past a broken lawnmower that hadn't seen a blade of grass in decades. The one small overhead light that somehow still worked was unqualified for illuminating all the nooks and crannies, and the beam from the open door didn't reach far. Perfect for harboring small animals and things that slithered.

A shifty-looking set of stairs led to the loft overhead. She'd explore that another day, when she had a flashlight and didn't mind the possibility of falling and breaking her neck.

She eased around, caution directing her steps, assessing the amount of work this would require and what she needed to bring with her. The mass of stuff to go through was overwhelming. Did these people throw nothing away?

She swiped the sweat layering her brow with the back of her hand. No air circulated in the old tin building. Another pair of doors stood across from the ones she had entered, but Peg told her they hadn't opened in years. With no way to circulate the air or catch a breeze, she'd only be able to work here early in the day before the sun heated the building beyond human endurance.

She stopped to pick up a green glass bottle, and a rat darted along the wall mere inches from her hand.

Maribel jumped back, bumping into an old wood stove, jostling the chimney pipes. She flung her arms up to cover her head as they came clattering down around her. Something struck her head. The last thing she remembered thinking was she hoped she didn't land on a snake.

A heavy weight pressed against her. A quilt? A thick black quilt. So hot, she had to get away from it. But it wasn't a quilt. It was darkness engulfing her, like drowning in a sea of black ink. She had to find her way to the surface. Panic exploded inside her until finally she recognized her surroundings. The knowledge she'd been unconscious came to her slowly, but how long had she been out?

She sat up and pain shot through her head. Something was off and it took a moment for her to realize it was darker than before. The overhead bulb no longer shone, and the door had closed.

Apprehension squeezed her insides. She rubbed her throbbing head, trying to think. She was in Peg's barn. She was sure of it. But there was no wind today, and the doors were too heavy and rusted for a breeze to blow them shut. It made no sense they were closed now.

She moved through the dark on unsteady legs, waving her hand overhead, searching for the string that attached to the light, hoping she could coax it back on. Nothing. She aimed her steps toward the thin slice of light around the door.

She needed to get outside so she could cool off. The lightheaded sensation brought on by the blow to her head and her rising body temperature made her move slowly, carefully. She placed her palms against the door and pushed. Nothing.

Not possible.

She pushed again. The door rattled but didn't open. She angled her shoulder against the obstinate door and threw her weight against it. Other than an explosion of pain detonating in her skull, still nothing.

Not good. Do not panic.

Had Peg closed the doors? She said she was having trouble remembering things, but still.

"Peg!" She pressed her ear to the metal and listened, then, ignoring the pain, called again. Still no response.

Her throat burned from the effort. She shook the doors as hard as she could, then beat her fist against the hot tin.

Panting now, she rested and contemplated her next step. Running her fingers around the edge of the door, she felt for hinges she could unscrew. No luck. They were on the outside and probably rusted in place. Never mind the fact she didn't have a screwdriver.

She pressed the back of her hand to her forehead. *Think.*

There were no windows, but she studied the walls for streaks of light, wanting to find a loose sheet of metal to pry open. She found none.

Could she dig under the door and at least find any cool air there? Groping around in the dark, she found a horseshoe and knelt to scrape the ground beneath the door. Packed firm by years of use, the dirt didn't give. Tossing the horseshoe aside, she sat back hard against the hot metal. She needed to be careful she didn't make her circumstances worse by overheating.

With no air movement and midday temperatures tipping over the one-hundred-degree mark, it didn't take long for the barn to become a furnace. Perspiration streamed down her body. A good thing, she knew. When it stopped, she'd be in serious trouble.

The slight gap around the edge of the door let in a thin wisp of air. Enough to tease her. Not enough to help. What was the probability someone would find her? Soon?

Who was there to even miss her enough to search?

Not encouraging.

She concentrated on relaxing, trying to slow her pulse.

The blistering air dried her lungs, making them feel stiff and papery—or was that charred—unable to draw in enough breath.

She closed her eyes. How long before she passed out and then what? Heat stroke? Death?

And what had her life amounted to? She stacked her failures one on top of another, like bricks in the wall surrounding her.

Sweat covered her now, but without air to move against it, it offered little relief.

Something skittered across her hand and she jumped to her feet. A wave of dizziness followed, making her head spin until she fell. Reeling and paralyzed by nausea, she lay sprawled across the hard-packed dirt floor.

Regret. That was what she felt most. She didn't want her life to end on the record she had now. Not only was there nothing worth remembering, the ripple of her existence had never been wide enough or strong enough to touch another with her love.

There had to be more to it. There had to be more to her. She wanted what others had, Mack, Peg, her aunt, and until this morning she'd thought maybe even Conner. She didn't know what it was, but there was an unmet longing pulsating through her veins, stirring a desire to live— even stronger than what she'd experienced yesterday.

Her skin felt dry now. Not good.

Goosebumps arose on skin that felt chilled even though it wasn't. Facts from an article she'd written in college blazed through her mind—extreme thirst, system shut down—the details blurred. What came next?

It didn't matter. She was in serious trouble. Her pulse sped. Pulling herself up, eyes closed to fight the dizziness disorienting her, she shoved against the door one more time.

She tried to be angry at the unfairness of it all, but there wasn't enough energy left.

Love would have been enough. The sincere I-see-you-for-who-you-are love that says you matter, you belong. You are enough.

Lord, why wasn't I enough?

She didn't know if the words came out in the sob that shook her body, or only vibrated in her head. She closed her eyes and curled up on the dirt.

You have always been enough for me.

Enough for what? To die a horrible death alone in a barn?

For God so loved the world, he gave his one and only son that whoever believes in him shall not perish but have eternal life.

The words her aunt poured into her, but she never understood. *God, I want to understand. I want to live.*

I want to hope.

***

Conner put his truck in park and hopped out to open the gate. He needed to check the last of Peg's cows. The heat of the day wasn't the best time to do this, but he knew he could find them now beneath the oaks that surrounded the stock tank on the south side of the pasture. Something had them spooked lately, and he'd have to get them calmed down before the truck came in a few days to haul them away.

Something out of place on the barn drew his attention. The lock and chain he expected to see hanging from the handle of what Peg called the tractor shed was missing. Odd since he and Peg were the only ones with a key. He couldn't imagine her going in there in this heat when she could send him after anything she needed. He'd only been in there a few times, but Mack and Peg both told him there were lots of items in the barn treasure hunters would find enticing—antique things worth big dollars to the right buyers.

Instead of the gate, he shifted his attention to the barn.

He opened the door to check inside and jerked to a stop. A body lay sprawled in the dirt at his feet.

Something whooshed over Maribel's skin, causing her to shiver, a sudden breath of air that chilled her. Light made the insides of her eyelids glow.

A voice speaking her name tried pulling her thoughts toward consciousness. Things touched her body. Then she was floating. The air stirred around her bringing relief. Heavenly—although she didn't expect that to be the door to eternity she was allowed through.

Struggling, she fought through the dark, dead ends of her thoughts, frantic to find the door to coherence and understanding of what was happening. She should have told them how she felt. Peg, Daylee, Conner. She should have told them they mattered to her. Was it really so hard to speak the words? If they received her admission with indifference, so what? At least there would have been a proof that she could love unconditionally. And it would have mattered if they'd only known.

"Maribel!" Recognition broadsided him, unbalancing his thoughts. Not again. He wasn't going to fail someone again.

And not Maribel.

That his feelings for her were far deeper than he realized became a searing truth when she didn't move.

He reached her arm, feeling the dry skin. He pressed his fingertips against her throat, "God, please let there be a pulse. Please let her be alive." His choked words burned their way from a throat constricting in fear.

A tiny, fragile flutter beneath his fingers—she had a pulse. He released his breath and scooped her up, hurrying her into the fresh air. The water trough by the fence caught his eye, and he ran to it.

Lowering her in the tepid, moss filled water, he held her head from going under. She roused, struggling with little strength. He lifted her from the water to lay her on the grass. Stripping off his own shirt, he dipped it in the water and dabbed it against her forehead.

"What are you doing? What happened? What's that smell?" Her voice was a hoarse murmur as she batted her hand weakly at his wet shirt.

"You passed out in the barn." Why had she closed the door? She was a runner. She knew what that kind of heat could do to her.

She moaned, rolling over to vomit in the grass.

When she had finished, he wiped her face gently with his wet t-shirt. She pushed his hand away. "That smells terrible."

"I'm taking you to the hospital." He gathered her in his arms and lifted her as if she were weightless.

"Stop. I can walk." Her faint protest didn't faze him as he covered the distance to his truck in long, quick strides. Water still dripped from her as he deposited her onto the passenger seat.

Maribel sobbed as she lay over in the seat, pressing her head between her arms. She mumbled something that sounded like "Please, let me die."

CHAPTER THIRTY

M aribel hadn't needed to use the restroom this bad in a long time. The IV they hooked up in the emergency room must have been connected to a fire hydrant. Conner found every bump and pothole as he drove them home.

The pain medicine for the crushing headache kicked in. She hoped it didn't relax everything before she made it to the bathroom. Maybe she should ask him to pull over on the side of the road. An embarrassing place to handle the matter, but she was already about as embarrassed as she could imagine being.

The doctor wanted to keep her at the hospital due to the mild concussion he diagnosed, but she'd be a lifetime paying for the ER visit alone. Besides, she felt vulnerable there. Not that she should feel any safer with Conner, should she?

Maybe this was a bad idea.

Conner was quiet. In fact, he'd been acting strange the entire evening. Of course, this was not a normal evening out. She remembered him hesitantly picking moss out of her hair while they waited on the doctor to arrive. Her face warmed.

When he spoke, breaking the silence, his words sounded unsure, as if they stumbled over his tonsils on their way out. "I don't know what's going on with you, but people here care about you and would do anything to help you. Whatever happened in the past, ending your life won't change anything, or make it right."

"What?" The sound came out far too loud, and she flinched.

"Killing yourself. It's wrong. You matter." The manner of his stare caressed her soul and took her breath.

She felt the drowsy effects of the medicine making her body heavy and lethargic. Her head sank back against the seat that was still damp from her earlier trip.

"You matter to me." The husky tone of his declaration resonated in the air between them.

Tender vulnerability wrapped around Maribel and held her fast for a moment. If she hadn't seen the file he kept in his room, she could have believed he meant it. But the absurdity of his first statement pushed that moment aside.

"Wait. You think I was trying to kill myself?" Sometimes she thought about it, wondered why Alexander had done it. But the knowledge it solved nothing, only made everything worse or meaningless, repelled her from the idea. It didn't undo the past. It only eliminated the future. The pain hadn't pulled her that far under yet, but could it?

"You shut yourself in the barn in the hottest part of the day. You're a runner. You can't tell me you didn't know that was a set-up for a heat stroke. You could have died."

"I ... you ..." Maribel drew in a breath to settle the emotions clashing through her. She waited until she could enunciate the words with the proper amount of indignation. "Why would I do that? What a horrible way to die. I certainly wouldn't do that on purpose."

She waited, wondering if he might give himself away. After all, he already had all the answers in his file.

"Then why was the door closed? When you got hot, why didn't you come out?"

She stared at him, wondering if this was his idea of a joke. "I didn't close the door. And I didn't open it because I couldn't. It was stuck." Even with the medication relaxing her, the idea this was an intentional attempt to harm her

190

sent waves of anxiety over her. "The door was held shut. I think there was something wedged in the handle."

She swallowed, the medicine pulling her farther under than she wanted to go and making her words thick.

Conner shook his head, suggesting there was more he didn't want to say. His voice was soft when he said, "There was nothing in the handles, nothing holding the doors closed. And you asked me to let you die."

"I said, 'Don't let me die.'" She whispered the response, not caring if he heard or not.

Maribel shifted to stare out the window. Either he thought she was crazy, or he was a liar. The only reason to deny there being something holding the door closed was because he put it there or knew who did. After what she found this morning, she knew Conner Pierce wasn't who he pretended to be.

But there was another truth overwhelming her heart with conviction. If she truly did not want to die, why wasn't she living—really living?

CHAPTER THIRTY-ONE

Sunlight filled the room, but Maribel didn't move. A drug and exhaustion-induced sluggishness kept her nestled under the covers. For the first time in months, she had slept a dreamless sleep.

What was that smell? She sniffed again. She smelled like a water trough—cow slobber and algae. A shower would be great. But her body contented itself to be a prostrate lump between a scratchy blanket and the plastic mattress that had never been more comfortable.

She was sure Conner had still been there when she fell asleep last night. The effects of the medicine had overridden her fear. Or maybe she hadn't really been afraid to start with. In the relationships she'd experienced in the past, there had always been a sense of misgiving she'd convinced herself to ignore. Not a life-and-death sort of misgiving, but the constant feeling something didn't fit right. It pinched too closely here and gapped too much there. All things best ignored to have a chance at a relationship.

Yet not with Conner. It made no sense to feel safe with him. But she did.

It was a feeling she'd never really felt before.

But she couldn't forget about the file.

Her stomach growled. When had she eaten last?

If she intended to think with a clear head, she needed food first. A half-empty bottle of Gatorade sat on the nightstand. Conner had insisted she have it, even after the gallons of fluid the hospital forced down her. She groaned her way upright, her head still hurting, and took a sip.

Her face shriveled. Not coffee. And not a morning flavor.

A banging on the front door jolted her from her bed.

"Please, stop." She staggered as her feet hit the floor, trying to find her equilibrium. She glanced at her attire. The same thing she wore yesterday—athletic shorts and a t-shirt. Acceptable in appearance, if not in aroma.

"Maribel." Great. Conner first thing in the morning. Where was the coffee? And the pepper spray?

"Stop banging and come in."

"I can't. My hands are full. And it's locked."

"Locked?" She fiddled with the knob. Locked.

She opened the door to find Conner holding a tray loaded with enough food for five people. He handed her a large Styrofoam cup of coffee. "I brought the sugar and cream on the side, because—"

"You didn't know how much I use." She smiled despite how miserable most of her body still felt.

"I was going to say because you use too much, and I couldn't bring myself to ruin your health like that. I went through a lot of trouble to save your life last night, you know." He slid the tray onto the table, then scrutinized her as if she were a science experiment. Given the smell still lingering on the clothes she wore, she wouldn't judge.

"I didn't ask you to go through the trouble," she pulled her arms across her chest, rubbing her shoulder with her left hand, "but thank you."

He didn't make eye contact but nodded as if something bothered him.

"So, how'd my door get locked?"

"The replacement for yours hasn't come in yet so I switched it with mine last night."

She stared at him, too moved to hide her surprise or how much his actions touched her.

Shifting her gaze to the side, she cleared her throat. "And the key is ...?"

"In my pocket in case I needed it this morning. Plus, I checked on you a few times last night." He didn't offer her the key.

"Checked on me?" Her eyes narrowed, and she frowned.

"Yes, checked on you. You had a concussion, remember?"

"Slight concussion ... as in barely a concussion at all. And the doctor said nothing about my needing to be checked on."

He ignored her comment as he rearranged the tray of food. "You have no idea what the doctor said after the pain meds they gave you. So, besides difficult, how are you feeling?"

"Hungry." The aroma of bacon and warm cinnamon rolls drew her. She put the table between them, protecting him from the odor that clung to her, and her from any more of his scrutiny. "And ready for a shower."

"Well you're supposed to take it easy today. Good news, though. There's a chance of rain again, so it shouldn't be as hot. You need to stay out of the heat."

She surveyed her sparse furnishings. Not a place anyone would want to be confined, although she had more of Peg's papers to work through.

"I can't stay now. I gotta get things set up for the presentation this morning. Evan wants it moved to the tabernacle because of the forecast. But I'll take your tray back to the cafeteria for you later. There're some things I want to talk to you about." The weight of his words convinced her it would be a conversation she wouldn't enjoy. "Are you going to be okay for a while?"

She nodded. The urge to say yes because she meant it fluttered in her heart. But her brain hadn't warmed to the idea yet. All because of one stupid, unexplainable file.

A file she couldn't tell him she had seen because she was afraid of ... of what? Of what he might do or of having to admit it contained the truth?

He stared at her for longer than was necessary for a proper goodbye among friends, as though he didn't want to leave her.

Warmed by the scrutiny, her hand settled at the base of her neck.

Maribel was used to feeling alone. She was okay with that. But it was lone-liness that swept into the void he left as he pulled the door closed behind him. And that was not the same—and not okay.

"Wait, the key!" Her hand frantically touched all around her neck. The chain Peg had given her was gone, and with it the key to the locked box she'd been asked to protect.

CHAPTER THIRTY-TWO

R est and recovery were not going well. The quickening in her veins made it hard for Maribel to be still even though her body begged for rest. She had to find the key. She'd searched her cabin and found nothing. Had it come off in the barn or had Conner taken it when they were at the emergency room? Would she have remembered that?

But he did say he'd checked on her last night.

She replayed everything she could remember from the day before and kept circling back to the idea someone had tried to kill her. Irrational perhaps, but the feeling wouldn't let go.

But who?

It was possible Conner had a secret infatuation for her. That might explain the file. He could have set this up so he could play the hero. Stranger things had happened, right? But that explanation felt all wrong. She just couldn't come up with another.

At first, she'd been furious he thought she was trying to commit suicide. Then she remembered how frantic he'd been driving her to the hospital. He'd prayed aloud the entire time. She didn't know why he didn't share his suspicion that her trauma was self-inflicted with the doctor last night, unless he already knew the truth. And there she circled right back into the midst of indecision. Good guy or bad?

But it didn't add up. The way he'd spoken the words when he'd brought it up on the way home, full of such hurt and compassion, had kindled something in her. A feeling she didn't want to dwell on—not with an unknown someone trying to kill her for an equally unknown reason. But could she believe Conner might be a murderer?

And no matter how hard she tried, she couldn't convince herself it was anything but attempted murder.

She needed to get back to Peg's and search for the missing key.

Slipping on her shoes, she headed first to check on her car and verify Peg's box was still locked safely in the trunk. As far as she knew, no one was aware she'd put it there. Then she'd go to the office to retrieve her computer. A small step but at least it was something to do.

The girls gathered beneath the tabernacle and she angled her steps it that direction, drawn by a sudden urge to see Daylee and know she was all right.

Squeals splintered the air, arousing her curiosity. The girls were on their feet, the back rows standing on the benches for a better view and blocking Maribel's. She moved to the side and inched along the edge toward the front, scanning the cluster of pony-tailed heads for Daylee.

She was so focused, she nearly collided with someone.

A small, thin man, not much bigger than Maribel, stood beside her. A large snake draped over his shoulders. Maribel froze, cold fear clamping down on her.

"May we help you?" His question startled her, and a quick shake of her head was all she could manage.

"Can we hold her?" one of the girls called out.

"No way. Totally against camp policy." A counselor promptly squashed the idea.

"Ask him if you can hold her, Maribel!" Daylee's voice ripped through the air.

The crowd of young faces spun toward Maribel. Her stomach flipped and settled somewhere around her knees, which now felt as sturdy as warm Jell-O.

"How about it? Would you like to hold Mercy?" He moved even closer to her, close enough Maribel could touch the snake if she wanted. Which she most certainly did not.

She just stared, speechless. First, who names a snake Mercy? Second, why was the world starting to spin at an odd angle?

And who glued her feet to the ground and her tongue to the roof of her mouth?

The snake man's smile grew. "Ophidiophobia. The fear of snakes. The best way to overcome your fear is to face it. You'll realize you have nothing to fear when you handle them correctly. Allow me to show you. You can hold her. She's very friendly—and well fed. No need to be afraid in front of all these girls."

"No really, I'm supposed to be resting. Doctor's orders." She backed away, the words stumbling out of her mouth like they were drunk and disoriented. A round of giggles erupted from the girls. No doubt about it, she looked like a coward. A shame she could live with. No way she was getting any closer to the snake for any reason. Fear was its own boa constrictor.

The girls began to chant "do it, do it." Snake guy watched her as if the peer pressure of a bunch of teenage girls might change her mind. The blood drained from her head to churn in her stomach. The sudden onset of light-headedness set the tabernacle spinning even more off kilter.

"I don't think so. Miss Montgomery is supposed to be resting. Instead of setting a poor example of following doctor's orders for the campers." Conner stepped from the back of the crowd, walking toward them. Her knight in shining armor, although he wore cargo shorts and tennis shoes. But the expression on his face was an unveiled reprimand. "How about you show me how to handle Mercy?"

Maribel scooted herself out of sight as snake man walked over to Conner. She'd seen enough.

She leaned against a post, waiting for her legs to grow sturdy enough to get her up the hill to her cabin.

"Not much of a snake person, huh?" Sheriff Griger watched her, a bemused expression on his face. His presence surprised her.

Maribel shook her head, her eyes moving back and forth between Conner and the snake he held. The snake man pulled another smaller, though no less wicked looking, snake from a different container.

"Can't say I blame you. Hope he doesn't give these girls any bad ideas. Hate to see anyone get bit. The closest hospital with antivenom is a good hour away." Griger moved to her side. "That's a cotton mouth he's getting out right now. Good for the girls to learn what they look like, especially the poisonous ones like that." As if on cue, the snake opened its mouth, revealing the stark white inside that gave it its name.

"I never understood Milton's interest in snakes, always collecting and keeping them. His family always had a few rats in the attic, if you know what I mean. 'Course, that can be said for several of the families around here."

"Were you born around here?" Maribel regretted the question as soon as it was out.

"As a matter of fact I was. No rats in our attic though. We always steered clear of houses with attics." Sheriff Griger chuckled. "I hear you had a little excitement yesterday."

Maribel licked her lips. The idea someone had done that to her deliberately wouldn't leave her alone, but she wasn't ready to confess those thoughts to the sheriff. "I don't know that I'd call it excitement. I'm just thankful Conner found me when he did."

"So, just an accident, huh?"

Maribel nodded, an uncertain and jerky movement as though even her head couldn't tell a lie. Thankfully the sheriff let it drop.

"Do they know yet how Tracy Morgan died?" Maribel expected him to tell her it was too soon, but anything was better than talking about snakes.

"Too soon for the results of the autopsy."

"What about the girl, Leah? Do you have any idea what happened or where she might be?" Maribel was pressing her luck knowing even if he knew anything he probably wouldn't share.

"No news there either."

"What about her parents? Why aren't they here?"

"Full of questions today, are you? I hope you're not thinking of becoming an amateur detective. That's a good way to get yourself in trouble."

"Just concerned. Shouldn't there be more of an effort being made to find her?"

"We're having the milk cartons with her picture printed as fast we can, darlin'." Sheriff Griger leaned over and spit.

They watched as Milton held the poisonous snake on a long piece of equipment he referred to as a snake tong, explaining the correct use of his apparatus and proper handling of the reptiles by trained professionals only.

"It's a miracle he's never been bitten. I reckon it's just a matter of time, though. When folks start messing with stuff they shouldn't, sooner or later it gets 'em hurt. He used to try to get me to go snake hunting with him." Sheriff Griger shuddered. "No, thanks. I'm scared of the things myself."

Maribel regretted having come this way for a number of reasons now. Sensing a threat in the sheriff's words was almost as unsettling as being face to face with the snake.

"Well, I'm gonna mosey over and see if your boss is in yet." He dipped his head to her, the brim of his hat shielding his eyes. The way he accented the word boss insinuated he knew it wasn't true. "I'll be seeing you. And watch out for snakes. They're everywhere."

From a distance, Rock Griger stood and watched as Maribel walked back to her cabin. She was a complication. Whether she'd be a useful one or just a hinderance, he didn't know yet. She'd lied to him when he asked if the incident in the barn was an accident. It might have been, but her reaction to his question indicated she didn't think so. He was still waiting on some phone calls to be returned, then he'd decide what to do with her.

Until then, there was always Evan to keep off balance. He headed to the admin building, mentally bracing himself for Becca's greeting when he entered.

"Good morning," Becca's squeaky voice didn't disappoint. "To what do we owe the pleasure of a visit from the sheriff this morning? Please tell me you've got some good news on that poor child, Leah."

"It's still an ongoing investigation. I'm afraid there's nothing new to tell just yet." He removed his hat and held against his midsection. "The boss in?"

"He's around here somewhere. Said he was going to take a walk and would be gone for a while."

"Happen to know which way he went?"

"He turned right when he went out the door, but that's the last I saw."

Turned right. Great. The bulk of the camp lay to the right of the front door. He didn't have time to wait, or the patience to wander around until he found Evan. "I'll just try to catch him later then."

"You want me to give him a message?"

Rock held his tongue. There were plenty of things he'd like to say to the weasel, but none fitting for a lady to relay. "No, thanks."

Tipping his head, he put his hat back on and reached for the door.

"Oh, Sheriff Griger, I've been meaning to ask. Did you ever send in your DNA sample for the genealogy test? Some of my ancestors were Vikings. Can you believe that?"

"Uh, no. I haven't quite got around to that yet."

"Aren't you curious to know where you came from? Evan's been a real dud with his, keeping it all secretive."

He pushed the door part way open, adjusting his hat more firmly on his head. "Already know more than I want to."

CHAPTER THIRTY-THREE

The image of Conner with a snake as thick as a man's arm wrapped around his neck refused to leave her head. Maribel rubbed her neck, tugging at the collar of her t-shirt, thinking not of snakes but ropes and the marks they left. She lowered her head, pressing her palms into her eyes. Good guy or bad guy? Why did it have to be so hard to know? She longed for answers instead of more questions.

The urge to get out of this suffocating cabin and breathe pressed against her. The desire to check out the barn pressed even harder.

Late morning and a growing cloud cover kept the temperature a few degrees below normal. She wasn't one hundred percent recovered, but she'd go slow. She might have to talk herself out of a lecture if she got caught, but she could worry about that later. The look Conner had given her when he caught her at the tabernacle told her he wouldn't be too pleased to find her at Peg's either. And for some reason, he seemed to have appointed himself her guardian—which she didn't need.

She grabbed the half empty bottle of Gatorade and took it with her for good measure. Besides, she didn't intend to walk right down the front drive where Conner might see her.

Sounds of a game in progress came from the rec hall. Good, everyone would be in the gym. She cut across the hill behind her cabin, using it to keep her out of sight until she could reach the road undetected. She remembered the sheriff's warning about snakes and antivenom and took her time watching where she placed her feet.

Even with her hypervigilance the walk relaxed her, pulling her thoughts into a more peaceful direction as she moved away from the noises of the camp. The only sounds around her now were of nature.

Above her, a buzzard floated in idle circles. Peg's warning flitted through her thoughts. But was there really some metaphoric buzzard trying to blind her? Did it blind her to the truth? For the first time it occurred to her it might be self-doubt. It was the one thing that stopped her no matter which way she tried to go.

There was something Conner said on that first day as they rode to town. Something about the Pool of Siloam being a place where a man had his sight restored. She wished she hadn't stopped him from telling her the story.

She didn't stop to visit Peg. Explaining her mission would require worrying the woman with what happened last night. She left the road and skirted through the trees, hoping Peg wasn't watching out her window.

Someone had closed the door, chain and lock securely back in place. The ever-responsible Conner would have seen to all of that. She hesitated. Did she dare try this again?

With eyes closed, she drew in a long breath, trying to recall the details of yesterday. What had she missed when she'd gone in the barn?

She dug the key from her pocket and released the lock from the chain exactly as she had the day before. It took effort to pull the door open, something she might not have considered yesterday, but did now. It convinced her the door could not have closed by itself or as a result of the wind.

A piece of board lying on the ground caught her eye. She picked it up to wedge between the door and the ground for good measure. Instead she closed the door back and slid the wood into the handle. An easy fit and a perfect way to secure the door from opening. It was also obvious this board had not been outside for long. It still held the creamy yellow color of un-weathered lumber.

Assumptions had gotten her in trouble before, though.

Moving to stand in the shade of a tree, she shut her eyes and mentally retraced her steps from yesterday. Had she seen this board when she first came to the barn? After a while she gave up and told herself the only way to recall more was to go inside.

And she needed to find that key. Pulling out her cell phone, she clicked on the flashlight feature only to find the battery almost dead. She eased over to the string that dangled from the light bulb and reached to grab it.

"Hey, there."

Maribel jumped, her startled scream amplified in the metal barn. Her hand pressed hard against her chest as she labored to catch her breath.

Conner. Why was he here?

"Didn't mean to scare you. Of course, I'm not going to say it wasn't kinda fun." He made his way closer to her. "Unless you've found another dead body? Or are trying to be one again?"

"I'm not." Her words were sharp, heavy with annoyance.

"You're not going to stay put and rest today, are you?"

"I have work to do." She put her hands on her hips and gave him a look she hoped said please-go-away. He either didn't understand or chose to ignore her implied request. She huffed and reached again for the cord to the light fixture. She paused as she stared up at an empty socket. "I don't understand. There was a bulb in here yesterday. I turned it on, and it worked."

Conner stared up at the empty socket, then back at her with skepticism. "Hang on. I got this."

He darted back out and returned before she had time to miss him, flashlight in hand.

"I'm not crazy or making things up. Something's not right here." Anger crowded her thoughts.

He studied her for a moment longer. "All right then, if I help you snoop around, then will you go back and rest?"

She wanted to do this alone with only her thoughts in her head. "You think I'm imagining things—what? Because I got a bump on my head?"

"I think the count of blows to your head in recent days was a little higher than just one." He settled his hands on his hips and dared her to argue.

"How did you know I was here?"

"Peg saw you walk up and wanted me check on you."

Peg trusted him. That was encouraging, right?

"So, you're here to babysit me?" Maribel gave him her fiercest glare of annoyance. She wanted time alone. "And why does Peg think you needed to check on me? You didn't tell her what happened, did you?"

"It's Peg's place. And I prefer to think of myself as well-being facilitator, but if babysitter works for you, I'm game." He grinned, his mischievous dimples exacting an adverse effect on her pulse. "However, this is against doctor's orders. I really have to question what you're doing here."

"I needed to make sure there's nothing else I need for the ... project I'm working on." *Investigating my attempted murder* didn't feel like it would get a positive response from him.

"Quite the dedicated employee you are, huh? You know Peg would send you home if you told her that was your reason for being here?"

Maribel hesitated, watching the buzzard of self-doubt swoop in circles around her. Taking a chance, she told Conner about the missing key.

"You weren't wearing it when I found you."

"You're sure?"

"Quite. Soaking you in the water trough—let's just say I remember the details extremely well and leave it at that." He looked away as if the admission embarrassed him.

Maribel felt the heat of a raging blush blistering her face.

Conner cleared his throat and clicked on his flashlight. "Okay. Where do we start?"

"Thanks, by the way," she said.

"You're welcome, but it's only a flashlight." He pondered the light in his hand, for once giving the impression he wanted to change the subject to something less intense.

"Not for that. For yesterday, and for this morning."

He gave her a questioning look.

"With the ... you know." She stared at him, eyes wide, imploring him to read her mind.

"Oh yeah, the snakes." He shuddered and frowned, surprising her.

"What? You didn't like that?" The male hubris he held in excess should have feasted on the opportunity to impress the girls with his fearless masculinity.

"Nope."

"Then why did you do it?"

"Because it seriously looked like you would like it a lot less. I have never seen anyone turn white as fast as you did." He continued to examine his flashlight as if it were new to him. "It was no big deal."

Maribel thought differently.

She surveyed the objects around them, then stepped to the last place she remembered before she lost consciousness—the first time. The stove pipes that had fallen were still scattered about, but they'd fallen on the far side from where she remembered waking up. That didn't mean one of them hadn't hit her on the head, though. She scanned the ground, searching for the missing chain and key.

"So, I'm guessing this is more about coming to see for yourself than it is about finding a key." Conner came to stand beside her.

Ignoring him, she worked through the details of everything that happened yesterday. "Conner, something fell on me and hit my head. I think it knocked me out. But I'm positive the doors were still open, and the light was on before I blacked out."

She scanned around, more confused. "What does that mean?"

"Tell me what you remember." Conner's troubled eyes held her gaze. He wasn't hiding anything. He didn't know.

"A rat ran by and I jumped into this old stove. The stove pipes came loose and fell on top of me. I think that's what hit me. But how did the door get closed and the light—someone had to take the bulb out."

Conner moved his beam of light to the loft. She knew he processed all she said, but his doubts still existed. "Show me where you were standing."

"I was reaching for a bottle," she pointed, "the green one here." She moved to stand beside it, then stepped back into the stove, more gently than she had yesterday. "Here. I was standing here."

Conner peered up again at the loft. "Maybe the jostling knocked something loose from up there."

Flashlight in hand, he edged past her and headed for the stairs. "Let's see what's up there. Might give us a better perspective on what could have happened at least."

"Do you think those stairs are safe?"

He gripped the rail and shook it. "I doubt it. You wanna go first?"

She started for the first step, but Conner put his arm out to stop her. "I'm kidding. I'm going first."

Old cookware, saddles made of drying and cracked leather, and scraps of various things deemed too broken to use, but too valuable to discard filled the loft. Curiosity and a nostalgic heart overrode her fear once she saw there was nothing but old relics up here. She poked around.

"Why did Peg send you in here?"

She wiped her hands together, brushing off the dirt. "She didn't send me. Just wanted to do something with it and I offered to help. She doesn't want to leave it to happenstance after she's gone."

"Lighter fluid and a match would probably be the best—and easiest—solution." Conner obviously didn't share her interest in history and antiquity.

He stepped closer, moving to the center where the roof was tallest, so he didn't have to duck. It brought him so near, she had to tilt her head back to peer up at him, but piles on either side of her kept her from moving. "There are other things that shouldn't be left to happenstance either. I reckon now is as good a time as any to have that talk."

And now back to intense. No thanks.

"Here? Now? This isn't a place I want to spend any more time than necessary in case you aren't aware."

"Great. The sooner we talk, the sooner we go. Tell me what's going on in your heart, Maribel."

She attempted to step around him, but he shifted, blocking her path.

He clicked off his flashlight, leaving them in darkness.

"Turn that back on."

"Nope. Not until you answer my question," he teased, but it didn't hide the compassion with which he spoke.

Maribel crossed her arms over her chest and glared at him. She refused to admit he scared her—or made the blood flow through her veins with a pyrogenic hum. "You're acting like a five-year-old. And what difference does it make?"

"Maybe I'm just a very curious guy."

She swallowed, her dry mouth. She didn't feel threatened, not physically, but there were other things she needed to protect.

The only escape route was the stairs, which he blocked, and she couldn't manage in the dark anyway.

When he spoke again, his words were quiet, his tone solicitous. "What happened in your past you don't want to talk about?"

"What makes you think something happened?" She recoiled at the tight sound of her voice.

"Only guessing. You seem broken."

"Is this because of what I said the other night? That I didn't think God believed in me? Or is it because you think I tried to kill myself?" He might not have meant to be abrasive, but his words rubbed her raw. Her shoulders pulled back, stiffening, arms still crossed like a shield.

"Both, I guess. You can trust me, Maribel. I want to help."

"I'm not your do-good-works-and-get-into-heaven project. I don't need your help."

"You're right. It's not my help you need. But you also don't want my help. There's a difference. What you said about God not believing in you. That's not true, you know?"

Maribel's hair brushed against her neck as she shook her head. "No. I don't know." But the words fell uncertain.

"He created you, Maribel. Of course, he believes in you. What if I could prove he does love you?" He placed his hand on her shoulder, both his touch and his voice soft and warm. But she wanted the words to be true too desperately to risk finding out they weren't.

"No."

He turned the light back on "All right then, tell me why you were in my room yesterday?"

CHAPTER THIRTY-FOUR

M aribel shifted away, feigning interest in the nearest object she could see in the dark. "Why do you think I was in your room?" She cringed. Answering a question with a question was never a good defense.

He laughed. "You told me so last night."

She spun to face him, mouth open but no words coming out.

"The medicine they gave you for your headache loosened you up. By the way, thanks for the compliment. But even though you think I'm hot, I don't think we should get involved since we are co-workers."

The heat searing her face rivaled what she had experienced yesterday. "I ... I didn't mean to ... the medication ... I don't usually refer to men as hot. I mean you're very nice looking, handsome, but I ... I didn't ..."

Conner laughed as her words burbled out like a pot boiling over, sizzling on the hot cooktop. He ducked his head and peeked up with a devilish glint his eyes. "Okay, you didn't say that. It was just a guess. A very impressive and satisfying guess." He offered her a flirtatious grin. "But now we have that out of the way—by the way I think you're hot too—let's hear why you broke into my room?"

She inhaled, studying the ground as she tugged at the hem of her shirt. "I didn't break in to your room."

She pushed past him and headed to the stairs.

"Not so fast." Conner grabbed her arm, pulling her closer. "I know the medication can make people talk out of their heads. But you were in my room, Maribel. The medication doesn't make up the details of what you saw."

The nearness of his body radiated heat throughout her, the kind of heat that makes one's knees unsteady. She watched him, more afraid to deny the truth than of what his wrath might be. "I was just curious, that's all. I saw where you keep the key and I let myself in."

"Usually when people are curious about someone they just ask."

"You're right, but I didn't know if I could trust you."

"You don't trust me? After what you pulled the other night, you're the one who doesn't trust me? You broke into my room to spy on me?" His voice held the incredulous tone it rightly should. What had she been thinking?

"I'm sorry. It was a stupid thing to do, but I don't have the best judgment sometimes—clearly. I just needed to know." She lowered her gaze. And she did now, didn't she?

"Well, did you find what you were looking for?" He didn't curb the note of sarcasm in his tone.

"I need to go. I'm not feeling well." She tried again to edge past him.

He held her tight, forcing her to look at him. "What else aren't you telling me, Maribel?"

His breath was hot against her face, but his eyes held only hurt, no fury.

"I saw the file." There. She said it and whatever happened, happened.

"What file?"

"The one about ... the one about me."

He released her arms and stepped back. "What are you talking about?"

A clap of thunder vibrated the walls surrounding them.

Conner sighed. "I don't want to be stuck in here in another storm. Let's get to the truck before the bottom falls out." He took her hand and headed to the stairs.

"Conner, stop. Someone else's been up here."

"What makes you think that?"

"That jar has been moved recently. Look, there's no dust where it used to sit."

"Okay, could have been Peg or someone else she sent to look for something." Thunder rattled the roof above them again. "Now let's get out of here."

They hurried down the stairs and back outside. He moved to close the door behind them, kicking the wood she placed against it aside. Then he stopped and picked it up, flipping it over in his hands, exposing writing.

"I found this outside this morning. Someone could have used it to barricade the door yesterday."

"Where did you find it?"

She pointed to the spot.

"And it wasn't there yesterday?" The skepticism in his voice had the effect of a cheese grater passing over what little pride she had left.

"I don't know. I wouldn't really have made note of a piece of wood. I wasn't expecting anyone to use it to kill me."

The expression that passed over his face hinted at confusion and consternation.

Drops of rain began to fall. Conner hustled to close and chain the door. They sprinted to the truck, jumping into the cab seconds before the downpour began.

He started the engine, then sat for a moment before turning to Maribel. "You really believe someone tried to kill you?"

Maribel stared straight ahead. When spoken aloud, the words made the idea sound crazy.

The rain beat against the cab, creating a metallic roar. The sound, accompanied by the thick wall of water falling around them, blocked everything outside the cab. It gave her the perception of being isolated in a world of their own.

"I don't know." She was quiet for a second. "Do you believe in karma?"

"No. I believe in a broken world desperately in need of the grace and mercy only the Creator offers."

Maribel wrapped her arms around herself, pulling her shoulders in tight, chilled by her thoughts more than the rain. "Grace and mercy, huh? I don't deserve either."

The shush of the rain beating against the truck was the only sound. Then Conner chuckled. "I don't think you understand the meaning of the words. If you did, you'd know their power is because no one deserves them. They're a gift."

He rested his head against the back glass. "I took you for a better grammar perfectionist than that. And yet you don't know the meaning of grace and mercy."

Maribel faced the side window. Yes, she knew the definition of the words, but maybe she didn't actually understand their meaning.

He sat, tapping his fingers on the steering wheel. "For all have sinned and fall short of the glory of the Lord. You aren't the only one, Maribel. We've all made mistakes and bad choices. But God gives us what we don't deserve through His grace and keeps us from what we do deserve through His mercy." His gaze shifted to her, unhurried and tender, gaging her response. "So, look it up. It wouldn't be grace or mercy if we deserved it."

"I don't know if I want grace or mercy. I don't deserve anyone's forgiveness." It was a lie. To believe there was true forgiveness available to her was something she desperately wanted.

"What is it you do want, Maribel?"

The question was too big and the answer too complicated. What did she want? Last night she thought about life and living. But in the daylight, the thoughts scared her again.

She remembered the file in his desk and her eyes misted. "I think I want to go back to the cabin and rest."

The light in his eyes clouded. Her answer had disappointed him.

"Okay, so we won't talk about grace and mercy. Let's talk about why someone wants to kill you?"

She wiped the moisture from her eyes, hating that he might see her vulnerability and think her weak. He brushed a strand of hair from her face, then took her hand in his. She wanted to pull it back, but oh, how much more she didn't. She glanced at him and the tender concern on his face was almost her undoing.

But she couldn't forget what she'd seen in the file. He already knew.

Maribel watched the rain run down the windshield in crooked paths, impossible to predict. Just like life she had discovered. Her gaze went to where his hand still held hers. Why did the person who brought her the most comfort right now have everything pointing back to him as the source of her problems?

When she was able to speak, she answered. "No reason I know of. But that doesn't change the fact something, or someone, trapped me inside. What I don't know—was it on purpose?"

"That piece of board is mine ... or one I used recently, anyway. I recognize the notes I'd written on it. I left it in a closet in your cabin, so I'd have the measurements when it came time to repair the roof. But Maribel, it wasn't in the door when I found you." Conner spoke slowly, as if the admission troubled him.

"Are you saying you don't believe that I couldn't open the doors?"

Stillness filled the cab as the question hung between them.

"You had been knocked unconscious. Is it possible you only imagined you couldn't open the door?" Conner stared straight ahead, not making eye contact.

Self-doubt rolled back in like the fog of early morning. She didn't know what she thought, much less believed right now. "I don't know."

"Well, either way, someone still took the board from your cabin and left it at the barn. So, the questions are who took it out and why?"

Unless the obvious answer was the one right in front of her. Why did everything keep pointing back to Conner?

Reluctant to leave her alone, Conner loitered as long as he could reasonably justify. He'd checked her cabin inside and out and given her instructions to stay put and rest. The distrust in her eyes as she watched him hurt, but he tried to be patient. He made sure she locked the door behind him, thankful and

215

surprised she hadn't demanded the key from him. A minor lapse in prickliness on her part he was certain she would soon correct.

On the seat beside him lay the board with his handwriting scrawled across it. He remembered the day he'd written those notes when he couldn't find a notepad. And he remembered where he'd left it afterwards—nowhere near Peg's barn. He'd wanted it to be handy when the materials for the new roof came so he'd stuck it in a closet in the cabin where Maribel was now resting—alone.

How did it end up at Peg's? Unless Maribel took it there?

Would she have set up the entire thing yesterday to look like someone was trying to kill her? He didn't think so, even though the evidence led his thoughts in that direction.

Not wanting to worry Peg anymore, and with Mack in Houston for his checkup, Conner pointed his truck toward town and the sheriff's office. Maybe Rock could brighten the darkness of his thoughts. Either way, the sheriff needed to know.

He drove a little faster than he should.

CHAPTER THIRTY-FIVE

M aribel attempted the nap she said she wanted but gave up after half an hour. The incessant dripping from the holes in her roof twisted her already-worn nerves into angry knots. The edgy restlessness held on even after the rain stopped.

Maybe Peg was right. Maribel needed to get this work wrapped up. What Peg hadn't said but Maribel felt was that she needed to get away from this place and these people who were confusing her thoughts and making a mess. Only one box remained to sort through, and she wasn't sure she felt up to it.

So far, all Maribel had seen had been the typical letters, documents, and newspaper clippings one expected from a family like the Morelands. Business deals good and bad, along with records of their benevolence and compassion for others and their love and devotion to their family.

Thunder interrupted her thoughts. More rain was coming. Her stomach growled, reminding her she hadn't eaten lunch.

She scavenged the loose change from her backpack and hurried to the rec hall, anxious to beat the rain. Long past lunchtime, she headed to the vending machines, keeping her eyes on the darkening horizon. She dropped coins into the slot for a Dr. Pepper, then deposited the last of her change for a package of peanut butter crackers with a Three Musketeer for dessert.

"Hey! There you are." Daylee's voice reverberated in the small enclosure that housed the vending machines.

"Yes, I am." Maribel stooped to retrieve her meal from the tray.

"I went to your cabin this morning to check on you after you nearly had a heart attack over the snake."

"I'm fine, thank you," Maribel replied, her words acerbic. Daylee apparently saw no irony in mocking Maribel's fears although she'd been the one expressing her own terrified thoughts in the shelter of Maribel's arms just a few days ago. "I wanted to hang around and wait, but Evan came over to your cabin, and I definitely didn't want to explain to him what I was doing, so I left."

"Evan came to my cabin?" He had no reason to be near her private quarters. She wasn't sure why the knowledge that he had been gave her a queasy feeling.

"Yeah. It was weird. He didn't knock or anything. He just tried to open the door and then looked mad when it didn't open. When'd you start locking your door, 'cause that's going to be inconvenient for me?"

"When Conner fixed it for me."

"I liked it better the other way." Daylee delivered her impish grin.

Maribel noted the poncho Daylee carried. "Where you headed now? Looks like it's about to rain again."

Daylee held up her phone. "I checked. It's going to miss us this time. Either way, I need to go for a walk. I can only stay cooped up in the cabin for so long."

Maribel could sympathize. "Well, don't stay gone long. I still think it might rain."

She watched as Daylee's lone figure walked away. Someone else feeling the effects of too much confinement, and too much uncertainty.

Maribel yawned, her eyes filling with water that trickled down her cheeks until she swiped it away. The effects of yesterday coming back to drain her again, leaving her sluggish and weary. Sugar was her best solution, or at least her favorite.

Three hours later, sugar and caffeine fix long gone and nap still unaccomplished, Maribel emptied the buckets of water for the third time. The rain fell hard, relentless.

She picked up her phone hoping music would help, then remembered it needed to be charged. Unfortunately, the charger was in her office, sprawled carelessly across the floor. The lack of organizational efficiency was unlike her, but this place did that to her—spinning her in circles. She struggled to stay tethered to the things holding her together.

The rain fell in a light shower now. She should take advantage of the reprieve to run over to the office.

She headed in that direction. The sound of country and western music bounced down the hall from Becca's office in the front as Maribel came through the back.

She clicked her computer on and tapped in her password. Might as well check her email for the highly unlikely possibility she had a job offer waiting somewhere less crazy. Drumming her fingers on the desk, Maribel waited while her computer warmed up.

Becca's head popped around the door frame, appearing to be the only part of her body with time for a visit.

"I just heard on the radio they're worried the dam on the conservation lake upriver will bust. Hope it doesn't wash out the crossing. I don't want to drive all the way around to the other bridge." She paused, out of breath, but definitely not out of words. She inhaled, refueling.

"How far away is the other bridge?" Maribel did not like the thought of being stuck here for any reason—trapped—even if she had nowhere else to be and no car to get her there.

"Takes another forty-five minutes to go that way. This has been such a weird, rainy summer."

"We'd be stuck here, unless we go all the way around to the bridge?"

"Yep. Always makes me nervous with all these kids here. You never know when someone is going to get hurt. Thank goodness the water usually goes down pretty fast, but I don't know what'll happen if the dam breaks." The phone rang on the front desk. "You missed lunch. Peg's grandmother's homemade spice cake recipe and fresh peaches. You better get over there and see if there is any left."

On her computer screen, the processing indicator still spun. She could sit and wait, or she could grab something to eat—spice cake and peaches—and most likely be back before the computer was ready for her. It was always good to use one's time wisely.

In the cafeteria, she talked the lady into giving her two pieces of cake and a glass of sweet tea. The aroma of cinnamon and nutmeg brought back recollections from her own days at camp. Not every memory of camp was as unpleasant as she told herself.

She headed through the doors to the tables, the glass of tea in one hand, the saucer of cake topped with a generous spoonful of fresh peaches in the other. Hands full, she changed directions to push the door open with her backside and found nothing but air. Then the sensation of falling. Not again.

Hands grabbed her waist, saving her backside and her cake, as her body collided with something solid.

"Whoa, there." The familiar male voice vibrated far too near her ear. Conner braced the door with his foot as he helped her right herself. "Impressive." He winked at her un-spilled plate of food.

"Priorities." Maribel popped back.

"Well you owe me one, again. Wait up and I'll join you."

Owed him one? What was the point of keeping score? And what was it about him that made her want his company and dread it at the same time?

The warmth of his hand holding hers this morning spread up her arm like heated honey.

"I stopped by your cabin to check on you, but you weren't there." Conner soon returned from the kitchen with a plate piled high with cake, settling himself into the seat across from her. He obviously had a different effect on the ladies than she did. Dimples and blue eyes—go figure.

"Oh? Where was I?" When had her cabin become Grand Central Station?

"I'm not sure, but I plan to find out and when I do, you'll be the first to know." He stabbed a peach from her plate and popped it in his mouth. "And I will figure it out."

Maribel shifted on the plastic chair, railing at her body for betraying her by fidgeting. The intensity of his stare moved her body as if he were using mental telepathy.

Why was it always so hot in here?

But he appeared willing to let go of the conversation from earlier today. For that, she was thankful—she thought she was, anyway.

"How's the roof holding up?"

"Like a sieve. Why haven't they fixed it before now?"

"Rarely rains much this time of year. They probably didn't think it'd be an issue, or they would have fixed it sooner. Of course, if the camp is closing, there's no reason to worry about it. But you'd probably know more about that."

"Why do you think it's closing?" She ignored his insinuation about her job. From what Peg had told her, no one knew about the coming changes to the camp.

"Just a hunch."

"That's an odd thing to have a hunch about." She prodded, hoping he'd share his source and satisfy her curiosity.

"You don't get to pick your hunches, Maribel." His eyes danced in enjoyment, not taking her bait. "Are you telling me you only have hunches when you want to?"

She raised an eyebrow. "I'm a—I used to be a reporter. Facts are important." And hunches without facts were slippery slopes at best.

"Come on. I bet you have a hunch about something right now." His eyes taunted, inviting her to duel.

"As a matter of fact, I do." She leveled her gaze on him and held his stare. Why did men always want to make a battle out of everything?

221

"So now you're attempting to gather facts to support your hunch, right?" His enjoyment of the moment crinkled around his eyes.

"Already got 'em." She stabbed a piece of cake from his plate and moved it to hers. He watched, eyes narrowed, moving his fork into a defensive position in case she reached for a second piece.

"First of all, if you've got the facts, then it's not a hunch anymore." He set his fork aside and took a drink. "And second, are you sure?" he asked, returning his glass to the table, his eyes never leaving her face.

"As sure as I need to be." Hard to believe this was the same man who … rejected her "advances" just days ago. His flirtations were confusing her. This was the same guy who saved her life yesterday. The same guy who said he believed her when she claimed someone had tried to kill her. The same guy with the hidden file full of information about her.

The confusion should have been enough to cement her belief he was trouble. So why couldn't she believe?

"Suit yourself." He shrugged, an indifferent little motion that poked at her ego. He was confident and far too impressed with himself, and yet content to just be who he was. "But one day soon you may have to prove whatever it is you think you know."

The side door burst open. Shrieks of wet girls racing in from the rain filled the building. They ran to Conner, all shouting the same thing at once.

"We can't find Daylee."

CHAPTER THIRTY-SIX

M aribel flinched as Conner snapped to attention. "Are you sure? When did you last see her?"

"After the snake guy. She wasn't with us at lunch. We thought she went back to the cabin, but she hasn't been there all afternoon."

Conner was on his feet now. "Where have you checked?"

The girls recited a list of expected places, then waited, eager for instructions. "Do the counselors know?"

They nodded in unison. "They're trying to find Mr. Beck, but he's not here."

"Go back to your cabin and stay there. Do what your counselors tell you."

As they scattered out the door, Conner's expression confirmed he felt the same alarm Maribel felt.

"Wait," Maribel called as he headed for the door. "I saw her heading toward the river before the rain." Becca's news about dams breaking and flash floods thundered in her ears. "Conner, Becca said the dam might break."

Fear for the girl shot through Maribel in a rush of adrenaline that overpowered her tiredness, propelling her out the door behind Conner.

Together, they raced to the trail. The path skirted the camp and led to a wide field nestled in the river bend.

A burst of cold rain soaked them as they ran, calling for Daylee through the heavy rain.

"Are you sure she headed this way?" Conner paused at the top of the ridge scanning over the field. Water ran off his face in rivulets, spluttering from his mouth as he spoke.

Was she? The old familiar voice whispered in her ear, reminding her of past mistakes. Doubt yourself, it said. If she was wrong, they could be wasting valuable time. Daylee's life might be in danger.

But this was the way Daylee had gone. She was sure. "Yes."

"You check at the boat dock. I'll take the trail by the bluffs and meet you there."

Maribel watched Conner sprint away, then took off toward the river, the possibility of a flash flood fueling the panic hurling her toward the water.

She topped the bank above the dock. Pressing a hand to the stitch in her side, she refused the urge to double over as she gasped for air. The effects of the heat yesterday had ravaged her stamina more than she realized. Someone sat on the end of the dock, legs dangling over the rising water. The army green rain poncho hid the identity, but Maribel was certain this was Daylee.

She called, but the girl didn't move.

She yelled again. Still no sign Daylee heard her.

Fast steps carried her the rest of the way over the slope and across the wooden pier, until she stood behind the girl. She seized the girl's shoulder and Daylee jerked to face her, the neon green cords of her earphones trailing from the sides of her head to the phone in her hand.

"What are you doing here?" Daylee asked, warily leaning away from Maribel's dripping form.

"Looking for you. No one knew where you were and it's pouring rain. They're all a little freaked out."

"They're all?" Daylee's sarcasm did not amuse Maribel. "I was under the boat shed. Might as well be there as trapped in that smelly cabin with a bunch of girls acting like idiots."

"Come on. You need to get away from the river." Maribel hurried off the dock then turned back to find Daylee stopped, fiddling with her phone, earplugs still in. A churning line of frothy foam raced over the already turgid surface of the river. She searched upriver. An angry wall of water rushed toward them. Daylee didn't see it.

"Daylee!" Maribel screamed, lunging for the girl and taking hold of her jacket. The giant wave sped toward them. The roar increased, deepening, drowning out every other sound. There was no time to move. Nowhere to go.

Her fingers clenched Daylee's jacket as the surge knocked her feet from under her. She fell. The gritty splash of muddy water hit her face. She clutched at Daylee, refusing to let the torrent rip the girl from her grasp.

Daylee screamed, cut short by a mouthful of water. The river sucked them off the pier with savage strength.

The rope swing stretched out, tugged across the top of rough water. Lifted away, Daylee swept toward the rope.

Grab it Daylee, Maribel wanted to scream. But everything happened too fast.

Maribel flailed her arm, reaching for the rope with her free hand. Panic raged through her, tightening her grip. Strained between the rope and Daylee, who pulled her like an anchor, Maribel refused to let go.

The girl disappeared beneath the water. A terrified sound erupted from Maribel. Then Daylee resurfaced, both hands clamped to the rope.

With only one hand holding the rope, Maribel struggled against the momentum of the water. She wouldn't let go of Daylee.

She let the force of the water sweep her legs forward until they wrapped Daylee in a firm hold. Muscles shaking but grip firm, she released the girl's poncho and caught the rope with both hands.

With her hands clutching the rope above Daylee's own white knuckles, Maribel prayed for a miracle, certain the wide-eyed terror in Daylee's eyes mirrored her own.

A log swept past. She would have screamed if she had oxygen to spare.

Where was Conner? Would he find them in time? And if he did, what could he do but watch?

She held so tight to their only lifeline it felt as if her bones might snap. The rope cut into her flesh, digging deeper with each bit the water pulled her away. The burn raced up her arms letting her know she still held fast.

"Maribel!" Conner's voice broke through the din engulfing them. He ran toward them, stopping at the river's edge, which now stretched so far away. His hands were empty. He couldn't save them. "Don't let go!"

As if that needed stating.

"I'll get you. Just hold on." A strained urgency replaced his usual drawl. Even tough guys can't always hide fear.

The water bobbed her, jerking her around, obscuring her view. She spotted him in snatches as he searched the banks for anything to use to save them. The emergency rescue pole by the canoes flashed in her mind. Even if he found it in time, what was there he could use?

Her legs were strong. No fear of losing Daylee, not yet. But the water pushed against her, twisting her, fatiguing her. The girl clung tight. If they went, they'd go together.

"It's gonna be okay. Conner will get us out." She spat the words out wet with the filthy water splashing into her mouth. She didn't know if Daylee heard.

She searched the bank, frantic to see him.

Dread filled her. He would watch them both drown if the water tore them away or sucked them under. Even with muscles aching, she couldn't let go. She couldn't do that to him.

He reappeared, shepherd's hook in hand. Sliding down the muddy bank, he found a place to stand within reach of them. Planting both feet, he thrust the hook toward them, shoving it through the swift water. The pole was too short.

His eyes met Maribel's, and they shared the same thought. Daylee had to reach for the pole.

"Daylee, Conner will get us out, but you have to turn and grab the pole." Maribel strained to make herself heard while keeping her voice calm, as if the rescue were a done deal. "Look over your shoulder. When you see the hook, reach for it."

Daylee's eyes met hers, wide and confused.

"Do you understand? Over your left shoulder. When I say go, reach for the hook. Don't worry. I'll still have you." *Lord, let that be true* she prayed. Her legs shook, fighting the water trying to pull them apart. Blood smeared the palms of her hands now, making it harder to keep from sliding.

Daylee blinked, her response sluggish as Conner maneuvered the hook closer.

"Can you see it?" She thought the girl nodded. "Reach for it!"

Daylee started to let go, panicked, and clung tighter.

"Conner will pull you out, but you gotta reach and take hold." *And do it soon.* Maribel's own grip slipped a little farther on the rope. "Remember what you said the day we met? When I asked how you found cell phone signal? You said you gotta want it bad enough." Maribel shouted, but the roar of the water surging past made it hard to know if Daylee understood. Water filled her mouth, choking her words. "Come on Daylee! Want it bad enough."

The girl reached a hand toward the hook, splashing before latching on. For a moment she hung bobbing between the rope and the pole.

Maribel had to release her legs so Conner could pull the girl to safety, but fear held her fast. She searched for Conner, needing reassurance, but with Daylee between them she couldn't see him.

Trust. She had no choice.

"Hold tight." Conner yelled. "I've got you."

"I'm letting go, Daylee." Maribel loosened her legs, not yet ready to let go. The water ripped what hold she had left. Panic gripped her before she saw Daylee in Conner's hook. Relief hummed through her, her body buoyed by the lessening of Daylee's weight pulling her down river.

A survival instinct must have taken over. Daylee kicked herself toward the bank as Conner strained, pulling her closer. When she was within arm's length, he dropped to his stomach and, leaning over the water, seized the girl's wrist, dragging her from the deadly water. He lifted Daylee onto the shore, then sprang up, pole ready for Maribel. He stared upriver, his eyes widening with alarm.

"Maribel hold on!" His voice strained with urgency, his eyes fierce, terrified.

Something hard struck her from behind, rolling over her, ripping her hands from the rope and forcing her under water. The rush swept past her, carrying her.

Panic seized her. This wasn't happening. She couldn't think. Couldn't tell which way was up. Couldn't remember how to breathe, even though her lungs burned for the next breath.

Then a jerk. Something tangling around her middle, crushing her ribs. She tugged but was powerless to remove it.

Submerged, she fought.

Air. Oxygen-starved lungs screamed in agony. She kicked hard. Arms lifted her. Her head broke through. Gasping, water seared her lungs. She thrashed, searching for something to hold. But something bound her. Strong arms held her, rescuing her. She relaxed, ensconced in a shelter she couldn't see.

Realization came. The shepherd's hook was around her waist, grasping her fast. Conner had her.

Conner pulled until she was within reach. His fingers closed around her wrist like steel bands, her arm stretching as he dragged her one way and the river fought to take her another.

Then there was ground beneath her, and she lay on her stomach, coughing out dirty water from lungs that burned like white-hot coals. She rolled onto her back, her body numb, depleted. And grateful for the mud beneath her.

Conner sank next to her, laboring to catch his breath.

She tried to sit. "Daylee? Is she okay?"

The girl latched around her before the words were fully out, the embrace of a child clinging to her mother after a nightmare. Maribel closed her eyes, returning the embrace just as fiercely.

The raining had ceased. The sun poked glowing fingers through tiny gaps, prying the clouds apart.

Daylee would be all right. That certainty comforted Maribel, but it came at a cost she wasn't sure she could bear. Maribel felt more broken and vulnerable than ever before. The protective shell she worked to build crumbled around her. After everything she told herself, she knew what she had wanted wasn't possible.

Every heartache she experienced was worth this one moment, wrapped in the love and arms of the girl she helped save.

Maybe perfect love really did cast out fear.

And maybe the imperfect love of imperfect people could too.

CHAPTER THIRTY-SEVEN

C onner flipped the menu open, ran his eyes over both sides, snapped it shut, and slid it between the ketchup bottle and the napkin holder. Streaks of dried mud he'd missed when cleaning up lined his face and crusted his hair. Fatigue dampened his usual mischievous disposition and melted his smile at the corners. Dark circles Maribel knew must match her own, shadowed his eyes.

The emotions of this day—this entire week—washed her with a weariness that soaked all the way to her bones. Unexpectedly, she thought she might be okay with that. Or maybe she was just too exhausted to care. The feeling she had experienced in the river stayed with her. She couldn't explain the sense of security and peace she felt in that embrace. If her father had been the kind to comfort, that was how she imagined what curling up in his lap as a little girl would have been like.

She closed her menu and wedged it in place next to Conner's. She started to square the edges together but didn't. It wasn't the sore hands wrapped in gauze, but the absence of a need for control that stopped her. For the first time in a long time, she trusted that whatever might happen would be okay. Resting back against the chair, she let the truth bring understanding. Control had never been in her hands.

Daylee was fine. The ambulance brought her to the hospital even though it had been a long ride since they'd had to take the far bridge. They were keeping her overnight for observation. She was cold and scared, but nothing rest, ice cream, and rockstar notoriety from her friends wouldn't heal. The girl's parents hadn't yet been located so a camp counselor stayed with her. She requested Maribel, but Evan vetoed that.

Conner rested his hands on the table, but his eyes were busy darting to Maribel every few seconds.

The restaurant was full and Cindy ping-ponged from table to table before she bounced up to their corner, notepad in hand. She surveyed them with skepticism. "Wow. Look what the cat dragged in but refused to eat. Y'all look terrible."

"Rough day at the camp." Conner answered.

"Everything okay?"

"It is now." He ordered water.

"Large Dr. Pepper." Maribel added.

When Cindy left, Conner faced Maribel. "What happened out there?"

"I don't know. She said—"

"I'm not talking about her. I'm talking about you." His eyes held an emotion she hadn't seen in a while … respect. It seduced her already tenderized heart. Whatever was happening frightened her, but she was powerless to stop it. There was too much inside her that didn't need to come out. If she released a little, she wouldn't be able to stop the rest. One dam bursting in a day was enough. But the trumpet blast that brought down the walls of Jericho was nothing compared to the warmth in his eyes as he watched her in a way that ravaged her ramparts.

"Anyone would have done the same." Maribel shifted in her seat, flicking at the edge of her placemat and avoiding eye contact.

"That's not true."

"Here ya go. Ready to order?" Cindy set their drinks down.

When Maribel ordered the chicken fried steak with extra gravy and a side of French fries, Conner shook his head. "Do you ever eat anything healthy, or at least not so fatalistic?"

He didn't wait for an answer but turned to Cindy and placed his order. "I'll have the same."

"Salad. I'll have a salad too. No dressing." Maribel blurted out before Cindy hurried away. To be honest, she wasn't doing well with the diet on which she'd been existing. The idea she might have a purpose brought with it guilt.

She turned to find his tired eyes filled with a generous glitter of amusement.

"The same, huh?" she asked.

"It's been a long day. I need the extra carbs." He slumped back in his chair and dragged his fingers through his hair, knocking loose clumps of dirt and leaving the jagged peaks of a rough plowed field. "You did good today. You saved her life, you know. And I'm wondering where that woman came from. She was fearless." His blue eyes became like crystal, earth-movingly earnest. "I liked it. Confidence looks good on you, Maribel."

She avoided his gaze. The tears pooling in hers distorted her vision. She didn't want him to see this side of her, too drained to even accept a compliment. She wanted a friend, an experience she hadn't enjoyed in a long time. But not him. There were too many things unanswered between them. While her heart softened, telling her to let him in, her brain reminded her of every fear and every wound she'd ever gotten by trusting.

"I know you think I'm a hypocrite, but you really can trust me." He smiled, lopsided and friendly, an olive branch of good intentions. "Talk to me, Maribel." His urging tone had the scratchy depth of exhaustion but still held enough compassion to melt her bones.

Resting her head in her hands, she closed her eyes. She wanted to trust him. Someone. The weight of carrying everything by herself was crushing her. She wanted a fresh start. Would the compassion still be shining back at her after she told him? When she confessed to the parts that even his file of information didn't contain?

Tears, warm and wet, dropped from the corners of her eyes to slide down her cheeks. She hated her tears and, unlike Peg, couldn't blame them on medication. With her hands clenched in her lap, she met Conner's gaze with uncertainty. In her mind, she saw not the present but the past.

"A boy killed himself because of me." The statement hung in the air like a toxic gas and she waited for the words to dissipate like the poisonous vapor they were. After several long moments, the rest of the story flowed, absent of the fear of judgment that often made her speechless.

"I was dating a man I thought loved me, but he was just using me to get at someone else, because I was a reporter." She studied Conner, searching for the disgust he must feel, but saw none. "I did what no good reporter ever does. I trusted him and didn't check the facts. He lied to me and used me." She swallowed, trying to keep the pain and shame from clamping her throat shut. "I was so stupid. And selfish."

She paused, letting all the memories spin through her head in painful succession. With her fingertips, she nudged the utensils, lining them up in parallel lines.

Conner reached over and took her hand in his, stilling the constant arranging. His hand was firm, but warm and tender as he held her. The gentle squeeze came unexpected and was her undoing.

"I wrote an exposé based on false documents he gave me, and it destroyed a man's career. It almost destroyed his marriage and led his teenage son to hang himself." She attempted to swallow but emotion constricted her throat. Her words came out broken and forced as she finished. "I was the one who found him—hanging from the bar in my closet." The ultimate retaliation. If he'd only killed her, her suffering would've been over.

Tears flowed unchecked as Conner stroked his thumb across her fingers. Someone was comforting her, and she was allowing it. Oh, how precious the message. She hadn't allowed herself to receive comfort since the day Alexander died, and she wanted to pull away now. What right did she have to find forgiveness while the boy lay in a grave because of something she did? But Conner's touch—loving and not condemning—was too reassuring and valuable to let go.

They sat in silence, her hand in his, unmoving as the sincerity of his friendship filled her heart.

"I felt someone holding me when I thought I was being swept away." She stumbled through the confession, allowing her eyes to flicker to his, needing to see his reaction but fearing it as well.

Conner smiled with understanding and squeezed her hand. "Yeah, I knew I had some help out there."

Setting platters spilling over with gravy on the table, Cindy pretended not to notice the tears on Maribel's face. She gave Conner a pointed, accusing glare as she deposited his plate. Conner held tight to her hand, refusing to release her as he prayed over their meal.

It wasn't a long prayer. He thanked God for saving Daylee and asked for her full recovery. But then he thanked God for Maribel, asking him to help her accept the forgiveness God wanted her to know. When he asked for the strength she needed to forgive herself, something burrowed inside her, hollowing her out to make room for the hope flowing in.

She wanted to hear him say those words again. She wanted to pick each one up and examine it for truth.

Her chair scraped as she stood in a hurry, excusing herself to the restroom. She needed to get control. Alone in the restroom, she thought about what he said, that she needed to forgive herself because God already had. She splashed cool water on her face and patted it dry with the rough paper towels from the dispenser. Her reflection in the mirror told her what she already knew. She was a disaster, inside and out. But did it have to be permanent?

Cindy was refilling Conner's glass when Maribel walked up unnoticed.

"You know Katy's back in town." Cindy paused, leaning close to Conner and lowering her voice. Just not enough so Maribel couldn't hear her say Katy was pregnant or see Conner's face harden.

He opened his mouth to speak, but Cindy cut him off.

"It's not yours, is it? Is there something you haven't told me?" The threat in her voice was as clear as the one in her eyes.

Disappointment razored through Maribel. Tracy wasn't the only one, and his distant past wasn't all that distant.

"When I gave my life to God, I changed everything. I'm not going back." His words dropped through the air like stones, hard and heavy. "And whether or not the baby could be mine isn't the issue here."

He sat for a moment, then slammed his fist against the table before storming out the door.

Cindy stared at his retreating back before noticing Maribel. "I ..."

"It's all right. I'm fine." Maribel stopped her. There was nothing more she wanted to hear.

Maribel reseated herself and stared at her plate. The world swept away from her, leaving her untethered, back in the raging waters with no rope to hold. She had just started to think she might have found solid ground beneath her, but now the merciless waters of doubt and distrust knocked her feet out from under her again.

The name of the song from a few nights ago materialized in her head. Oh, What Firm a Foundation.

More like Oh, What a False Hope.

CHAPTER THIRTY-EIGHT

Sleep ran like a fugitive from Maribel's exhausted body as her brain rushed from one thought to another, unstoppable. When her eyes closed, she saw Daylee's frightened face trying to stay above the murderous waters. It morphed into the face of the body in the river, and then the boy hanging by a noose. Conner with the snake around his neck. Her own hands rattling the closed door of the barn.

The ride home with Conner had been in silence, but Cindy's words had echoed in Maribel's head.

She reached for her phone, hoping music might distract her. Dead. She never got around to retrieving the charging cord from her office. Becca had distracted her with food, and from there the day careened downhill in a hurry. The clock read 1:40 a.m. She should have accepted the doctor's offer of something to help her relax. But then again, the last thing she needed right now was to be unprepared for whatever was coming next.

And an awareness that something was coming was a feeling she couldn't shake.

She slipped on the first shoes she found and stepped onto the porch. The night held a peace the day had mercilessly avoided. Stars winked against the ebony curtain stretched above her. No rain clouds lingered, but the rich smell of damp earth hung thick and satisfying in the air.

From the river bottom, a whippoorwill called. Maribel hugged herself against the unsettling emotion the sound stirred. The cry called to her as surely as if the bird had spoken her name. Overwhelmed, she sat on the steps.

He calls his sheep by name and leads them out.

She rested her head against the wooden post, aware of the roughness against her skin, and closed her eyes.

Am I one of your sheep, Lord? Are you going to call out to me and lead me from this darkness? Do you even know my name?

She stayed there, letting the spin in her head slow as the whippoorwill repeated its lonesome call.

The crunch of gravel intruded, distinctly out of place with the quiet sounds of the night. The security lights glinted off a vehicle creeping into the parking lot in front of the office, lights off. Was the sheriff patrolling more vigilantly thanks to the recent string of events haunting the camp?

But it wasn't the sheriff's vehicle that trolled the parking lot. It was a silver Lexus. A silver Lexus like the one Ava drove. The car stopped in the lot. No one got in or out.

Whether it was leftover adrenaline—which she doubted she had—or a fatigue fogged brain, Maribel was on her feet, slinking into the shadows and creeping closer. She dodged the lights and made her way down the hill. Halfway there it occurred to her she had no plan if this was something criminal.

She rounded the back corner and slid closer, sticking as near as she could to the building.

At the front, she pressed her back to the wall and peeked around the edge in time to see Evan climb into the passenger seat. Something was off, though. She studied the scene for a minute before it came to her. The vehicle's interior lights weren't working. No bright flash illuminated the inside when he opened the door. The secrecy of this meeting felt premeditated.

The fluorescent bulbs suspended from their poles in the parking lot gave off enough glow Maribel could make out two figures sitting in the darkened interior. Ava and Evan. She watched as they talked, Ava more animated than Evan. Then Evan reached over and caressed Ava's face. Maribel shuddered at the manipulative suggestion of his touch.

A moment later the door opened, and Maribel froze. Evan climbed out, then pivoted back to Ava and nodded his head before closing the door. Ava didn't wait for him to move, but rolled away, lights still off.

He returned to the building. Maribel watched for several minutes before he came out again and walked to his car. He turned and stared straight toward her hiding place.

Did he see her? Her heart beat as though it were full of shrapnel. She remained frozen in place, having no choice but to trust the shadow hid her.

He started his car and drove away, leaving her with the impression there was far more to this than she understood.

CHAPTER THIRTY-NINE

A pounding on her cabin door awoke Maribel. Even with the curtains drawn, the room was bright with sunlight. She'd finally slept, but for how long?

"Stop knocking." The words fell out crackly and dry. She cleared her throat, trying to swallow enough moisture to lubricate her vocal cords. "I'm coming." She tried again.

She rose from the bed, her movements resembling a rusted tin man. Yesterday finally made its effect known, and she struggled to drag her tired and sore body to the front door. She swept a flop of hair from her face and unlocked the door.

"Good morning," Conner greeted her as she squinted against the light.

She rubbed her eyes. She wasn't ready for him, but the cup of coffee he offered was something she wouldn't pass up.

"I thought you didn't approve of my choice of drink." She took the cup and let him follow her inside without invitation.

"After the last couple of days you've had, I thought you earned it. And honestly, I'm not sure you're going to live long enough for it to matter."

"Gee, thanks." She sipped the coffee, strong and sweet. Nice.

"Is that what you usually sleep in?" His eyes roamed up and down with a curious glint.

Maribel surveyed her attire, unable to recall. Nothing unusual about the athletic shorts and a t-shirt, so it was probably the hiking boots she hadn't bothered to remove when she returned from the office that had him curious.

"I thought it best to be prepared."

"For what? The apocalypse?"

"After the last few days I've had, doesn't sound too unreasonable."

"Can't argue with that. You seem to have a gift for impending doom." The expression on his face said he'd found her unique in that way, at least.

"Yeah, well be careful. It's not always my own."

"I'm not scared."

"Foolish man." Maribel moved across the room and sagged her stiff body onto the sofa, careful not to spill coffee.

"No. Just confident about a few things." He stuck his hands on his pockets and leaned against the door frame

"Any news on Daylee?"

"I called the hospital first thing. Apparently, she's driving them crazy. She's ready to get out of there. I can see why you two get along so well. So, how about you and I head to town for lunch? The parts for your car are in and I can pick them up. And if she's still there, we can stop by and pay her a visit."

"Yes! Ugh. Is it lunch time already? You could have mentioned that before I sat." She reached a sore hand up and let him pull her to her feet.

He lifted me out of the pit ... No, she wasn't going there.

He looked so genuine standing here this morning, handing her coffee and inviting her to lunch, the trouble of last night no longer present in his demeanor. Maybe she had overreacted to what she'd heard at dinner.

"Can I change and brush my teeth?" She paused and considered telling him what she saw in the early morning hours, but she didn't. Not yet. They needed to reestablish some ground between them before they strolled into someone else's territory.

"I would appreciate it if you did. I'll be outside."

Changed and ready, she hurried out the door, coffee sloshing from her cup as she reached his truck.

"Don't spill that in here." Conner warned her as he assisted her beat-up body into his truck.

"Want me to get rid of it?"

"No. But I don't want to smell it for the next six months. I'm still trying to get the water trough smell out."

She blew across the top, wafting the smell in his direction, then grinned at his reaction.

He shook his head in response to her attempt to annoy him. "Well someone is in a good mood this morning. Wish you got as excited to see me as you do to see coffee."

She wasn't sure how to take his comment but leaned back in the seat and closed her eyes, deciding to savor the moment instead of analyzing it. The windows were open as they headed to town, creating chaos with her hair. The heated wind whipped against her skin. She inhaled the distinctive smell of summer that only a rain brings out—sweet, pungent, earthy, and hot. In Texas, even hot has a smell. The tension loosened, slipping away until the wind whipped it out the window, like a ribbon blown from her hair. He could drive her like this all the way to the next state and she wouldn't mind.

After a while, he cleared his throat. "Cindy told me what you heard last night ..."

"It's fine. It's none of my business. Seriously."

"No, it's not, but I'd like for you to know the truth."

Maribel faced out the side window, staring at the passing landscape and seeing nothing. The moment was gone as Conner ushered reality back into her thoughts.

"I didn't handle myself well last night and I apologize for that. The truth is my past is like a giant garbage dump. I don't live there anymore, but sometimes the wind blows from just the right direction and the stench creeps back in." Conner paused and Maribel resisted the urge to glance at him, afraid she couldn't handle what she might see.

"Katy and I were in a relationship that ended about a year ago. I kicked her out." His speech was slow. "I kicked her out knowing she'd end up back with her drug dealer ex. That's where she's been and he's probably the father of her child. My fault."

Maribel shifted to meet remorse-filled eyes that mirrored her own regrets. "You didn't make her go back to him. It was her choice." Her words came out choked as her memories mocked her contradiction.

"Was it? And even if it was, what kind of life is that child going to have. If I hadn't kicked her out maybe …"

"People make their own decisions. There's always another way." Her voice filled with uncertainty. That was the truth she'd been missing, wasn't it?

"Maribel, I've been forgiven. It doesn't mean I don't still wish I'd done better for those I've hurt. There are pains that won't ever go away. But holding on to the shame and guilt is just like being in bondage, chained to the same garbage dump I'm trying to climb out of. God's given me a new life—he's set me free—and if I don't do something with it, I'll slip right back into that same old prison."

"So, what changed you?" And could it change her?

"I guess you wouldn't know, would you?" He rested his wrist on the steering wheel and scratched his chin with his other hand. Lack of a recent shave gave the gesture a raspy sound. "I got myself in trouble a little over a year ago. And Mack got me out."

She tucked a strand of hair behind her ear and the wind pulled it loose again just as fast.

"I was living wild and free and completely self-centered. And so was Katy. We were a disaster waiting to happen. What changed was an accident that saved my life. I went to a party one night like I always did. But that night I tried to do something right and unselfish. Unfortunately, it was while I was wasted at two in the morning with an underage girl and an open container in the car with me." The happy-go-lucky drained out of his words like used motor oil.

"Oh." Disappointment churned inside her and she was glad she hadn't eaten yet.

"Just so you know, I wasn't interested in doing anything with the girl. I was a jerk, but I was never a creep. We were at a party she definitely shouldn't have been at and things were about to get ugly for her, so I put her in my car to take her home. Then I wrecked the car before I got her there. And that's how I got to know Mack. I ran the car into the fellowship hall at his church." He placed both hands on the wheel. "Second best thing that ever happened to me."

A cataclysm of jagged, razor-sharp conviction came crashing around her. She had done to him last night the very thing she feared he might do to her. She had taken what she heard and judged. She knew, as well as anyone, the action observed didn't always show the heart's true desire. She hadn't wanted him to think less of her when he heard what she had to say. But she'd been quick to be his judge and jury. The slice of hypocrisy cut deep.

"That's what straightened you out?"

"You might say that." He stared at her, and the intensity in his eyes shot through her flesh and bone and lasered her heart. "Or you might say it brought me face to face with the one who straightened me out."

Maribel stared at the passing countryside without seeing. Conner, Mack, Peg, her Aunt Rachel. They all had something she wanted. But they didn't know what it was to carry responsibility for the death of an innocent person. To live with the sound of parents burying their child and be the one responsible.

"That's nice. I'm happy for you. Was the girl all right?"

"A little banged up, and a fractured wrist, but yeah she was okay. Because I uhmmm ..." He rolled his lower lip between his teeth, then licked them both before continuing. "I had an open bottle of beer in the car, I was charged with several things, including providing alcohol to a minor. Her parents were merciful about it. They knew what would have happened to her if I hadn't gotten her out of there. They spoke on my behalf before the judge. And Mack," the words knotted up somewhere inside him and he paused before continuing.

"The forgiveness they showed me ..." his voice trailed, choked with emotion. He glanced at Maribel. "And the rest is history, I guess."

"Pretty amazing story. Pretty tolerant people." Questions rambled around in her head, but she didn't know how to ask them. "A preacher was that easy going? Was there much damage?"

"I believe the word is forgiving. And yes." His tone said understatement. "It wasn't like I got off with nothing. I have worked every spare minute since then to repay and restore the church. And as you've found out, Mack and the sheriff both use this for their benefit as often as possible. I don't mind. I'm fortunate to have a second chance. Thank goodness for what Peg did for Mack. It saved his life, and he saved mine."

"What Peg did for him?"

"They haven't told you?"

"No. I wondered how they came to have such a strong friendship, but I never asked."

"Well it should be a story for them to tell, but I'm still working on the patience thing." Dimples were one thing, but the crinkling lines radiating out from the corner of his eyes expressed a deeper joy. "You know Peg had a son who died in an accident, right?" He watched her, waiting for a response.

He continued in an it-could-have-been-me tone. "Mack was the drunk driver who hit him." The words, spoken as softly as the blooms of the cotton-wood that float in the spring breeze, tore through the air and slammed Maribel breathless.

"Mack killed her son?"

Conner nodded.

"But she ..."

"Forgave him?" Conner had somehow perceived this was the stumbling stone for Maribel. That level of forgiveness was something she didn't know. "Yes, she did." His words slipped through the space between them, satin smooth and confident to her ears.

Forgiveness. Must be nice. She faced out the window. When she spoke, her voice was so soft she wasn't positive he would hear her over the sound of the rushing wind. "But how could he forgive himself?"

Conner was quiet, and she thought he hadn't heard her question. Finally, he answered, "I think he came to understand that everyone has sinned. No one is perfect. He still had a life, and he owed it to Peg and her son—and to God—to do something with it."

"But he took a life he had no right to take. He killed Peg's only child and look at her now. She is fighting cancer alone. She's going to die all by herself."

"If you think she's all by herself, you need to look again."

CHAPTER FORTY

They drove through town, the silence rising like a wall between them as they sat preoccupied with their thoughts.

Conner wanted to say more. He wanted to find the words fitted for her heart. The desire not to let the moment pass gripped his chest so hard he ached. But fear thickened his tongue, the words sticky in his mouth. The wrong words might destroy any ground gained. She needed to get free from the prison she had locked herself in. The key was hers, and it was shaped like forgiveness, but only she could reach out for it.

He'd come clean with her about his past, but still she held back, refusing to let go of her own deep regret.

On a sudden whim, he pulled into the drive-through for the Dairy Queen. This wasn't what he had in mind when he invited her to lunch, but this might be his last shot. "Are you up for a little adventure today?"

The glare she gave him was not a credit to his intelligence.

He laughed. "Okay probably not a good question, considering the past few days. Just a picnic. I want to show you something."

She didn't say no, so he proceeded, still not sure what his plan was.

Minutes later, the cab filled with the smell of cheeseburgers and fries as he drove them back to the river and the place known as the Pool of Siloam. He had no idea what to do or say once they got there. But he knew more than one blind man had his sight restored at a place with the same name.

Maribel wasn't in the mood for a picnic, but she wasn't in the mood to argue either. It wasn't her recent string of near-death experiences that crippled her emotions. But she knew she was standing on the brink of something unknown, unable to change her course until she saw what was on the other side. It made her knees ache and her heart hopscotch.

Peg had been right. She hadn't been seeking—she'd been running. Hiding. She couldn't live this way forever. Deep inside she understood the step she had to take, but she didn't know how.

They headed in the camp's direction until Conner steered them onto an unfamiliar road. Soon they were rolling along shaded, narrow country roads, country music coming from the speakers and Conner as he sang along.

He pulled to the edge of the road where the earth appeared to fall away on the far side of a loosely constructed cedar rail fence. A hundred feet below, the river rushed by. The ugly, muddy waters of yesterday had receded, but the river remained brown and shaded in treachery.

"Oh, good. The river. Didn't get to see enough of that yesterday."

A flicker of his eyes bounced her way, acknowledging the comment but saying nothing. She wished he'd said something.

He backed the truck under an oak tree, and they got out to eat their lunch. Conner lowered the tailgate and unwrapped their burgers while Maribel walked over to the rail.

She stood a few feet back from the railing. Her knees locked, the drop-off bringing the familiar paralysis.

Except for a few scrubby bushes that grew out of the side, it was a straight drop to the rocks below.

Judging by the ground worn bare on the roadsides, this was a frequent stop for visitors. "Let me guess. Lover's Leap?" Didn't every small town have something of that nature?

Conner pulled out a burger and handed it to her. "Not exactly, but close. Mostly just a make out spot." He pulled back the paper on his. "But it is where Mack came when he was thinking about killing himself." He took a bite, chewing and staring into the distance as if nothing noteworthy slipped from his lips.

Maribel's head snapped in his direction. "He planned to jump off and kill himself?"

"Nah, don't be ridiculous. It's not far enough down to guarantee death. He brought a gun."

"I ..." She opened and then closed her mouth, fiddling with the wrapper on her burger, but no longer hungry. "I can't imagine him doing that."

"He was a different person then. The guilt was killing him."

"What stopped him?"

"Peg. She found him. And how he tells it, she set him straight on why the world didn't need two senseless deaths. Mack says she told him to man up and do something worthwhile with his life—so he became a preacher." He took another bite of his burger while Maribel chewed on his words.

"So, you still think I'm suicidal? Is that what this is about?" Tempered by her sudden anger, her words came out caustic.

"No, I don't, and this isn't about dying. It's about not living."

"That doesn't make sense."

"It makes perfect sense, but you, Maribel, are doing your best to ignore it—to run from it. What will it take to convince you that hiding from life doesn't make you less dead?"

Maribel looked away to stare across the river, aware of her inability to focus through the tears in her eyes.

"I don't know how she did it. How she forgave him. I saw how much Alexander's parents hurt. How could I have the nerve to even ask for their forgiveness? I just sent everything I had in my bank account to the funeral home and hoped ... I don't even know what I hoped." She sank onto the open tailgate beside him.

Conner reached a finger to wipe the tear that had slipped to her cheek. She flinched at his touch, and he dropped his hand to his lap.

"You know, there were a lot of events that conspired to make things happen the way they did. What made Mack drink so much that night? What happened in each of their days to put them at that exact spot at the exact time? It's never as simple as we want to make it."

The intensity in his eyes pierced her as he continued. "Do you know why Peg's son was on the road that night?"

She waited for him with an uneasy feeling he might say something that could fracture her heart. And terrified a part of her wanted him to.

"Peg had forgotten to shut off the coffee pot at the church after bible study that night. He offered to go back, so she didn't have to."

She let her gaze wander with no need to see, letting the slight breeze lift her hair, but not her thoughts. "That doesn't change the fact it was our mistake. Mack chose to drink too much that night and drive. I chose to ignore what I knew was right, to ignore doing what I knew I was supposed to do for my own selfish purposes."

"True. But none of us are perfect. The consequences may be different, but we're all guilty. Some by choice, but many by accident. Maybe you both acted selfishly, but neither of you set out to cause a death. You hold on to the guilt like it's the only thing you have, and it will eat you alive."

"I don't deserve better."

"None of us do. But all the guilt and unforgiveness and regret isn't going to change a single thing from the past. The question is, what good will it be if it destroys the future as well? You have a choice, Maribel." Conner wadded up his wrapper and tossed it behind him in the truck's bed.

Then he walked away.

CHAPTER FORTY-ONE

Maribel stepped out of her cabin the next morning to find her Falcon parked in front, keys in the ignition. He'd been right in his estimation of the time needed, but he must have worked through the night.

She headed to the maintenance barn. She could thank him and ask the questions refusing to leave her alone. Instead, she found the barn empty and his truck nowhere in sight.

"Becca, do you know where Conner is?" She charged into the front office on the way to retrieve her phone cord, eager to find him.

The expression on Becca's face said answering made her uncomfortable. The woman cut her eyes toward the hall and cocked her head to the side, listening for something—or someone. She spoke to Maribel in a lowered voice, forcing Maribel to lean close to hear.

"I'm not sure he's here ... anymore." She said the last word like all heck might break loose if the demons heard.

"I don't understand?"

"He had a meeting with Evan yesterday afternoon, then he stormed out. He looked pretty mad." Becca chewed her bottom lip.

"But you said anymore?"

"He said he'd be back for his things later."

"That doesn't make any sense. I thought he worked for Peg. How could Evan get rid of him?" And why? "Any ideas where he went?"

Becca shook her head, "No, but I'm sure going to miss those blue eyes and dimples."

Maribel headed to her office for the charging cord. She snatched it from the wall with her free hand and spun back to the door. Her eyes widened and she shook her head. On her desk lay a pencil covered in smiley face motif and the words *If not now, when?* Her pencil. The one she'd dropped and left by the river. A sticky note lay beside it, and in the same blocky letters she recognized from the file in Conner's room was the word SOON.

Her pencil. Even if she tried to reason to herself there were other pencils out there just like it, the familiar teeth marks kept her from believing in that possibility.

Her pencil. Not just found by someone near the river, but by someone who knew it was hers. Someone who had seen her drop it. And left her a note. Was this someone's idea of a joke? Not someone … Conner. The handwriting was the same.

Despite the summer heat, chills raced over her. Unnerved and shaky, she reached for her chair only to realize it sat askew from the way she always left it. The computer mouse, too, had been repositioned.

Maybe her obsessive-compulsive organizing had served a purpose after all.

She placed a tentative hand on the mouse, clicked her computer to life, and typed in her password. Immediately, as if some rogue program had been engaged, a slide show of pictures popped open, filling the monitor with images she had taken of Conner lurking around that night at the bonfire.

And then came pictures she hadn't taken. Pictures of her and Conner together that night in the cafeteria … her in his arms as he caught her from falling, both of them standing far too close together on her cabin porch, and him leaving her cabin later that night. The time stamps displayed across the bottom could be misinterpreted to imply something they shouldn't.

But they did make her think one thing. Those pictures weren't taken by Conner, but they were planted on her computer.

She didn't wait around to make sure the computer shut down but hurried back to the car. Unlocking the trunk, she exhaled to see the box still there. The key to the box was still missing, but one way or another she was going to find out what was inside it today.

And she needed to find Conner.

The joy of being back in her car, windows down and foot a little heavy on the accelerator, was overshadowed by an urgency to locate Conner, especially since she wasn't sure where to look. Her first stop would be at Mack's. If anyone knew where Conner might be found, it would be Mack.

Fortunately, Conner hadn't gone far. His truck was parked behind the café. Maribel swerved into the parking lot faster than she intended. She stomped on the brakes. The combination of excessive speed coupled with somewhat unresponsive brakes threatened to land her right through the wall. She killed the engine, then sat, wondering what she truly wanted from him, and what happened with Evan.

Glancing at the back floorboard, she studied the locked box sitting there. It had been a relief to find it still safely locked in her trunk. Storing it in the trunk of her car while Conner was making the repairs had been a risk, but her options had been limited. She'd moved it to the back floorboard because today was the day. She was tired of the secrets. Someone was playing a dangerous game with her life and she wasn't going to leave anything unexamined.

Peg said she'd know when to open it and now felt like the time. It—whatever it was—ended today. She still didn't hadn't found the key, but she'd find a way.

She left the windows rolled down a few inches to offset the heat that would be cooking the interior when she returned.

Inside the café, she spotted him at a far table, alone. Other than Conner, the place was empty.

She walked over and stood waiting for him to acknowledge her. He was ignoring her, so she pulled out the chair opposite from him and invited herself to sit, forcing him see her.

He arched an eyebrow but said nothing.

Sweat trickled down the sides of the tea glass. Maribel felt the same. "Hi," she said, somewhat disappointed in her sudden lack of conversational skills.

Conner picked up the glass, swiveling it around so the ice rattled. He chuckled as though something struck him as funny.

"Hello, Maribel." He lifted his eyes to meet hers. Despite his laugh, Maribel ached at the hurt that stared back at her.

A waitress other than Cindy approached, and he signaled for a refill.

"Sweet or unsweet?" she asked.

"Sweet," he answered, "and a coffee with a lot of extra creamer and sugar for this one."

Maribel didn't want a coffee, but he was in a mood she didn't wish to argue with. Hearing him order her one pricked her heart. Where was the lecture about making healthy choices? She cleared her throat, now drier than usual. Fear was very dehydrating to the vocal cords. "What happened?"

The cold stare he gave shredded her confidence, cutting her courage to the core.

"I don't know, Maribel. You tell me."

"Becca told me you and Evan had a disagreement." She studied her hands resting in her lap, afraid eye contact might transform her into a pillar of salt. Were the pictures a part of this? He'd left her that note and her pencil, so it was possible he'd seen the pictures. Had he misinterpreted their presence on her computer?

"I guess you could say that." He picked up an unused coaster, holding it lightly between his thumb and forefinger and spinning it by thumping it with his other hand.

"So, what else could I say?" Her hands slid between her knees, and she pressed them together, so she wasn't tempted to knock the coaster from his fingers. The air between them quivered with an unspoken tension that confused Maribel. Without moving, he was farther away, as if an invisible force injected distance between them.

He set the coaster back on the table. "How about saying why you had quite the assortment of pictures on your computer that looked really bad for me?" The intensity in his eyes gouged holes in her heart. "Or the papers in your desk. When were you planning to file them?"

She recoiled, stunned. "What are you talking about?"

"Again, why don't you tell me?"

"File what? I don't know what you're talking about." Confusion replaced her fear, and she stared at him, baffled.

"Sexual harassment, Maribel? I never thought you would stoop that low. Nice work by the way, splicing the recording. I sound like a real piece of work in it."

"What recording? I have no idea what you're saying. But Conner, listen to me. There are pictures on my computer I didn't take. I didn't even know about them. Someone else put them there. I don't know anything about a recording or sexual harassment charges, but I'm being set up. I would never do that to you, Conner."

Did she really mean that? How stupid could she be to trust him when the more she learned the less she knew him?

"Wouldn't you? Isn't that kind of your pattern?" His words cut through her.

She flinched as tears burned her eyes. But she refused to give in. There was too much at stake to let his cruelty stop her from finding the truth.

"I don't know what to say. Did you see the file?" She stuttered, wanting to see anything but the coldness in his eyes. "Conner, I've been set-up. We've been set up."

He threw his head back and laughed. "Yeah, like someone set you up by leaving the board from your cabin by the barn you claimed to have been trapped in. Or by planting the file you supposedly found in my room." He leaned forward, folding over his arms on the table, until he was close—too close for the anger she felt radiating towards her. "Funny thing, Maribel, I tore my room apart and never found that file."

The distorting effects of the tears that filled her eyes blurred her vision of him. She started to speak, but he put up his hand to cut her off.

"Just stop. I don't even know if you know the truth anymore. Bugging your own cabin to record our conversations? Is this all some game to you ... destroying people's lives for fun? Get some help, Maribel, before you ruin any more lives. Or maybe that's your goal."

The shopkeeper's bell dinged as someone entered. The waitress laughed at something the cook said. The world continued to spin as usual for everyone else. But for the two battered souls at this table, everything changed.

He pushed away from the table—and her—and crossed his arms. "I think you'd better go now."

CHAPTER FORTY-TWO

B ack in her car she sat, sweat forming as she tried to calm herself. She gripped the steering wheel too tightly and winced as pain jolted up her arms from her injured hands.

"I really believed you were different, Conner. My mistake. Again." She mumbled the words in the empty interior of the Falcon. Squeezing her eyes closed, she denied the tears that wanted to fall. She refused to cry over him. Instead, she let the hurt fuel the hot rush of anger that came in place of the pain.

Forget him. She stomped too hard on the accelerator as she left the parking lot, sending gravel flying.

Was Evan the one behind this? He had access to her computer. But what reason did he have?

The board. How oblivious had she been? It was Conner's handwriting on the board they'd found by the barn. He said so and she'd seen it. And it looked nothing like the handwriting in the file or on her desk. He could have done that on purpose, but she couldn't come up with a justifiable reason, and he certainly wouldn't have planted pictures to get himself in trouble.

They'd planted a fake file in her desk, couldn't they just as easily have planted the one she'd seen in his room and now the note? She and Conner were being set up, and the one person who could help her now couldn't stand the sight of her.

Okay. What next? It probably wasn't safe for her to be at the camp. What would Peg think? And what about Daylee? Leah?

She didn't care about the rest of her job. But she cared about Peg and the girls. She'd find Leah herself if she had to.

Who was she kidding? She didn't know the first thing about any of this. All she had was a bunch of things that made little sense. She was playing detective. If she'd been serious, she would have taken it all to the sheriff before things had gone this far. Maybe that was what she needed to do right now.

Like a flare in the pitch black of night, the image of the shovel lying in the sheriff's truck bed came to her. It was there when they had loaded her belongings into his pickup that first night. There was green and yellow paint like Daylee had described. Was that the same shovel Leah took from the maintenance barn? And if it was, how did the sheriff come to have it? Was Daylee right when she thought she saw the sheriff carrying it away from the river?

Too many questions.

Trust no one.

A shimmer of movement caught the corner of her eye. A dark and shiny ribbon spilled along the floorboard from beneath the passenger seat. Maribel froze as it coiled itself mere inches from her. Terror grabbed her throat, choking her.

A horn blared. She looked up in time to jerk the wheel hard to the right, avoiding a head on collision. Responding to the tug of the wheel, weight of the car shifted, leaning too far. Momentum nosed it into the ditch, the earth no longer holding the back end to the ground. And then she was rolling.

She screamed in panic but couldn't say whether it was from the fear of the crash or the snake loose in the vehicle with her. The vehicle rolled once and came to rest against a tree. Her head hit hard against the glass, her last thought before the darkness took over—she hoped the wreck killed her before the snake did.

Conner drained the last of the tea from his glass and set it back on the table a little too aggressively. What was wrong with him? Did he really believe Maribel could do the things he had just accused her of?

Nothing about her convinced him she was capable of deliberately hurting another. It was possible she was right they were being framed. But the idea was so absurd, he just couldn't buy that either. For starters, there was absolutely no reason he could think of why someone would.

He frowned. But what if she was the target? He needed to find her and hear what she had been trying to tell him.

He'd let Tracy down and now Katy as well. He wasn't going to let Maribel go down without fighting for her. Whatever—or whoever—was behind all this, she needed a chance to let grace and mercy work in her life.

Sounds, vague and detached, floated to her from a place far away. The voices came first, then the pain. Her head, side and shoulder. Voices and pain-wracked nerves. So confusing. Maribel heard her name and mumbled a response, her eyes still closed. She crawled through the dense fog, uncertain how to reach the voice—a voice she knew. Conner. He'd be so mad at her. She didn't know why, because he didn't have to be here. Why was he here?

Her car rocked as they worked to open the passenger side door. A hand settled on her shoulder. She was certain it was Conner's as his words whispered smooth and calming in her ear, ordering her to hang in there. A lessening of pressure as the seatbelt released.

Then the sound of air being sucked in, followed by a harsh expletive.

"What's wrong? We need to get this away from the tree so we can get her out of here." Conner's voice was urgent.

"Mister, we need to be real still here for a moment and think." Maribel didn't recognize that voice. She did, however, hear the second expletive shatter the air from beside her head as Conner's grip on her shoulder tightened.

The voices spun together, talking all at once and making no sense.

Sirens screamed. Were they for her? She recognized the sheriff's voice as she faded back toward the dark.

"Everybody stay calm. Conner, you keep her still, you hear me? The last thing we need is for you to do something and make her move. Someone get Milton out here. And you, call the hospital and tell them to have the antivenom on the way. Tell 'em it's a cottonmouth."

Maribel relaxed. It wasn't her. They were talking about someone else.

"Hey, Maribel." Conner spoke so calmly.

"I'm sorry. I didn't mean to make you mad." Maribel mumbled.

"I'm not mad—just stupid and taking my anger out on you. I'm the one who should be apologizing." He rubbed her cheek with tender, hesitant fingers. "Listen, can you hear me?" An urgency crept in and mixed with the softness, pleading. "I need you to do something for me Maribel. I need you to stay perfectly still. Okay?"

Maribel stirred her head, blinking open her eyes, trying to focus. "Conner?"

"Shh, don't move. Just close your eyes and stay real still."

"No. I want to get out," Maribel felt a flush of panic. She hurt, and she needed to get out of the car. She needed a doctor to clear the mush making it hard to think. His hands pressed into her shoulders and pinned her firmly to the seat.

"Maribel, please, don't move." There was an insistence in his voice she didn't understand. Something was wrong.

"Why can't I get out?"

"First, try to tell me where you hurt without moving." Conner coaxed.

"My head and my shoulder, my sides a little."

"Nothing too bad then?"

A gradual shake of her head. "I can't remember what happened."

"That's all right. It doesn't matter. Just try to relax and be still."

Maribel rested for only a moment before her eyes snapped open as the memory exploded.

Conner's hands gripped her as he first ordered, then begged her not to move. He pressed hard against her shoulders and she winced in pain, surprised at the whimpering sound that escaped her. Her pulse raced, roaring like a waterfall in her ears. His hands held her upper body in place, but they did not stop her from tilting her head forward enough to see the snake curled between her feet. The viper head and dark coloring. She was one small thread away from possible death.

"Breathe, Maribel. Don't freak out on us. Stay calm. He's not going to bite if you don't move. Milton is on his way."

Not bothering to hide her terror, her eyes met his, hot tears sliding down her face. She began to mumble words she didn't know she knew. "What's that story? The one where someone gets thrown in the lion's den? 'My God sent his angel, and he shut the mouths of the lions.'"

Her eyes searched Conner's, pleading. "He can seal the mouths of snakes too, right?"

Conner's smile didn't stretch to the concern in his eyes when he responded.

"Yes. Yes, he can." He cleared his throat and quoted his own part of the verse. "No wound was found on him because he had trusted in the Lord."

"It's been a long time since I trusted God, Conner." Maribel cried, her soul aching.

"I know, Maribel. But it's never too late."

"You think he cares—you know—since I've been mad at him for so long?"

Conner loosened his clutch on her shoulder but didn't move his hands. "I know he does. He caught you in the flood, didn't he?"

Maribel closed her eyes again, focusing on the sensation of her hand in his, warm and strong. Assurance flowed up her arm and radiated through her body.

A new voice entered the mix. Milton. "That's a cottonmouth all right. Only aggressive when they feel cornered, which I'd say he probably does right now." He lowered his voice, but Maribel still heard. "Has she been bitten yet?"

"We don't think so, but hard to tell." The sheriff answered Milton's question.

"The venom here attacks the blood, as in hemorrhaging and inability to coagulate. If she's got any internal injuries ..."

"How about you shut up and get it out?" Conner spoke his words as though he ground them through clenched teeth.

"I'll do the best I can, but I can't make any guarantees."

Something cool and smooth moved against her ankle, a slow sliding motion. And the world went black.

CHAPTER FORTY-THREE

onsciousness came back slowly at first, a heavy curtain being dragged apart, then yanked wide in a moment that caused Maribel's heart to lurch. Her brain caught up to the gut reaction—the last of the fear that hadn't found its way out of her body before she lost consciousness. The snake, the car rolling, the snake again. And Conner, calm, determined, angry. And still the snake. The shiny black coil between her feet. The triangular head. Maribel's first conscious breath was a gasp.

In an instant, he was beside her, hovering, caressing, calming her.

"Hey, it's okay. You're all right. We're at the hospital." His voice was a whisper, suggesting he expected more of her might come undone if he spoke too loudly. "How ya feeling?"

She tried to speak but found her mouth dry and her body sluggish in its response. He retrieved the cup of water a nurse had left and held it for her to drink, positioning the straw and holding it steady for her. Her ribs protested as she worked to lean forward and sip the liquid.

"I've been better." She worked at a smile but wasn't too confident in the results. "What happened?" In her mind she saw the events in jagged, disjointed clips but she clutched at the hope these were drug-induced hallucinations, and it hadn't happened at all as she remembered.

"Do you remember anything?"

Brow furrowed, she sorted through her thoughts like searching the junk drawer for a pen that still worked. "Rolling. Crashing."

"Do you remember right before the accident? What made you swerve?"

Her body reacted even before she formed the answer, her pulse quickening, and fear vibrating through her veins. She nodded. She tried to move, searching her body. "Those memories are real? Did it bite me?" Even through the fog of sedation the image terrorized her.

"It's okay. You're okay. You weren't bitten." His hands rested on her shoulders urging her back against the pillow.

"I'm afraid of snakes, Conner."

He chuckled. "I'm aware of that."

She glanced up at Conner. "How … how did it get in there?"

Conner shook his head and pulled his chair up close beside the bed before sitting. "I'm not sure. Did you ever leave the windows down or maybe the doors open while you ran in somewhere?"

She nodded, her vision blurred by tears. Her fault.

Conner leaned forward and took her hand in both of his, rubbing his thumb across her fingers.

Maribel stared at the board on the wall. The details of her existence boiled down to marks on a whiteboard. "Conner, you said one time that if I ever wanted to get rid of the car, you might be interested. I think I'm ready to take you up on that." For more reason than one, she might be ready to let go. Of course, she'd be happy if he exploded the thing and pushed it off the highest cliff he could find. That might be hard to accomplish since the cliffs of central Texas weren't near tall enough for what she had in mind.

"Well, how's our snake charmer?" A nurse dressed in emoji covered scrubs flounced into the room and tapped on the keyboard. She took Maribel's pulse and gave Conner an appreciative smile. Such was the life of a hot guy. "What's your name, sweetie?"

"Maribel Montgomery." Conner blurted the answer.

"Are you the husband?" the nurse asked him.

"Uh … no." Conner shifted in his seat, releasing Maribel's hand.

"Well, I will need her to answer for herself." She spoke to Conner, a pleased smirk on her face.

Maribel didn't miss the glimmer of renewed hope in the nurse's eyes. She adjusted herself, trying to sit up without exposing herself. An unexpected possessive feeling made her voice arch when she stated her name for the nurse's benefit.

The woman lifted Maribel's arm with soft, cold fingers, checked the name on the plastic band, then pressed her fingers against Maribel's wrist to take her pulse. She turned back to Conner. "So then, you are the fiancé, brother ...?"

"No. Just a ... a good friend." Conner picked up her hand again, staring at the dry erase board. Maribel wondered if he was seeking the nurse's name. But after a few seconds he appeared oblivious to others in the room.

"Oh, well then ..." The nurse performed her routine check of Maribel's vitals. She went back to clicking away at the keyboard, recording her observations, including which of the round faces Maribel most resembled in terms of pain. Maribel was aware there were no faces for frustration on their chart. "If you need anything, press that call button." The nurse gave her final instructions. "Or send blue eyes down to the nurse's station."

Fat chance, Maribel thought.

Conner waited until the nurse was gone. "I called Mack. He won't be back in town until tomorrow, but he's trying to get in touch with your aunt. We weren't sure how to reach your parents."

Maribel thought about her family. Had time and distance—and history—stretched them that far apart?

"I can save you some time. Aunt Rachel is in remote backcountry in Mexico right now. My dad died of a heart attack a few years ago. And my mom and I don't talk much." She faced away, embarrassed.

"But she'd want to know, to be here, right?"

"I'll call her later." For the first time in longer than she could remember, she wanted to talk to her mother, but not in this condition. What she wanted to say had nothing to do with being in a car wreck.

"I didn't know about your dad. I'm sorry."

"Well, it's not the stuff a person wants to share right off, and we've only known each other for a week."

"A week, is that all? I have to be honest, Maribel, it seems like much longer." Conner teasingly implied he was exhausted.

"I'm uncertain how to take that so I'll just let it be for now." Her laugh was weak and came out as more of a happy breath as the sharp pain in her sides shut down further movement. "My mom was success-driven, always climbing the career and social ladders. And my dad, I don't know. He just became distant. We weren't a close family." She admitted the truth to herself as much as to Conner.

"I'm sorry to hear that. They missed out." He continued to caress her hand, but it was the shine in his eyes that swept her away. "But you were close to your aunt, right?"

"Yeah, she was always there for me." She'd been blaming her aunt for not being here when she needed her, but the truth was Maribel hadn't been honest with her about the events happening in her life lately.

He reached up and brushed a strand of hair aside from her face. "Maribel, I need to ask your forgiveness. I had no right to say the things I did to you at the café. I'm mad at myself because I knew better. I should have realized something else was going on."

She fidgeted with the strip of plastic around her wrist.

"If you'll forgive me, we'll sort this out together. Something bad is definitely going on around here. I want to figure it out before you—or anyone else—gets hurt."

Maribel nodded. "I forgive you. Please believe me I had nothing to do with the file or the tape. I took the pictures, but I didn't even know you were in them until later."

"I believe you." He looked as if there were more he wished to say, but he rose and slid his chair back into the corner. "I need to go take care of something. Will you be all right until I get back?"

Her brow furrowed. How had this happened? When had she let him care about her? "I'll be fine. I don't know why they even have me in here. The doctor will probably release me soon." The wall was heavier than usual this time as she struggled to get it back in place.

Conner laughed. "I don't think so, kiddo. Pretty sure the doctor plans to keep you overnight. You had a good head injury ... again." He winked at her with the blue eyes that sparkled more than they should. "If you'll behave and follow the doctor's orders this time for a change, I'll bring you some ice cream."

"Why?" Maribel wasn't talking about the ice cream.

"Why not?" He smiled, not the fabulous cocky smile she expected, but something softer.

"Conner, I need to tell you I'm sorry too."

"So then tell me."

"Tell you what?"

"That you're sorry."

"I just did."

"No. You said you needed to. Not the same." His lips twitched, insinuating he was trying not to smile.

"I have a head injury and I'm medicated at the moment." She huffed out mock exasperation. "Conner, I'm sorry."

"What exactly do you have to be sorry for, Maribel?"

"I think I may have been wrong in the conclusions I came to."

"You broke into my room and then accused me of things I didn't do."

"No. I used your key. That is not the same as breaking and entering." She picked at the hem of the sheet.

He lowered his head for a moment, then stared back at her with earnest and hopeful eyes. "Since we now have more than one mysterious file causing

269

us trouble, I think it's safe to say someone has an agenda and for some reason, we're a part of it."

Maribel nodded.

"Shall we work together to get this straightened out?" He stuck out his hand to shake, but at the last minute pulled it back and kissed her on the forehead instead.

It was powerful medicine that made her forget the pain in her body, aware only of the ache in her heart.

"And, Conner, thank you for holding my hand while they were, you know, trying to get me out of the car with that—thing."

Confusion registered on his face. "I didn't hold your hand. We couldn't reach your hands, and we couldn't risk having you bitten if we tried."

She shifted away and told herself it was the medication that caused her eyes to water. Someone held her hand. She wasn't mistaken about that.

"Conner, wait!" Her face tightened in pain as she tried to sit up, a memory detonating inside her aching head. "The box. It's in the car. You have to get it."

Concern shot out of his eyes, so she lowered her voice.

"Peg's box. She said I'd know when to open it and I was thinking it was time, but I still haven't found the key. I think we need to know what's in it." The words streamed out sounding insane even to her own ears. She leaned back, closed her eyes, and replayed the events of the day before the accident.

"Maribel?"

She opened her eyes to find him still staring at her as if he might need to press the panic button at any moment.

He stood closer, brushing his hand over her hair and across her cheek.

"I need you to get that box." She wiped the wetness from her cheeks and turned to appeal to him with eyes that surely reflected the desperation she felt.

His nod was almost imperceptible. "I'll see what I can do, but I don't know if they are treating the car as a crime scene or not. If so, I can't take it out."

"A crime scene?"

"Sheriff Griger is just ruling out all possibilities. He thought the brake cable might have been undone."

"I was driving too fast and slid in the parking lot. That's probably my fault."

"Then nothing to worry about. Get some rest."

Maribel nodded, trying to smile, but her cheeks felt heavy. She nestled into the hospital bed and let the medication pull her into a dreamless sleep.

CHAPTER FORTY-FOUR

Rock scratched his head and shoved his hat back on top of a skull full of jumbled and concerning thoughts. He drained the last of the cold, stale coffee from the Styrofoam cup and tossed it in the trash can with the accuracy that earned him the position of defensive tackle—not quarterback—on his high school football team.

He stooped to retrieve the cup with all the sound effects that came from four years of hard tackles and thirty-plus years in law enforcement. Retirement was sounding good.

But not until he straightened out the mess in front of him. Maybe it was a pride issue, but in all his years he'd never had anything before him as unclear as whatever was going on right now. He and Peg were never close, although they were related in some very distant way. Her son's death should have brought them closer together, but if thinking there was always time to get around to that one day was a crime, he was guilty.

Something connected all of this to her, or at least involved her family and the camp in some way. It was partly a gut feeling he'd learned not to ignore. But more than that it was a growing list of occurrences that didn't make sense.

Crime in Turnaround was pretty straightforward. It didn't take much to know who the perpetrators were. One only needed time to collect the evidence, and the cunning to catch them—which wasn't usually a lot. This business of sorting out disappearances and murders was something else.

And attempted murders. He couldn't get that idea out of his head. If Milton was right and the snake in Maribel's car was the one that showed up missing from his collection, the odds of it escaping Milton and finding its way to her car were unbelievable. Microchips in snakes, what was the world coming to?

His background check on Maribel hadn't uncovered anything too troubling. There had been the case of libel against the newspaper and the subsequent wrongful death lawsuit. But no one had brought charges against her. Just sloppy, irresponsible work was all he could tell. The timing of her arrival here in the middle of all this raised concerns. But his conversations with both Peg and Mack had satisfied most of his questions about her.

So, had someone really attempted to kill her with the snake in the car? And what about the undone brake cables? Who and why were pretty big mysteries.

A knock drew his attention to Conner standing in his doorway. "You got a second?"

"Come on in." Rock nodded toward the empty chair opposite his desk, easing himself into his own chair while Conner took a seat. He waited for Conner to initiate the conversation.

"Any news on Maribel's car wreck?"

Interesting question. And the bouncing knee led Rock to think Conner was nervous. Did he know something? "Such as?"

"I'm not sure how to say this," Conner peered over at him, "but Maribel ... I mean, is it possible someone put the snake in her car on purpose?"

Now that the words were out, Conner's stare locked on Rock.

"It's possible. But why would someone go to that kind of trouble to harm her? A pretty sick way to get rid of someone, don't you think?"

Rock had considered retaliation from what had happened with the newspaper. He had someone checking on the whereabouts of certain parties during the past few days, but that might take a bit.

"I don't know why someone would want to harm her." Conner's leg stopped its hopping as he leaned forward. "But I do think there's something going on. Too many unusual things have happened to think it all a coincidence."

"A missing girl, a dead woman, and a possible assault with a deadly snake. Thanks for the heads-up you think something's amiss here." Rock didn't bother to bring up the mysterious board and barn incident Conner had told him about the last time he visited the sheriff's office. Rock pulled a package of antacids from his shirt pocket, flipped the one on top—a green one—into the wastebasket, then popped the next one—purple—into his mouth. He offered Conner one before dropping the dwindling supply back in his pocket.

"Fair enough." Conner leaned back in his chair and let out a long breath. "There've been a few things that point toward—well they seem prearranged. Like we're being set-up."

"I see." Rock crunched on his antacid while he spoke. He listened as Conner explained about the files.

"How well do you know this woman, son?"

"In terms of anything concrete, not that well. But my heart tells me she's on the right side."

"So, there's a wrong side?"

"Look, Sheriff, I'm not claiming I can make any sense out of this. But I'm afraid Maribel is in danger. And there's something else. There's a box Maribel had in the car. She's convinced she needs to see something that's in it."

"The woman with the head injury?"

"Yeah, the same." Conner smiled and shook his head. "So, can I? Get the box and let her see?"

"Well, you're right it's possible the snake in her car was no accident so as of now, it is being viewed as a crime scene. I can't let you near it. But I can tell you there was no box." Rock paused and cocked his head to the side. "You care for her, do you?"

Conner squirmed the way guys did when confronted with a truth they thought they had hidden. "Yes, sir. I do."

"Then take care of her. You're not wrong to be concerned for her safety. The car's definitely a crime scene. That brake line wasn't just undone. It'd been cut."

After Conner left, Rock had gone back to noodling things, letting the thoughts float around and collide at random in his head. It was how most things came together for him. Peg had told him she'd hired Conner as an extra set of eyes around the camp once she'd refused the offer from the real estate developers. No one was supposed to know what he was doing.

Wasted money in Rock's opinion. All Conner had dug up was a piece of lumber possibly used to barricade a barn door. He hmphed and popped another antacid from its wrapper.

Evan and Ava's strange behavior at the accident, now that was worth considering. It wasn't too surprising they found out about the accident and arrived almost before the ambulance. Everyone in this county had a scanner, but they'd arrived together almost as if they'd been planning an outing. It hadn't occurred to him then, but later as he processed through the events of the scene, that was the feeling that niggled away at him.

He settled back and closed his eyes, trying to sort through what he'd seen, breaking each aspect apart for individual consideration. He'd never known Evan to come to an accident scene until the body of Tracy Morgan surfaced and now Maribel's wreck. But maybe he was just trying to impress Ava, because she had been keen to see it all ever since she arrived here. When was that? Eight months ago.

He thought it was an interest in him that brought her out when the scanners announced a need for law enforcement, but he was sure now that wasn't the case. Still, she had always been solid with her emotions, undisturbed by the scenes. Until today. And that was something that needed further exploration.

She and Evan had hung back until they had gotten the snake and Maribel out of the car. Then Ava had gone into hysterics about the snake. She'd gotten the attention of everyone who wasn't busy situating Maribel in the ambulance. And while she was having her episode, where was Evan?

When Rock had spotted him, the car was between them. Rock had ordered him away from the car and then Ava fainted. Something he wouldn't have believed if he hadn't seen for himself.

Now Conner had showed up asking about a box belonging to Peg that was supposed to be in the car.

The image of Evan standing on the far side of the car kept jigging into his thoughts. He'd had time to remove something if he knew what he was searching for.

He tapped his computer to life. Just because he didn't enjoy using it didn't mean he didn't know how. And something told him he needed to scrutinize a few things a little harder.

CHAPTER FORTY-FIVE

Conner returned with a large ice cream sundae in one hand and a large chocolate shake in the other. No box.

He set both on the rolling tray by her bed and told her to take her pick. Then told her he hadn't found a box in the car.

"It could have gotten wedged under a seat during the accident ... or fallen out. Did you check where the accident happened?"

"Sheriff Griger went through the car and there was no box. And yes, I went to where the accident happened. No box there either." He pulled a chair close to the bed and sat.

"You're barely looking at me. You think I imagined this, or it's because I hit my head." She pressed her fingers against her temples, eyes squeezed shut. She wasn't wrong. She wasn't imagining this. And it was important. Yes, it was a hunch, but a good hunch. She knew this.

"Maybe you left it in your cabin and forgot. It's been an eventful day." He leaned so his elbows rested on his knees, fingers interlocked.

Maribel said nothing for a minute, then "Yeah, maybe you're right." She didn't think so, but it had to be somewhere. She studied him. "What aren't you telling me?"

"I think you need to rest, and we can talk more in the morning."

"No. I want to know whatever it is you aren't telling me."

Conner sighed, avoiding eye contact for a moment. Then he came to sit on the edge of the bed, taking her hand in his. "I think someone deliberately tried to harm you."

Maribel shifted her eyes to focus on the white board. The emoji faces at the bottom looked ridiculous as she contemplated what her gut had been telling her ever since she woke up in the hospital. Someone had tried to kill her.

"Your brake lines had been deliberately cut. And I know for a fact they were working when I left the car at your cabin last night." He ducked his head as if talking himself into saying more. Finally, he met her eyes. "And the snake belonged to Milton."

"Milton? Why would he ...?

"The sheriff doesn't think Milton is responsible. He reported the snake missing before any of this happened. But it was one of his. Apparently, he has microchips put in them."

"This doesn't make any sense."

"You said it was Peg's box, right? I think I need to talk to her and find out exactly what's in it that might make someone kill for it." He leaned over her, the concern in his eyes melting her resistance to being loved. "The sheriff has a man watching the hospital. Will you be all right while I'm gone? You won't try anything crazy like running off, will you?"

"No promises." Maribel's smile was weak. "But I need one from you. Promise me you'll find Daylee and get her somewhere safe. She saw something—or thinks she did. I'm afraid she might be in danger too."

Trying to not compromise her ability to think, Maribel refused any more pain medicine. Still she drifted in and out of sleep. It was the sound of Becca's Minnie Mouse voice, mere inches from Maribel's face, that prodded her from the fog.

"Yoohoo, Maribel?" Becca whispered, which only increased the squeak in her voice.

Maribel blinked a few times to focus, remembering where she was.

"Oh, there you are," Becca said, like a parent playing hide-n-seek with a toddler. She patted Maribel softly on her shoulder. "How are you feeling? Well I guess that is a silly question, but what does one ask at times like these?"

Maribel swallowed and tried to draw some moisture into her mouth. She motioned for Becca to hand her the drink cup and she sipped the cool water.

"My goodness, you've had a rough go since you got here. And I've been an awful friend. I was thinking about how alone you must feel right now." She plopped into the empty chair and pulled a ball of multi-colored yarn and her knitting needles from an oversized canvas bag.

"I'm fine, really. Just sleeping. You don't have to stay here." For once Maribel's argument was only half-hearted. She didn't mind the company.

Becca's needles began to click in smooth and steady meter.

"What are you working on?"

"Oh this? I'm knitting scarves for Christmas this year. Not that it ever gets cold enough around here to need a scarf, but I'm all out of ideas. What color would you like? Sorry, I guess that won't be much of a surprise now." Becca gave her a grin not unlike the impish one Daylee used.

"I'd be honored with any color you chose, but I if were to choose ... I'd like red." The memory of Conner saying red paint would suit her car—and her—brought a smile and a blush. She might never see her car painted red. She'd gladly settle for a scarf.

"Red it is. You remind me of Peg. Everyone always picks some plain, basic color so that it goes with everything." Becca bobbed her head in an imitation of haughtiness. "Not Peg, she likes what she likes and isn't afraid to stand out."

Even better. Maribel sipped some more of the water and wished it tasted like a Dr. Pepper.

"I'm sure going to miss her." Becca's needles paused their clicking, as she wiped her eyes with the back of a hand.

Me too, and I hardly know her Maribel thought. What would her life have been like if she'd had someone like Peg around sooner? Aunt Rachel had tried, but apparently it took a team.

"I'm just all out of ideas for people these days." The knitting needles picked up their rhythm again. "Last year I thought I'd found a fun one. I bought everyone one of those genealogy tests where you send your spit in and they tell you where your ancestors are from. I thought it'd be interesting, you know, for everyone to see and then we could share our results. I thought it'd be chance for us to talk about the world and not just our little corner of it, you know?" Becca paused, glancing over to Maribel.

"Anyway, it was supposed to be just for fun. I personally don't pay those things much mind. I mean, the Lord knows who I am. All that other stuff don't matter to Him. But anyway, Evan refused to share so I give up."

"Did he do the test? I mean does he actually have his results?"

"Oh, yes. He was the first to send it off I think."

"It's odd he won't talk about his results. Like you said, none of that matters really." Wasn't that what Peg had told her? The past doesn't have to define the future.

"Oh, Evan can just be that way, kind of secretive. I think he has always believed he was related to Peg—on his mother's side I think it was. The connection goes way back so I don't know how much truth there is to the story." Becca stopped her knitting again to ponder the thought. "Anyway, he's getting a scarf this year."

"Becca, did Evan say why me?"

Becca eyes gazed down as she thought. "You know, he didn't, and I never asked. He just said he thought the community should have a record of all Peg's family had done and that Mack and I were the only ones who would be able to talk her into it. A few days later he brought me your information from that job search site."

"Becca, I never posted my information on a job site. That's why I don't understand why me."

"I saw the entry. It was sure enough there on that website." Becca's hands went back to orchestrating the dueling needles she held, but the tempo was slower this time. "Well now, that is curious."

A nurse popped her head in and announced visiting hours were over, and Becca packed up her yarn and stood, but instead of leaving she lingered.

"Is there something you want to tell me, Becca?" Maribel could see the conflicted emotion on the woman's face.

"I don't like to speak ill of anyone, but I've got to say something to somebody. I just can't believe they aren't turning this county upside down to find that poor Leah. I haven't hardly slept a wink since she went missing. Evan told us we had to go on like normal around the camp, so we didn't mess up the investigation. But it's ... it's just like nobody cares. I can't stand thinking about that poor girl out there alone or in trouble."

"If she did run away, I think odds are good she may be a long way from this county by now. What about her parents?"

"Oh, Maribel, it's so awful. They just said she's done this before, and she'd be back." Becca's hiccupped sob shook her body and tore at Maribel's heart. "How can parents be so heartless?"

CHAPTER FORTY-SIX

Maribel pulled her bruised and sore body from the hospital bed. After her conversation with Becca, she couldn't sleep. She needed to move, or she'd go crazy. Conner had stationed himself in a chair outside her door. How he'd managed to talk the hospital into letting him stay was a mystery, but she was confident it involved blue eyes and dimples.

She didn't want company right now, just time to walk and think. She didn't concur with the doctor's assessment that this was where she needed to be. She could rest at home as well as—probably better than—here. Only she wasn't sure where home was at the moment, and they all knew her record for following doctor's orders. After tallying up three hospital visits in less than a week, they weren't inclined to grant her much freedom right now.

And if someone was really trying to kill her? Well that was another reason she needed out. Something inside her told her she alone held all the pieces of the puzzle, but she wasn't going to solve it from a hospital bed.

She found her tennis shoes and a pair of dirty socks in the large plastic bag they provided to hold her possessions. She pulled the neon yellow hospital gown that labeled her a fall risk up over her head and tossed it on the bed. After pulling her own clothes on again, she sat in the chair to work the tennis shoes onto her feet. One lap around the tiny room convinced her she had to have more space, or she'd pass out from dizziness. If she was careful, she could slip by her sleeping bodyguard.

She didn't know where she was going, only that she needed to move around, trying to let her battered body keep up with her racing mind.

An instant before her hand touched the door, Conner's cell phone went off. She froze, all of her except her heart which was running like a thoroughbred at the Kentucky Derby.

"Yeah, I'm at the hospital. I can't—," Conner's lowered voice was the only part of the conversation she picked up, but someone must be asking him for something. "What? I can't hear you."

She squinted at the clock. Three forty-five a.m. An odd time for a call.

"Hold on. I'm going outside to see if the reception is better."

"Okay, mister. I let you stay because you promised to keep it quiet. But you're going to have to leave now." The stern voice of an unhappy night nurse sent Maribel tiptoeing back to the bed.

Conner tried to reason his way into her mercy and when that didn't work, he tried to charm his way into her grace.

But she didn't budge. "No way, I could lose my job for this. Besides the sheriff's deputy is still here watching the building. I only let you stay because you looked so pitiful, but at 4:00 in the morning everybody looks pitiful. Now, you don't have to go home, but—"

"—I can't stay here." Conner finished her sentence for her.

"Bingo."

Maribel had slipped back under the covers, hiding her wardrobe change. She lay perfectly still, eyes closed, anticipating the one last check he would do. The harsh wedge of light as he opened the door made it challenging not to squint, even with her eyes closed. And then the light shrank as the door closed and he left.

She allowed several minutes to pass before she stepped into the now vacant hall.

She had seen people post hip replacement surgery moving with more agility than she felt as she ambled her stiff body away from the room. She needed to get out of this town. Forget this entire experience ever happened. But there were two things that restrained her from running as far away from this place as she could get. First—she wouldn't do that to Peg and Daylee or to Conner. And second—she was too close to something about to happen. She'd been brought this far out of the pit she'd spiraled into. If she didn't see this through, she might never get out.

There was also the notion that if someone really was trying to kill her, what was to say they wouldn't follow her? No, this was the place to take a stand.

She passed an oil painting at the far end of the hall and stopped for a closer view. A flock of fluffy white sheep grazing in a lush green meadow. It felt peaceful. Words written in elaborate scroll on the metal plate attached to it said, "Come to me all who are weary ..."

That was what she was. Weary. The heavy guilt she carried had become an impossible burden. She thought of Mack and what he did. But he hadn't laid down the rest of his life or given it over for no purpose. No, he kept going. He lived a good life, a loving life as he cared for others. He wasn't letting guilt keep him chained to the past, but judging by the compassion he had for others, he hadn't forgotten.

And what about Peg? Did she ever blame herself for forgetting to shut off that coffee pot? For sending her son out on the road that night? That's what Maribel would have done, blame herself. But she wouldn't have wanted that for Peg.

In this world you will have trouble. But take heart! I have overcome the world.

Peg knew that. Mack knew that. For the first time, understanding began to reach into Maribel's own heart.

Footsteps alerted her to someone walking in the hall and she slid into the stair well to avoid discovery. She needed fresh air, so she worked her way down the steps to the first floor.

She exited the stairwell on the first floor on the end of the hospital reserved for the radiology department, straight across from an emergency exit. Her hands were on the bar when it occurred to her an alarm might go off if she opened this door. She risked it.

The night air was hot and muggy, thick with the dampness that lingered from the heavy rainfall. A dog barked in a back yard somewhere nearby. How did people sleep through that? She wanted a dog. A constant and loyal companion filled with unconditional love, but not if it was going to bark at nothing all night.

Trash dumpsters on one side and air conditioner units on the other surrounded her. In need of a private refuge, she thought it would be nice to sit, secluded in their midst. She could live with the smell from the dumpsters, but no air circulated around them, and the heat was stifling.

She moved away from the noise and found a forgotten bench near a row of overgrown shrubs. A few cigarette butts littered the ground so this must be where the employees took their smoke breaks. Lowering herself to the metal seat, she closed her eyes and rested. She'd have to get back to her room before the nurses came by for another check and she wasn't sure how long that'd be. But a moment alone, that's all she needed. She inhaled the night filled with the scent of hot asphalt and freon from the air conditioners.

The headlights from a car rounding the corner startled her and she realized she'd dozed. She shook her head to wake herself up and watched as the car headed out of the parking lot, stopped, then reversed back. It turned on the side street nearest Maribel. She didn't move, hoping whoever it was wouldn't question her presence here if they spotted her.

The car slowed as it neared her, and the driver's side window lowered. Maribel recognized the car—Ava's.

"Maribel, thank goodness I found you. Daylee's missing. When I came here to get you and you weren't in your room either, well you about scared me to death. I thought something had happened to you too."

"Daylee's missing?" Panic catapulted Maribel's emotions from wariness to alarm. Was that what Conner's phone call had been about? But why was Ava the one coming to get her?

As if she read Maribel's mind, "Evan sent me to get you. He said you knew her best. He's already got Conner searching."

Everything felt off, but Maribel couldn't take the time to think or make sense of what was happening. She had to help find Daylee. She ran to the car and climbed in the passenger seat. Ava hit the accelerator and they were flying down the dark alleyway before Maribel could ask any more questions.

Ava bypassed the intersection that would have headed them out of town in the direction of the camp.

"Where are we going? I need to get to the camp." When Ava didn't answer, Maribel turned to stare at the gun Ave held pointed at her head. "What are you doing? Are you crazy?" She swallowed, probably not the best question to ask at this moment.

"Shut up. Open the glove compartment and take out the handcuffs." Ava's voice was calm and steady as if she were a surgeon giving orders to the OR nurse.

"Ava, what is this? You've got to slow down. You're going too fast. You're going to get us killed."

"Then hurry up and do as you're told so I can give my attention back to the road." The lack of any emotion—fear, hostility, nervousness—in Ava's voice wrapped Maribel in a cold, dark blanket of fear.

Maribel obeyed, pulling the set of handcuffs from the glove compartment. Ava instructed her to reach down near her feet and find the chain she'd secured beneath the seat. Next, she had Maribel attach the set she held to her left wrist, then fasten the other end to the set below her feet. It left Maribel in a hunched position, with Ava's gun still pointed at her head.

"Where's Daylee, Ava?" Stay calm. Reporter training had taught her to build a connection with others, to gain their trust so they would talk, but it hadn't prepared her for this. And she didn't want to gain Ava's trust. She wanted to find Daylee.

"How should I know?" The woman laughed, but she lowered the gun to her lap. "You're the one I want, Maribel."

The evil in Ava's eyes radiated across the open seat, burning like glowing embers against Maribel's skin. With her free hand she gripped the edge of the seat to keep from shaking. Her jaw moved mechanically as she spoke, but she managed to keep her tone even.

"Is Daylee all right?"

"That's up to her. But honestly, Maribel, do you really care?"

"I don't know what this is about, but I'll do whatever you need. Just leave the girl alone."

"Trust me, you have bigger issues to worry about right now. Enough talking. You'll ruin my surprise."

CHAPTER FORTY-SEVEN

Maribel sat quietly, but her mind jumped back and forth between praying for a way out and trying to figure out why Ava was doing this.

She wasn't dead yet. She couldn't let herself think that like. So, she prayed.

And in her heart, she heard God ask *do you trust me with your past as much as with your present and your future?*

She closed her eyes, not sure she understood.

Trust me with it all.

She didn't know how far they had driven. They were on a road Maribel was unfamiliar with, and judging by the sparseness of lights, they were passing fewer and fewer houses.

The car bounced over something and Maribel's head hit the dash. Pain arrested her and she gasped. The sound seemed to please Ava.

The car slowed but continued to jostle down a driveway that hadn't been used or maintained in a long time. The recent heavy rains had washed deep ruts that kept the car bouncing and Maribel wondered if they might get stuck.

A house materialized from the darkness. The faint light of pre-dawn was softening the dark, but not enough to help Maribel get her bearings.

Ava stopped the car and again pointed the gun at Maribel. "Open the door slowly. Don't get any ideas and decide to try something stupid. I'm already getting tired of this car, so it really won't bother me to if it gets a little blood on it."

Maribel had no doubt the woman meant what she said. She'd never been this close to the level of wickedness and hatred that dulled Ava's eyes. She waited as Ava came around to the passenger door.

"If you want to see Daylee again, keep following my instructions." Ava handed Maribel the key to the cuffs. "Use the right hand to unlock the cuff from the chain. Drop the key on the floorboard, then slowly get out and turn around." She stepped back and braced her gun so it pointed squarely at Maribel.

For a very brief moment Maribel would be free, but she'd never get to Ava before the woman had a chance to pull the trigger and inside the car there was nowhere to go. Maribel wasn't going to risk it for Daylee's sake, anyway. She had to keep hoping a way out would present itself.

Ava snapped the empty cuff on Maribel's wrist, binding her hands behind her back. Then she slipped a blindfold over her eyes. "A little extra precaution. We're going to take a walk now, but don't try anything stupid."

Still caught in the lingering weakness of the pain medications, Maribel staggered as she got out of the car.

The woman grasped a hand full of Maribel's hair. Yanking hard, Ava held her head tight for a moment. Maribel felt the cold, hard metal of the gun barrel press against her temple. The erratic breathing, the almost jerky rise and fall of Ava's chest, belied the seething psychotic anger that filled the woman. She feared Ava might pull the trigger any second.

The emotion passed, or Ava gained control, subduing the beast a little longer.

With Ava steering her by the arm, they began the slow walk to wherever Ava was taking her. Questions raged in Maribel's head, but she held her tongue, waiting to see what came next.

She stumbled up the stairs where Ava shoved her, banging her shin against the corner of the step. Once inside, the floor creaked beneath their feet. The hollow sound of an empty house resonated around her. Maribel staggered along a corridor, bouncing off each wall as Ava pushed her further inside.

In a back room, Ava forced Maribel onto chair. She snatched the blindfold from over Maribel's eyes, her fingers tangling in a few hairs, ripping them out as she pulled. "Do you know who I am?"

Maribel flexed her jaw to be sure it still worked before speaking. "I know who you are. Your name is Ava."

The woman's laugh sounded like shattering glass. "You don't have a clue, do you? You ruin a person's life, you ought to know their name and their face, Maribel."

"How did I ruin your life? We've just met."

Ava ran her fingers through Maribel's hair, gently this time, twirling as though it fascinated her. "You really weren't a very good journalist, were you?"

"No. I think that fact has been established. I'm not a journalist anymore." Maribel spoke slowly, buying time. Thinking.

The room they were in was empty except for the chair Maribel occupied. The hardwood floors and dingy walls told her it was an old house. The stale smell mingled with rodent excrement told her it was abandoned. The lack of furnishings—no pictures on the wall or curtains covering the windows and a thick layer of undisturbed dust—also told her it was a house no one ever visited. Through the grimy glass windows, she saw past an old barn to nothing but pastures, open fields, trees. Isolation. Ava had put effort into choosing this place. No doubt it was the perfect location for whatever she intended. But the drive hadn't been long enough to take them far from town. They were still near the Pool of Siloam.

She could jump up, take Ava off guard, and run. She could outrun the woman, but having her hands handcuffed would make her slower. And the bullet from Ava's gun had all the advantage. If Maribel had a better idea of the layout of the house maybe, but Ava had brought her to this room blindfolded.

"You've gone through a lot of trouble to bring me here. I'm sure you have something you want to tell me." Maribel had to find an opening—even a small sliver—in this woman's delusion where she might wedge in enough sanity to survive.

"Oh, precious Maribel. It would take a lifetime to tell you everything I'd like to say to you. You ... so pretty and sweet. You've never known what it was like to not have people falling at your feet, have you?" Ava moved to stand behind her.

Maribel's senses were acutely aware, trying to anticipate Ava's next move. She let the question go unanswered.

"Even Conner couldn't stay mad at you after he found out about the things you'd done. Men are easy come, easy go for you, right, Maribel? At first, I thought to spare him for his ignorance. I tried to scare you away from him. It would keep things less complicated if you didn't have a hero coming to your rescue."

"You put the file in his room. You set him up, so I'd think he was the one stalking me."

"I wasn't sure you'd have the gumption to search his room. I admit I was proud of you when you did. But even after he found out what you'd done, he forgave you and kept right on being infatuated. That's when I knew he needed to suffer too. I'm sick to death of men who are too stupid to see what you are." Ava's chest rose and fell, her anger growing. She paused. Maribel could hear her working to regain control.

But Ava liked to talk. She was enjoying explaining herself and Maribel would encourage that as long as she could. Ava spoke like a woman betrayed.

Abandonment—that's what they had in common. Could she have slipped off the edge of sanity like Ava if things had been different in her life? "Who was he?"

Ava laughed. "He? As if there were only one." She ran her fingers through Maribel's hair again. "I guess we could go all the way back to my stepfather. He was the first to love me. Oh, and he loved me in a very special way. You know that little clicking sound the TV makes when you turn it off at night? I really hate that sound."

She came back around in front of Maribel. "I bet your daddy did what daddies are supposed to do—protect you." The shattered glass laugh echoed in the room, "But did he call you his princess? Mine did. I hate that word." Ava twirled a strand of her own hair around her finger now, working her finger in obsessive circles faster and faster until the movement radiated an action more compulsive than comforting.

"You know what other word I hate? Panties. I'm going to take your panties off, Princess, so you'll be comfortable." Ava's scream, a raw, primitive guttural sound, pierced Maribel's ears.

Her chest heaving, she slapped Maribel hard across the face.

Ava went to the window, her back to Maribel. "You always do that to me. You make me lose control. I almost messed up my own plans that day in the barn. Watching you walk around so perfect and innocent. Although having you die of a heat stroke in the barn wouldn't have been the worst thing either. But watching Conner so eager to save your life. Yeah, he deserves to suffer too."

Maribel watched as Ava now paced the room, waving the gun as she talked.

"The tape was a nice touch, I think. It took time online learning how to bug someone's house and edit the tape. It's not a great job of splicing. They'll figure it out soon enough, but by then it'll all be over. Did I ever tell you I have a degree in cyber technology? Silly me, of course, I haven't told you. I'm better at hacking into computers. Splicing the tape was a new skill for me to learn."

"It was you who posted my information to the jobsite. I just don't understand why."

"I did so much more than post your resume. I read every one of your emails. I studied your online activities, every transaction, every site you visited. I knew it all."

"You did a good job."

Ava spun to glare at Maribel. "Don't patronize me."

Maribel flinched and swallowed. Clearly compliments were not the way to make friends. How much longer did Maribel have? And why couldn't she find the words she needed? She still didn't understand why she was the target of Ava's hatred.

"Why do you hate me enough to go through this much trouble?"

"It's what I do when I want something bad enough, Maribel—I work hard for it. But not you. You cut corners. You take the easy way because you're lazy and selfish."

"You're right. I know that now. Let me make it up to you. I can fix it, but not if I'm dead."

"Fix it? You haven't even figured out what I'm talking about have you?" Ava's voice shot up in anger. "Does the name Richard Donevy ring a bell?"

Maribel tried not to flinch, but she knew the surprise in her eyes gave her away. Alexander's father. The man whose reputation, career, and family she almost destroyed.

"It does, doesn't it?" She brushed Maribel's hair back from her face with her fingertips. Under other circumstances it might have appeared to be a loving interaction between sisters. "You uncovered so many things that weren't true and what was true you completely ignored. And you did it because you were sleeping with Sam." Ava's amused laugh bounced off the bare walls. "That was so rich. You couldn't even see he was using you. I have a great deal of respect for Sam. The one man who didn't fall for you. He didn't even like you."

Ava was pacing again, enjoying the torment.

"Richard was going to leave his wife to be with me. You didn't know that did you?"

Maribel recoiled, leaning away when Ava reached to touch her. Ava withdrew, annoyed by Maribel's sudden aversion.

"But that mouse of a woman he had for a wife stood by her man in his time of need." She spat the words out, full of contempt. "And he went right back to her. Forgot all about me."

The source of Ava's hatred was coming out. Maribel just needed to know how to connect with her through it.

Ava continued. "Did you know that one of the leading causes of divorce is the death of a child? Terrible thing, though, after Alexander's death—which you caused—nothing went the way it should. Okay, technically I helped Alexander decide what to do and where—I thought your house was a nice touch. But the point is, it should have made Richard leave his wife so he could be with me. That's what grief is supposed to do. But not this time. And just like that, he threw me away like a piece of yesterday's garbage." Ava shrieked out the last of her words.

"How is that my fault?" Maribel's mind reeled at Ava's admission. Was it true, Ava was responsible for Alexander's death, not her?

Ava reached for Maribel's hair again, only this time she pulled hard enough to set her scalp on fire. "How is it your fault?" She yanked hard on the hair between her fingers, sending pain shooting down Maribel's neck, then released her hold. "You wrote that story about Richard and his stupid, devoted wife felt she had to come to his defense. I thought Alexander's death would be my last chance, but then I realized I had one more option. There was one more way I could prove I loved Richard more than his pathetic wife did." Ava walked over to the closet door and opened it.

The space was empty except for the noose hanging in the center. The loop at the bottom burned against Maribel's flesh without touching her.

"I mean, all she did was stand by him through that little mess up with his reputation. I'm willing to kill. I'll be avenging the death of his son. And for that he can't help but love me."

Ava motioned with the gun for Maribel to go to the closet. "Move. Now!"

Numb with fear, Maribel's steps faltered as she moved to the spot Ava indicated. A stool sat in one corner and Ava slid it toward her. "Stand on it."

Maribel hesitated. This was not how she wanted to die. She'd come through so much these past few days, she'd learned so much. Was it going to end like this, right now?

Ava jabbed the gun in Maribel's ribs, and she thought for a moment she might provoke Ava to shoot her instead. But the coldness in Ava's eyes said she wouldn't make Maribel's death quick. Ava wanted to see suffering that matched the hurt inside her. She didn't have to say it. Maribel understood in Ava's mind, pain was a constant.

"Ava, it doesn't have to be this way. There is help. Let me help you."

"Look around you, Maribel. Obviously, I don't need your help. And when Richard sees what I will do for him, he'll realize he loves me. Not her, but me." She pounded her chest with her free hand. "Now, get on the chair and face me."

When Maribel turned, what she saw knocked the last of the hope from her like a giant, angry fist. On the far wall, the one she'd had her back to until now, blown-up images of Alexander. From childhood to his final teenage years, a visual reminder of the life that had been stolen from him. But it was the enlargements of the crime scene—Alexander in death—that clamped her lungs shut.

"Surprise." Ava smiled as her hand made a dramatic sweep toward the display, but her cold eyes never wavered from where they pierced Maribel with malice.

"I didn't do that. I'm not the one who killed him. You did." Maribel didn't recognize her own voice, but the words were coming from her mouth.

"Maybe not exactly, but you made it all possible and necessary. Face it, Maribel, this is your fault and you're going to pay."

"Ava, please. You were just a child back then. Your stepfather stole something from you—don't let him take what's left of your life by doing this. You had no one to stand up for you—it's not your fault. But you have people who will stand up for you now, who will protect you. Ava, please, it's not too late. God wants you—he wants his daughter—back. He loves you."

Ava's crazed laugh filled the room, then stopped abruptly. She studied Maribel as if she were considering her words.

"No one loves me. Now enough talking. Put your head in and I'll make sure it's nice and tight." She moved the gun to her other hand, but kept it pointed at Maribel. "And don't think getting shot will make this go easier. If you make me shoot you, I'll make sure you bleed out slowly." She adjusted the noose until Maribel felt its pressure, the roughness of the rope digging into her skin.

How long would she suffer once Ava pulled the chair away? She also wondered how long it would take before they found her body and who would be forced to see her like that.

"Now for the fun part. You get to do this yourself whenever you're ready. You can make it quick and simple—get it over with." Ava snapped her fingers like she was performing a magic trick. "Or I will just leave you here and eventually you'll want what Alexander has—freedom from pain. Or perhaps you'll get weak and sleepy and nature will take its course. Either way I win. For once in my life, I win."

Ava stepped away and pulled her cell phone from her pocket. "Now smile for the camera. Conner might not enjoy seeing this as much as Richard will, but it'd be a shame for him not to have something to remember you by."

She clicked the picture. "Can you imagine how frantic he'll be trying to find you? Unfortunately, he'll be busy with other things. Evan should see to that."

Ava spun to go.

"I forgive you." Maribel didn't know she had the strength to speak the words, but she heard them come forth from her mouth and knew they were right. Maribel's father loved her too little, Ava's loved her in the wrong way. She willed Ava to meet her eyes and repeated what might be the last words she would ever speak. "You're not a piece of garbage Ava, and I forgive you."

CHAPTER FORTY-EIGHT

The notification on Conner's phone went off and he jerked it from his pocket before he remembered it couldn't be Maribel. Her phone was in his other pocket and uncharged. He had taken it from her hospital room when they realized she was missing. He was sure Rock knew he had it, but he had said nothing about handing it over yet. Whoever this was, it wouldn't be her.

He checked the screen. An unknown number. He clicked on the message anyway, desperate not to miss anything that might help him find Maribel. He recoiled at the image that stared back at him. Sickened, the world spun around him in a black cyclone. Conner slammed his fist onto the desk to silence the roar in his ears.

He jumped from the chair he occupied in the sheriff's office, running out the door before Griger had the chance to ask him what was up. The sheriff's chair crashed against the wall as the man jumped to go after him.

"Pierce!"

"It's her, Sheriff, and I know where she is!" Conner didn't stop or give the sheriff a second glance.

"Slow down, boy. You'll get somebody hurt. Hold up and tell me what ya got."

Jaw clenched, Conner thrust his phone out for the sheriff to see. Griger stared. A glint of steel settled in eyes that were both ferocious and grim.

"It just came through. Unknown number." Conner said.

"And you know where it was taken? It's a picture of an empty room."

301

"No. There's a corner of the window and out that window is a corner of a barn I painted when I was fifteen."

"You sure? It looks just like the corner of a lot of other barns."

Conner ducked his head. "Sheriff, you never forget the view from the window of the room where the homecoming queen let you get to second base."

Griger let out a long low whistle.

"She's at the old Tackett place."

"You sure?"

"I am, and we're wasting time here."

"If you're sure then get in. I'm driving. But Conner, we don't know what we'll find when we get there. You sure you want to be there?"

"Yes, sir, I am."

They took off from town. The drive to the old farm took about twenty minutes under normal driving conditions, but Sheriff Griger wasn't engaging in normal driving conditions.

Griger radioed to his office, requesting an ambulance en route. A few minutes later the scanner buzzed to life again. "Sheriff, I have someone on the line you need to talk to. Can I patch it through to you now?"

"I'm kinda busy right now. Can it wait?"

"No, sir. You need to take it now." The dispatcher put the call through on the radio, and a shaky male voice came on the other end.

"Sheriff Griger. This is Richard Donevy. Do you know a woman named Maribel Montgomery?"

"I do."

"Oh, thank God. I didn't know for sure where she had gone, but I think she's in serious trouble right now."

Griger glanced at Conner. "What makes you think so?"

"I received a picture you need to see."

Griger rattled off his cell phone number. "Send it through then stay on the line with my dispatcher. I want your contact information and every detail you have about what's going on here. No chance that picture came with a location tag?"

"No, sir. She must have turned the GPS off."

"Who sent it?"

"Ava Hardin. She's … she's an old mistress. I was aware she'd moved up there and when I got the picture, I was praying I could find the right person."

"How'd you know to look here?"

"I have kept track of Maribel ever since I found out about the money she gave away on Alexander's behalf. I've … I've been praying for her."

"Well you might ought to keep praying."

Griger slammed his fist against the steering wheel. The truck swerved, fishtailing around a gravel corner he took too fast. The same picture Conner received came through on the sheriff's phone. He took one look and tossed the phone on the seat in disgust.

"Mine came from an unknown number. Nothing to track." Conner's fist clenched and unclenched repeatedly.

Picking up the radio, Griger called dispatch back and issued an order to stop a silver Lexus.

Griger shook his head in frustration. "Ava Hardin. I should have seen it sooner, but it wasn't until last night when I was checking a little harder into Maribel's background. Ava's in the pictures from the trial. I think she knew who Maribel was before she got here. Got a call in to the Houston PD trying to find out what her connection to that trial was, but I haven't heard back yet."

He shot Conner with a warning look. "You know what they say about a woman scorned, right boy? Might be a good idea if you prepared yourself."

As the sheriff slammed to a halt in front of the old house, Conner didn't wait for the truck to quit rolling. Not willing to lose another second in getting to her, he didn't plan to wait for an assessment of what kind of danger he might be heading in to. Ignoring Griger's orders, he was out of the cab and running full speed into the house. Ava's car wasn't there, but that wasn't his priority.

He bolted straight to the room were the picture had been taken, jerking to a standstill at the sight of her tear-stained face and the rope around her neck. The anger that roared through him burned through his veins like liquid fire. But it was quickly overcome by relief to see her still alive.

Then he was cradling her face in his hands as his eyes drank her in. "It's okay, Maribel. I'm here."

He loosened and removed the noose from her neck, then lifted her into his arms, embracing her with a fierceness that threatened to crush her. She remained stiff, unmoving and silent. He shifted, still holding her and saw the pictures plastered across the wall. "Oh, dear God."

When Maribel told Sheriff Griger what Ava had said about Evan, the sheriff had sent men to find him. But Evan Beck was missing.

Conner had been the last to talk to him when Evan had phoned him at four in the morning claiming he was worried about Maribel and wanted an update on her condition. He let his fist bang against the wall of the sheriff's office where he leaned, causing the picture hanging there to rattle. "I can't believe I let him con me like that."

"But what about Daylee?" Maribel couldn't put aside her fears the girl was in danger.

"I called the counselors and Daylee is sleeping in her bunk. I told them not to let her out of their sight until we can get there."

"We need to get her somewhere she'll be safe." Ava's threats concerning Daylee had been empty ones, but it brought Maribel no reassurance. She swirled the coffee in her cup and stared into the pool of black liquid as if it might tell her something. For once it held no appeal.

"And you need to get back to the hospital. Get checked out again." Sheriff Griger squinted at Maribel.

"Thanks, Sheriff, but if I step foot in there again, they'll put me in a strait-jacket." She stared at Conner. "I'm where I need to be."

"Until we find Ava Hardin and Evan Beck, where you need to be is in hiding somewhere safe." Conner stood, feet planted, letting it be known he'd not tolerate an argument.

Maribel nodded. Maybe one day soon she could stop running, but until then she trusted Conner. She was still trying to understand what they'd told her about Richard Donevy, how he'd been desperate to help her—to save her life. She felt the overwhelming sense of responsibility to now live a life worth saving.

CHAPTER FORTY-NINE

The unmarked car Sheriff Griger had sent to pick up Daylee stopped in the main parking lot. Maribel wasn't sure the girl would go with them, but they promised to get her involved if needed. Conner and Sheriff Griger persuaded Maribel someplace safe meant a hotel room in Abilene until Ava and Evan were found, but only after they'd assured her they were doing the same for Daylee.

The female deputy they'd brought in from the next county over to pick up Daylee stepped from her car and gave Maribel and Conner a slight nod as they drove by.

"Are you sure this is safe? Can we trust her?" Maribel asked the question for the third time.

"Yes, for the third time, I'm still sure. Officer Waters is completely trustworthy." Conner reached over and squeezed her hand.

"What? Did you date her too?" Maribel asked and then wished she hadn't.

Conner sighed and gave Maribel a weary smile. "Are you kidding? Her dad wouldn't let me within ten miles of her. She's solid. I promise. As soon as we get you both situated, we'll arrange a phone call. Will you please just trust us right now?"

Maribel closed her eyes and nodded, wanting the nightmare to be over.

"I need to grab a few things from my place too." Conner had once again appointed himself her well-being facilitator and gotten a room adjoining hers. "Maybe we should go to my place first, then come for your things."

"Nonsense. It won't take but a minute. If we split up, we can be out of here faster. I'm afraid the longer we stay here the more likely one of the girls could get hurt."

Conner stopped the truck and handed her the key he'd kept in his possession. Maribel swung out of the truck and hurried to her cabin before he could argue.

She entered her cabin in a hurry, then stopped. Daylee stood in the middle of the room, wide eyes over wet cheeks.

"Daylee?"

"Yes, Maribel. Daylee's here waiting. Come in and join us." Evan's voice taunted.

A sob choked its way from her chest. Was Daylee about to die, thanks to her? No, no, no, no. This wasn't going to happen again.

"Let her go and I'll do whatever you ask. You don't need her."

"Oh, Maribel, of course I can't let her go. She's too much like you and she'll find a way to be a problem, just like you. Why you wouldn't die already I don't know, but this time your luck has run out." His tone had taken on an edge of insanity that sent an icy slush through her veins. "I knew I shouldn't have trusted Ava to get the job done. Three times she could have killed you. And yet, here you are. A perpetual, useless thorn in my side."

"I don't understand. Why are you doing this? What did Alexander's death have to do with you?" Maribel tried to maintain a calm that contradicted the chaos of emotions inside her. Keep him talking. Although, twice in one day was too many times for conversations like this.

Evan snorted his derision. "Maribel, you disappoint me. Surely you don't believe I'm so shallow revenge is what I'm after. No, I know you don't. You're a journalist. That's why you took those pictures and then broke into Conner's room."

"There's a deputy at the office now looking for Daylee. You won't get away, Evan. Just walk out now and we won't tell anyone we saw you."

"Having a hostage will help. I prefer to take the girl, but if you force me to shoot her I will." He reached for Maribel, grabbing her and she let him. Evan pulled her close, his arm pressing hard against her neck as she resisted the urge to fight. Not while Evan held a gun and Daylee was present. "Peg never liked Ava the way I planned, but she liked you. But you were too smart for your own good. It was only a matter of time until you figured it out. And the bonus would be that Ava got to have her revenge."

"So you're the one who arranged everything so Peg would hire me?" Keep him talking until Conner returned. And then what? He'd kill them all?

"Don't be silly. I had Becca do it for me. She's a remarkably easy woman to manipulate." He laughed. "Well, aren't you all? Did Ava tell you?"

"Tell me what?" Maribel licked her lips, her eyes on Daylee. Stay calm.

"She's my stepsister. I'm sure she told you all about the terrible things my father did to her. Yes, she's always been an easy one to manipulate."

"And you're a hateful coward," Maribel's anger rasped in her voice. "You could have helped her. Instead you're just using her suffering for your own benefit. What kind of monster are you?"

"The kind that holds your life in his hands." He jerked up on his arm, choking her. She dug at his arm with her hands. Daylee started toward them and he swung his gun to aim at her.

"Stop! Don't move, Daylee." Maribel's breathless voice stopped the girl. She quit fighting, and Evan lessened the pressure strangling her. "Tell us what you want. I'll do it. I'll take care of it. Please, don't hurt her."

"Ah, Maribel—and you call me the coward." His slimy voice resonated close to her ear, and she tried not to flinch. He motioned for Daylee to move to the table where the no longer missing box sat. "The box, open it."

Daylee looked at Maribel before moving. Maribel nodded.

The girl opened it and pulled out a worn bible, holding it out for Evan to see. The key Maribel had worn lay on the table beside it.

"Where's the rest of it, Maribel?" Evan growled in her ear. "I have gone through a great deal of difficulty to get this box and the documents that were supposed to be inside it. Where are they?"

"I don't know what you're talking about."

"Liar!" His word was a whispered growl that misted her cheek with spittle.

Too late, she heard Conner's footfalls on the porch a second before he stepped into the room.

"Maribel let's—" he stepped through the door and froze.

"Hands where I can see them, Conner. Don't be the hero."

Conner raised his hands and tried to position himself between Evan and Daylee.

"Stay right where you are," Evan said, his gun now pointing at Conner. "Now slowly, with your left hand, remove the gun you have concealed under your shirt."

Conner reached behind his back for the gun with deliberate movements, unhurried.

"Now slide the gun over here." Evan directed, and Conner complied.

The gun slid across the floor, and Evan kicked it away.

"Isn't this nice, Maribel? Now you have two reasons to tell me where the papers are. Three if you count your life as well. Although I've not had the impression you count your life for much." Evan motioned at Daylee with the gun, moving her to stand beside Conner.

"What papers? Why go through this much trouble to get them?"

"Those papers are the only things that stand between me and my inheritance. People really shouldn't confess things in letters. It just makes a mess for every-one else." Evan shifted a little and Maribel suspected his arm was getting tired. "But if you must know, my dear sweet however many greats grandmother wasn't very faithful to her husband and before she died, she felt the need to repent and confess her transgressions. Why do people do that?"

His words were hard and full of the acid of hatred that comes from a life of blaming others for your circumstances. And not an ounce of remorse for what he'd let Ava endure.

"So she wrote a letter to her husband telling him he wasn't the father. The father was a traveling medicine man. Can you believe that? She had her five minutes of fun and then ruined it for me with one stupid letter because she thought she had to confess." His words spewed out, showering her with more saliva.

"That's why you wouldn't share the results of the ancestry tests, isn't it? It proves you aren't related to the Moreland's."

"How'd you know about the letter?" Conner spoke without inflection.

Evan laughed. "The pain medicines they gave Peg after her first surgery were wonderful. She told me all the family secrets. Even had the nerve to tell me she was sorry to find that letter and know we weren't related. But did she offer to share her estate with me? Not by a long shot. That's when I knew I'd just have to make it happen myself."

He yanked Maribel, pressing her closer to him and crushing her throat. "Now last chance ... where are the papers?"

"Okay, okay. I'll tell you." Her words tumbled out as a hoarse rasp, but urgent and desperate. Her eyes locked on Conner's, willing him to realize what she planned to do.

"Where?" He jerked his arm.

Conner stood stone still, his eyes unblinking on Evan, showing only calculation and none of the fear he must have felt. He needed an opportunity, and Maribel could make that happen if she could first get Daylee somewhere safe.

"In the bathroom. The bottom drawer. There's a false bottom. Lift it up and the papers are there."

He motioned to Daylee. "Go get them."

While he talked, Maribel twisted, positioning her chin centered in his elbow while her hands came up to hold his arm firm. She waited for Daylee to be in the bathroom, then she dropped, her full weight coming down against the arm that held her. Evan staggered, made off balance by the shift in gravity.

The moment of distraction was all Conner needed. He launched himself toward them a split second before Evan's gun went off.

The three of them slammed to the floor, the impact knocking the gun from Evan's hand. Maribel kicked free, rolling away from Evan's grasp. She clawed across the floor, reaching for the gun. Her fingers closed around it and she spun to see Conner on his back. He grabbed his leg where a patch of red grew, struggling to stand.

Evan lunged for her.

If he got the gun, they would all be dead. She pulled the trigger.

CHAPTER FIFTY

The rain had ceased, and the calendar had rolled into August, bringing with it a sun that sucked the moisture from the ground, leaving the plants drying and withered, the ground petrified in places, powdery in others.

The orange beams of the late day sun shone through the veil of dust particles stirred by the cattle stomping in the loading pen.

Inside the pen Conner worked them into the waiting trailer with patience, as much for the benefit of the cows as for his own healing leg. The bullet had gone through without hitting anything major, but he still needed more time to recover than he was allowing himself.

Maribel walked to the shade of an oak tree and watched. She had seen little of Conner since he'd gotten out of the hospital. He'd been busy closing the camp and preparing it for the renovations it would need as part of its transition into a permanent home instead of a camp.

And she'd been away, putting some things to rest.

Her eyes drifted to Peg, a silhouette against the glowing sky. Sheriff Griger stood with her. Another family in healing, past resentments and jealousies laid aside in pursuit of something better. A treasure more valuable, lasting, and rare. Evan could have been a part of this, but his greed was insurmountable.

In the days following his arrest, they had learned of his plan to contest Peg's will as an heir. The only obstacle that stood in his way was the fact he wasn't a true descendant. The papers Peg kept in the locked box told the truth. Evan was desperate to destroy this evidence before anyone else could see it.

Only Peg had taken them from the box before she sent it to Maribel, hiding them beneath a stack of empty casserole dishes in her linen closet. She'd planned to destroy them herself and allow Evan the dignity of being included in the Moreland family tree. She'd even made stipulations for him to receive a small inheritance.

She gave Maribel the box with the bible in it and told her to keep it hidden for a reason even she couldn't exactly explain. She just said Maribel wasn't a person who could have the truth handed to her. She needed to search for it herself. It had never occurred to her that Evan might try to find it or that it might put Maribel in danger

Footsteps drew her attention as Mack walked up beside her.

"These are for you." He handed her two envelopes. Letters from Daylee and Leah. Peg was requiring handwritten letters from the girls now. It turned out that Peg had been hiding Leah with the help of Mack and the sheriff—and the consent of her we're-yachting-in-the-Mediterranean-and-can't-be-bothered parents.

"Did you hear Leah's parents have made a sizeable donation to the building fund for the new home here? They'd like one wing to be named after Tracy Morgan for saving Leah's life." Mack drew in a breath that said he was determined to see *the goodness of the Lord in the land of the living.* Even through the sorrow and suffering, the injustice and iniquity. Just like he'd said the first time they'd met. Might not be a bad way to live.

"It still gives me chills to think about what would have happened to Leah if Tracy hadn't been there." Maribel rubbed her arms. "Evan would have killed her too."

"Love of money makes a terrible master. And I'm sure the idea of finding a treasure was Tracy's incentive to join Leah in the hunt. But she did what was right in the end. *Greater love has no one but this, that he would lay down one's life for his friends.*"

They stood silent for a moment, each in their own thoughts. Even after all she had witnessed in the past few weeks, it was still hard to believe that people could be so cruel and selfish. But that darkness had become the backdrop against which a love that went beyond reasoning manifested itself.

Leah had overheard Evan and Ava talking about his plan to gain a part of Peg's inheritance by destroying the only real evidence that proved he wasn't related. And for that Evan decided to kill Leah. His story about a lost treasure buried near the river was well played against her background of unhappiness and lack of love from her family.

Maribel felt the miracle of Tracy being in the right place—although that place was smoking behind a building where they shouldn't have been—to befriend Leah, and ultimately save her life. That she'd also told her to never trust anyone but go straight to Peg if she ever got into trouble was further evidence of something greater at work in their lives.

"I'm just glad Sheriff Griger agreed to sneak the food out to Peg's for Leah. If Cindy had caught me buying any of that stuff at the grocery store, I'd never have heard the end of it." A mock fear captured Mack's features.

Maribel laughed. She'd had some concerns about Peg's pantry when she'd seen it. "By the way, how did the sheriff know where to find the shovel?"

"When Tracy thought she heard someone, she told Leah to hide. So, of course, Leah followed her instead. She was just close enough to see someone swing the shovel and see Tracy fall. It was enough to tell the sheriff where it happened, but not enough to know who it was."

"Tracy saved Leah, and Leah would have saved me that day at the barn. She told Conner she was the one who took the board out of the door and was about to go inside when she heard him driving up." Intertwined like a delicate tapestry, no life was unimportant.

Maribel looked at the envelopes in her hand and was washed anew with the knowledge that things could never go back to the way they were before. Her heart had not only changed but had been inhabited by two precocious teenage girls who needed everything she had to offer. And in terms of wisdom gained from past mistakes, she had a lot.

Both girls were back with their families now, but maybe once the new facility was finished, they would find a home here.

"How are things going with what we talked about last time?" Mack changed the subject.

"It's easier with Ava, but I'm not sure why. I still can't believe she turned herself in, but it makes me hopeful she'll eventually get help. Somedays I have to remind myself you said forgiveness is a choice, not a feeling." She glanced at Mack. "Seeing Alexander's parents was hard, but I really believe they have forgiven me. I may not have been responsible for their son's death directly, but I still made plenty of mistakes. Did you know his dad is working with a suicide hotline now and speaking to schools?"

"That's a good thing. God can work all things for the good of his glory—if we just let him. And how about you? Have you forgiven yourself?" Mack's voice was soft, his love and concern mingling in his tone.

"Most of the time, but sometimes that's still hard too." She folded her arms in front of her and watched as Conner worked the last of the cattle onto the trailer.

"Sometimes it's fear that holds us back … fear of letting go of our anger, fear of making another mistake, fear of being unworthy. But per—"

"—fect love out fear. I got it." Her smile came with ease today.

"We try to reason things out with our feelings, but the problem is, feelings aren't reasonable. Believe the truth, Maribel, and stand on it. You are loved now, and you always have been." Mack smiled. "Let yourself be freed, Maribel." He drew her into a fatherly embrace.

When they parted, Maribel wiped the tears from her cheeks. A Father's love comes in many forms.

"Thanks, Mack. Speaking of truth, I hear you have a date soon?"

She thought he blushed. "I think I'll go check on Peg." He darted off, ignoring her comment. No worries. Aunt Rachel would tell her all about it.

Conner slammed the trailer gate—the impact of metal clanging shut, harsh, final—and gestured for the truck to move forward, the cows shifting in the closed trailer, jostling and banging. Assured the latch was secure, he waved to the driver and the truck and trailer pulled away, a cloud of dust rising behind it.

And it was over. The moment lingered without expectation, an element of time frozen in place.

Maribel wiped her eyes again. Peg was at peace, but it didn't make the coming separation much easier.

Conner walked over to where she waited, a slight limp where he favored his injured leg and a curious expression on his face. He pulled off his hat and wiped a sleeve across his sweaty brow. "You look ..." He stared at her as if he couldn't figure out quite the word he wanted, or exactly how it was she looked.

"Happy?"

"Maybe ..." he answered, stretching the word as he set his hat back on his head. "I think the word I'm looking for, though, is beautiful."

Maribel laughed, rich and deep. "I think you got dirt in your eyes, cowboy. Or something else."

"Oh, really?" He inched closer, the heat of a grass fire sweeping toward her in his gaze.

She backed against the tree and put her hands against his chest, trying to keep enough room for Jesus in between them.

"I've missed you these past few days, Maribel."

"I've missed you a little too." She bit her lip, trying to curb the smile. "I went to see my mother."

"And?" He pulled back, his eyes searching her face.

"It went well. Better than expected, I guess. We'll just take it one step at a time."

"But you're happy now?"

"Yeah, I am." She let the soft smile say what her words couldn't.

He reached up and tugged a strand of hair that fell by her cheek. "How many times did you owe me for helping you out—shoot, for saving your life? I think I've lost count the number was so high."

"I didn't know I was being charged for your ... help. Whatever you did to help me, it was purely your choice. You said no strings attached."

"A string isn't what I want Maribel."

"Still—you said it. You can't just change the rules to suit your ... uhmm ... desires. You quite chivalrously offered your assistance with no payment requested." A blush scorched her cheeks and she refused to make eye contact. She pushed against his chest, a wasted effort since he didn't budge.

He studied her hair between his fingers, then stared until her eyes met his. "A choice I'd make all over again—even with no promise of compensation."

"You really are something."

"I've been told that before. Hopefully this time you mean it in a good way." The dimples dug into his cheeks—and her heart.

"So, Maribel, I see you got your stuff all loaded in the car." Mack's voiced boomed, and they both jumped, spreading themselves apart.

Mack, with Peg and the sheriff right beside him, stepped around the tree.

"Stuff loaded?" Conner's question drew everyone's attention.

Sheriff Griger rubbed his chin between his thumb and forefinger, averting his eyes, but clearly amused.

"I'm sure you'll miss your tarp-roofed cabin, but for everything there is a season, right?" Mack continued on. If he was aware of any sudden tension, it didn't show.

Conner pulled away from her, his sky-blue eyes becoming stormy. "You're leaving?"

Mack clamped a hand on Conner's shoulder. "You didn't think she'd stay in that cabin forever, did you?" He released his hold on Conner and faced the others. "Well, let's all head up to the house and celebrate. Cindy sent sweet tea and peach cobbler."

"I've got work to do." Conner wheeled and stomped back toward the barn.

"Aren't you going to help her unload?" Mack called after him.

Conner stopped, revolving slowly back to face them. "Unload?"

"Yes. Unload. But I can handle it by myself. You've got better things to do and I wouldn't want to be any further indebted to you since you're keeping score." Maribel crossed her arms over her chest.

"Bit of an overreaction there son, I believe." Sheriff Griger mumbled under his breath as he chuckled.

"Unload? Here?" Confusion narrowed Conner's eyes, and he squinted at her.

"Yep. Now that Leah's gone and the camp's about to be under construction, Maribel's moving in with me. We got a lot to talk about." Peg winked at Maribel, then took Mack's arm, pulling him toward the house. "Let's go get something cool to drink. I've had some thoughts about your next sermon."

"None for me, thanks." Sheriff Griger said. "I've got a few days off and a boat on the lake that misses me. But y'all be ready. When I get back, we're going to have us a fish fry to celebrate."

"Celebrate?" Peg asked.

Sheriff Griger peered at Conner. "You didn't tell 'em?"

Conner shook his head with an air of hesitation. "Not yet."

"Well it seems there's more than one secret that has been kept here. I may need to have a sermon on honesty soon." Mack eyes hopped from one person to the next.

Her turn for concern, Maribel stared at Conner.

"No rush," Sheriff Griger glanced at Peg, "but Conner has his next job waiting on him. And if I'm lucky, we're looking at my replacement right here." Sheriff Griger clamped Conner on the shoulder, clearly liking the idea. He was almost glowing. As he walked to his truck, his joints moved with new freedom, his step lighter. He stopped for one last comment, giving Conner a pointed stare. "And son, you'd better make sure I'm lucky."

"Well, that is a cause for celebration." Peg's happiness radiated from her wrinkled face. But when did it not? She amazed Maribel all over again with the peace and joy that sparkled in her eyes, even leaning on Mack for support as he escorted her back to the house.

Alone now with Maribel, Conner shook his head, but the glint in his eyes said it all. "So, you're staying?"

"Peg offered me a job at the home when it opens, and I think I'll take it. I'd like to stay here for a while."

"Any reasons in particular?" He squinted off into the distance as if pondering the possibilities, but his expression said he was confident he was on the list.

"I think I can make a difference here. I want to help the girls." She glanced around, taking in the house and the stately oak trees. "This place feels like home." *The home I never had.* "And I want to spend as much time with Peg as possible." The underlying truth that the time might not be long wove a melancholy thread into the moment and they were quiet.

"Anything else?" Conner prodded, inching himself closer until she could smell the faint woodsy scent mixed with dust and sweat.

"Mack has been really good to me. He's helping me work through everything." Maribel refused to satisfy him with the answer he wanted. She kept her eyes on anything but him, so she didn't turn to ash right here on Peg's lawn.

He moved closer still, his arms sliding up hers until they rested on her shoulders. "All good reasons, but I think we can find an even better one." He nudged the tip of her nose with his, tilting her head and exposing her lips. "I'll try to help you figure it out." His lips brushed against hers in a kiss soft, warm, and salty. It lingered on her lips even after he pulled back to gaze into her eyes.

"Well, let's go—you'll owe me one again." He winked and headed to her car. After just a few steps, he turned back and pointed a warning finger at her. "And this time I will collect."

Maribel paused, taking in the details, memorizing the moment. The ground no longer sought to crumble beneath her. Daylee's words came back to her. *I guess you gotta want it bad enough.*

And want it she did.

He set my feet on a rock and gave me a firm place to stand.

Questions for Reflection

1. Maribel's story begins at a moment when she feels stranded and alone. She has come to a very low point in her life and wonders if she can ever get back out of the pit she has fallen in to. Has there been a time in your life when everything seemed to be going wrong or falling apart? What did you believe about yourself at the time? What does God say is true about you?

2. Mistakes she has made in the past have filled her with a self-doubt that makes it hard for her to trust herself anymore. Have there been mistakes in your past that cause you to doubt yourself now? Have you made mistakes that cause you to doubt God can love you? How have you let past mistakes influence your future decisions? What does God say is true about this?

3. Running is an escape for Maribel. What activity do you turn to when you feel anxious, guilty, stressed, or afraid? Does this activity bring you closer to God or do you use it to distract you from the pain? What activity could you chose, or what could you change about your current one, that would help you see and experience it as a way to worship God? Do you think Maribel was aware of God's hand in the creation of the scenery she observed—the sunrise, the wildflowers, the vine covered trees—while she ran? What does God say?

4. Conner deals with his own kind of guilt and self-doubt throughout the story. How did his reaction to seeing Tracy's body make you feel? How about his reaction when he learned that Katy was pregnant? Do you think his feelings of guilt were justified? Why or why not? What does the bible say?

5. God often uses the world around us to teach of greater truths. The river is a central element in several scenes of this story. What might the river represent to Maribel? What truths could it share with you?

A FREE DOWNLOADABLE STUDY GUIDE BASED ON THE SCRIP-
TURES USED IN THIS BOOK IS AVAILABLE AT
WWW.LORIALTEBAUMER.COM